SNOWBOUND AT *Christmas*

WIND RIVER MAIL-ORDER BRIDES

SNOWBOUND AT *Christmas*

LACY WILLIAMS
PRESENTS

WENDY GALINETTI

WENDY KLOPFENSTEIN

TRACI SUMMERIL

sunrise
PUBLISHING

Snowbound at Christmas
Wind River Mail-Order Brides Anthology

Published by Sunrise Media Group LLC
Copyright © 2025 by Sunrise Media Group

Print ISBN: 978-1-966463-17-7

This book is a work of fiction. Names, characters, places, and incidents are either products of the author's imagination or used fictitiously. Any similarity to actual people, organizations, and/or events is purely coincidental.

All Scripture quotations, unless otherwise indicated, are taken from the King James Version.

For more information about the authors, visit their websites at lacywilliams.net, wendygalinetti.com, wendyklopfenstein.com, and tracisummeril.com.

Cover Design: Sunrise Media Group LLC

Wind River Mail-Order Brides

A Convenient Heart
A Steadfast Heart
A Secret Heart
A Dangerous Heart
A Forgotten Heart
Snowbound at Christmas

Heart's
SECRET HAVEN

— WENDY GALINETTI —

To my sister Tina Wieland, for her steadfast encouragement, amazing feedback, and hours on the phone talking about fictional characters.

One

A CHILL SLIPPED DOWN LILLY MURdock's collar.

It wouldn't be long now until the blizzard hit. She could feel its icy fingers already gripping the town of Calvin. She grasped the handles of the wheelbarrow heaped with hay and pushed it along the central aisle of the stable. Bandit, a scruffy ranch dog with a patchwork coat of brown, white, and black that some cowboy drifter had left behind, followed on her heels.

The almanac had predicted the snowstorm. Pa would've said he felt it coming in his bones.

She missed his dear voice.

She'd been up at dawn, hauling in bags of feed and filling the water barrels. With eight rental horses to look after and another five boarded for the town's residents, she was "riding with a full saddlebag." Another thing Pa used to say. Lilly took in a deep breath against the familiar tightness in her chest. Almost a year now since Pa passed. It didn't feel right that he was gone. Sometimes she would look up, expecting to find him mucking out a stall or sitting at the table repairing a bridle in their small living quarters.

As she passed by one of the middle stalls, a familiar soft nicker called to her.

There was work to be done, but she stopped anyway, letting go of the wheelbarrow's weight outside the stall of her mare, Fancy. Unhooking the simple latch, Lilly swung open the three-plank stall door by its diagonal cross beam and slipped inside.

Fancy was getting ready to be a mama for the very first time.

"You called, Miss Fancy?" Lilly let her gaze rake the horse's bulging belly.

The mare lifted her head for a soothing stroke between her eyes, then affectionately pressed her muzzle against Lilly's shoulder, her warm breath tickling Lilly's ear.

Fancy lipped and tugged at Lilly's braid.

"Stop that," but the words had no heat as Lilly pushed the horse's snout away gently.

The mare had been tugging Lilly's braid since they were both young fillies.

"You are worse than a schoolboy!" Lilly scolded. She inspected the mare, running her hand down her neck in gentle, rhythmic strokes. She placed a palm on the mare's belly, her gaze flicking to the hashmarks on the stall wall opposite. Each one represented a day in Fancy's gestation. Her beloved Fancy was almost a week late delivering her first foal.

A sharp rap sounded, and Lilly quickly slipped from the stall, Bandit padding behind her toward the big barn door that faced the street, already sliding open on its rail.

She met a body wrapped in a coat, hat pulled low, as the door yanked at her arm and snow sprayed into her eyes.

Danna O'Grady, Calvin's marshal, was there with her hat pulled low to shield her face and the collar of her coat pulled up. The marshal's chestnut mare snorted and shook her head, raining the accumulating snow across Lilly's boots as she pulled the door closed behind them.

Danna stomped snow from her boots and brushed wet flakes from the shoulders of her long duster and the legs of her wool trousers. Lilly admired the marshal's no-nonsense attire but couldn't quite bring herself to wear men's clothing.

"Mornin'!" Danna pushed her hat back a bit. "Snow's comin' on quick."

"Need to board this girl?" Lilly asked. The horse lipped the pocket where Lilly kept a stash of sugar cubes. She nudged the soft nose away. "Aren't you going home for Christmas?"

The marshal lived on a homestead out of town with her husband and two small daughters.

"With a storm like this, I may be needed in town—holiday or not. Especially after last year."

Lilly remembered the dust-up when a local rancher had tried to take revenge on Nick McGraw, shooting at him right on the street.

Danna tied off her horse in the aisle. "Expecting a train this morning. With half the hotel closed for repairs, we're gonna be hard pressed to find lodging for the passengers to hole up and wait out the storm. You may end up with an extra horse or two."

Lilly's neck flushed hot at the mention of the hotel. She set her jaw against the unhappy memories, refusing to let her expression change.

"The few boarding houses Calvin has will fill up quickly with this storm and the holiday," Danna said, unbuttoning a few buttons of her coat and loosening her scarf.

"I reckon." A thought struck Lilly. "It's almost Christmas, and there's no room in the Calvin inns."

One side of Danna's lips inched up. She scanned the livery, her eyes catching on a few empty stalls, then returning to her face. "You do remember where Mary and Joseph ended up?"

"I think the lesson is about making room in our hearts for the Savior." Lilly didn't want to think about opening her heart. It was still too raw. She would be alone this Christmas—the first one without Pa.

Danna didn't seem in any hurry to head back out into the snow and wind.

"You gonna be all right?" Danna tipped her head toward the lean-to Lilly used as her quarters. "You set to weather this storm?"

Lilly nodded. "I've got plenty of water, feed, and hay."

Danna sent her a pointed glance. "Wasn't asking about the animals. I know you will take good care of them. I was asking about you. You got enough food stocked for a couple of days?"

Lilly pictured the barren shelves above the dry sink.

"I'll be fine." This time the hot prickle in her eyes surprised her. It had been a long time since someone asked after her. "I'll be fine," she repeated, walking to the mare and moving to take off the girl's saddle.

"You've already got a couple of inches of snow on the roof." Danna motioned to Lilly's quarters again. "Want me to get someone to climb up there and sweep it off?"

"I'll get to it once the storm passes."

"If it piles up too much, you might get a leak—or worse."

"I know."

The list of things she'd been putting off for later just kept getting longer. At least she knew she had wood. She had bartered the use of a horse and wagon with one of the locals for cut wood for the stove. But she hadn't filled her wood bin yet. Another thing to add to the list.

Lilly moved to the horse's bridle and began unbuckling it. She tucked the horse into the nearest free stall and put the wooden bars in place. "I'll bring you back some water, Chestnut."

Danna raised one eyebrow. "I didn't know my horse had acquired a name."

Lilly flushed slightly. "I can't seem to help myself from giving them a nickname if they don't have one."

Finally, Danna headed toward the door. "You sure you don't need help?"

"I'm certain."

She'd learned independence from Pa. Or rather, living with Pa. She knew if she worked hard enough, she wouldn't need help.

Except there was a part of her lately that felt like she was being buried alive in a snowbank.

Danna turned back before she slipped through the door. "I'll check back when I can."

"It's not necessary, Marshal. I'm used to being on my own."

Danna nodded her farewell and stepped out into the wind and snow.

Lilly settled Chestnut with feed and water. Just as she was getting back into her chores, impatient thumps pounded against the door.

She left the wheelbarrow a few feet behind her and opened the door. A wiry man wearing a wrinkled black wool suit over a white shirt and a snow-dusted bowler hat stood before her.

"Ma'am," he drawled. He seemed to look through her, peering over her shoulder. "I'd like to speak to your man about renting a horse."

"The livery is not renting horses today. Not with the storm coming." She was used to strangers assuming there must be a man somewhere. She never outright lied. And tried not to let it bother her.

Bandit padded over and sat near her right boot, ears perked, eyes alert.

"The storm is why I need to get on the road immediately," he spoke slowly, as if explaining to a child. "Go fetch your husband," he ordered.

Lilly bristled but drew in a steadying breath, mustering a professional tone.

"We're closed for business. I suggest you find a room in town."

He scowled, his mustache creeping up like a caterpillar. "I aim to rent a horse," he said tightly.

"I said no."

His expression twisted into a sneer. "A girl like you probably can't tell a filly from a stallion. Does your man know you're turning away good customers?"

He moved forward as if he'd pass by her to enter the livery.

Bandit surged to his feet, growling.

The man startled and stepped back over the threshold.

Lilly acted on instinct, slipping behind the wheelbarrow, grabbing the handles, and rolling it forward across the threshold to create a barrier between them.

The wind whipped around her while the smell of manure swirled up from the wheelbarrow in a pungent cloud. Lilly tipped the wheelbarrow just enough to cause several clods of manure to fall on the man's boots.

"Oh, forgive me." Lilly tried for a bit of her father's north Georgian drawl. "This heavy wheelbarrow can be a bit unwieldy."

Bandit barked but faded back into the barn.

The man's fingers curled in tight fists, his mustache now an angry slash above his tightly pressed lips.

Unease prickled at the back of her neck. From the corner of her eye, she caught a glimpse of movement.

"Is there a problem, Lilly?" A deep baritone cut through the snowy silence.

Jakob Anderson.

Recognition flared, followed quickly by an involuntary wave of relief.

The man turned to Jakob even as Lilly caught sight of Jakob's wagon and pair of horses through the falling snow. When had he arrived? The wind must have masked the sounds of horses' hooves and jingling harnesses.

Bundled up in a tan coat and a black wool hat, covered in a layer of wet snow, he looked more like a large snowman than a successful farmer. He'd grown a beard, and it too was white with snow. His vivid blue eyes narrowed as they assessed the situation before edging his towering six-foot-four frame between Lilly and the angry man.

The man offered Jakob a strained smile.

"Finally, someone I can talk business with. Your man looks quite capable." The last words were thrown over Jakob's shoulder, aimed at Lilly, whose hands fisted at her sides.

"He's not my man."

Jakob let the sting of Lilly's rejection roll off as he used his body to block her from the man who'd looked like he was ready to take a swing at her.

Even without looking at her, Jakob felt the familiar pull of affection, an invisible cord that drew him to her. He might not be her man, but women should be treated with kindness and respect.

"You'll want to move along, sir." The man blinked up at Jakob, then scowled, but when Jakob didn't relent, he turned without another word. The fool headed down the boardwalk muttering about how he'd take his business to the other livery in town.

Leaving Jakob to face the woman he'd once wanted to marry.

Her cheeks were pink with cold, and strands of her auburn hair had escaped her braid to frame her heart-shaped face. And her green eyes flashed with challenge. He couldn't seem to look away now that the threat was gone.

"Why did you do that?" Lilly side-stepped Jakob and moved the wheelbarrow to one side of the big barn door. "I had things under control." She said the words over her shoulder as she heaved the big door all the way open.

Jakob wasn't so sure. He'd seen the wheelbarrow tip, watched the man stiffen with indignation and barely contained rage when she dumped the manure on his boots. Lilly was clever that way. When they'd been in school, kids teased Jakob for his height and awkwardness, and she'd found ways to defend him. Like putting crickets in Tommy Freedman's lunchbox. Part of him wanted to smile at this latest shenanigan, while another part wanted to scold her for provoking the man.

He realized she was standing in the open doorway with hands on her hips, waiting for his answer.

"I didn't do anything." He raised his hands, palms outward.

She seemed stumped for a moment, then sighed. Her eyes flitted over his shoulder to the pair of dark brown Morgan horses hitched to the wagon. Jakob followed her gaze to see Jorunn snort while Pia stomped and shook, rattling the harnesses and shaking off the accumulating snow.

"The storm is coming on too fast. I'd appreciate a place to keep the horses. If you've got room." The words rushed out of him, and he gave her his profile as heat crept up into his ears. All these months apart, and she still could still render him a foolish schoolboy. He ran a hand over his beard and worked to steady his heartbeat.

She nodded. "I'm surprised you came to town at all, with this weather threatening."

"I was roped into it against my better judgment," he admitted, moving to take Pia's bridle in one hand. He clucked his tongue, and the pair started walking slowly toward the stable door.

Lilly stepped to the side for him and the rig to pass by.

"It's Christmas." As if that explained everything. He felt Lilly's stare as he led the horses inside, and more words tumbled from his mouth. "I came to get sugar and flour and cinnamon for the cookies my new sister-in-law wanted to bake. Also, to pick up the gifts Mor ordered."

Lilly sniffed, and he went on, "It was foolish. I know. But Marta begged me. 'Please Jakob,'" he made his voice high in an imitation of his youngest sister. "'We can't have Christmas without cookies.'"

Lilly used her entire weight to tug the big door closed as the wagon passed inside. Was it sticking a little?

He gave a soft command, and the horses came to a stop. With the door closed, it was much quieter inside, and Lilly's voice carried.

"She won't have them now." She must've realized how sharp the words sounded, because she softened her expression. "She's still got you wrapped around her little finger."

He couldn't deny the affection he felt for his family, especially Marta.

"I should have stayed put. Albert said he's closing the General Store early, and all the boarding houses are full up."

Lilly didn't look at him as she moved behind the package-filled wagon and then near Jorum's side, where she started undoing the horse's harness. "The marshal told me. Where are you planning to stay?"

Her voice was cool. Almost stiff. The teasing Lilly of moments before had disappeared. Had she remembered how things were between them now? The awkwardness of a broken friendship?

Albert had suggested Jakob lodge here at the livery. With Lilly. The young man couldn't have known his simple suggestion would stir up such turmoil inside Jakob.

"I'll figure something out—"

"You should stay here."

Her words tumbled over his, leaving an awkward silence as they faded.

Jakob fumbled with the buckle on Pia's harness. Alone for a day or two to ride out the storm? Stuck inside the barn—or worse, her living quarters for all those hours?

"I don't think it's a good idea," he said.

Though he kept his eyes on the harness, he felt her glance like a spark across the horses' backs. "Don't be ridiculous. You can't sleep outside." She slipped the harness strap from Jorum's back. "I have my quarters, and you can bed down in your wagon out here. No one can say anything inappropriate went on."

Her tone was calm, matter-of-fact. Completely the opposite of how his stomach felt, twisted in knots.

When she glanced up at him again, he ducked his head and pulled off his stiff gloves, shoving them in his back pocket. Pretending it was his half-frozen fingers that slowed his task, not her outlandish suggestion.

Stay with Lilly.

The drumming in his chest quickened its rhythm. His mind whirled as he unbuckled the harness. He had harbored feelings for Lilly from the first moment they'd spoken. She had been his anchor in a new world when his family emigrated from Sweden and settled near Calvin. When she'd become engaged eighteen months ago, he'd distanced himself. Prayed desperately for his feelings to fade.

Now, after only a few minutes in her presence, everything he had worked so diligently to bury was rising to the surface, sharp enough to make him bleed.

Wind blasted against the stable door. His gaze snagged there.

Lilly's followed. "You cannot go back out in that blizzard, Jakob. Soon, you won't be able to see a foot in front of you."

He wouldn't risk the horses, and they both knew it. There seemed to be no other choice.

He couldn't look at her when he said, "Thank you, Lilly. You are a good friend to let me stay." There. They had been friends once. It would be enough.

Her brows drew together. "Are we still friends, Jakob? We haven't spoken in such a long time, and I . . ." Hurt chased the ghost of a smile from her face before she blanked her expression.

He had caused that hurt by his silence.

Regret thickened his throat. He rested one hand on Pia's back, waited for Lilly to meet his eyes.

"Yes, we are always friends," he said softly. Saying the words aloud, he realized they were true. He would always be her friend. "I'm sorry I didn't come after your father died." After the broken engagement, Jakob had wanted to come and see her. But he'd been exchanging letters with Astrid, and Mor had discouraged it.

"You're not the only one to blame," Lilly said softly. "I've been busy since Pa passed. We'll both forgive each other. All right?"

She didn't wait for an answer but led Jorunn to one of the empty stalls. Jakob followed her with Pia, settling her in the stall next door.

The quiet companionship he and Lilly had once shared seemed to be rekindled. Maybe he could make it enough.

He wouldn't hope for more. Never again.

Two

C OME INSIDE AND WARM UP. YOU LOOK as frozen as a snowman." Lilly threw the bolt to secure the stable door and motioned for Jakob to follow her.

Jakob looked down at himself. Snow still clung to his stiff coat and the front of his trousers. The outside of his brown leather boots had darkened with wet stains, the seams crusted with snow. Inside his boots, his feet were so cold they ached and were turning numb. He should borrow some blankets from Lilly, make his pallet in the wagon, and get out of his wet clothing. Instead, he found himself trailing Lilly to her quarters, the dog close to his heels.

"I'll make us some coffee," Lilly said over her shoulder as she opened the door. She flew into action, fluttering around her small living space like a chicken in a cramped coop. Jakob stood at the threshold, taking in the room. Had it always been so small? It'd been years since he'd been inside these quarters.

The room was still dominated by a black iron stove that had seen better days. The soot-blackened pipe appeared crooked and loose where it went through the ceiling. A tiny window above the dry sink let in the muted gray light of the stormy midday.

Lilly plucked a coffee can from the top shelf of the corner cabinet, then breezed by the bed in the corner, straightening the rumpled quilt on her way to the table. The small side table near the bed held a lamp and a stitching awl and several pieces of leather.

Jakob remembered that Lilly's father was always working on something in his spare time. Seemed Lilly had inherited that trait.

She set the coffee can on the table. Scurried to the stove for the coffeepot, turned, and motioned him in with the swing of the empty coffee pot in her hand.

"Warm yourself by the stove. Bandit, go lie down."

Jakob took a couple of long strides past the familiar oval farm table to stand before the stove. When they'd both been ten years old, Lilly had helped Jakob write English words on a slate and read from their primers. The dog trotted to the rug by the bed, circled three times and plopped himself down. Jakob side-stepped as Lilly sidled by him to the water barrel near the back door. Her skirts brushed against his pant leg sending a subtle warmth through him that had nothing to do with the stove.

"Pardon me," she whispered. Her eyes cut to him and swept up and down his tall form before turning her face away, but he saw the blush climbing up her neck and into her cheeks.

He was clearly in the way. It had always been so in the schoolroom. On a church pew. He'd sprouted up early, and towering over his schoolmates had always made him feel self-conscious. His accented words had been another difference. He'd thought he'd long since buried those old insecurities, but here he was, feeling out of place and awkward again.

While Lilly ladled water into a tin coffee pot and placed it on the cookstove, he stalked to the wood bin next to the water barrel. He reached in and grabbed one of the two split logs left in the bin and brought it to her in two long strides.

He knelt to add the log to the stove, trying not to notice how close it put them. "I'll haul in more wood before your pile is buried in snow."

She frowned. "I can fetch my own firewood."

"Of course you can. But if I'm stuck here, I'd like to help."

Stuck here. She gave him a sideways glance as he flushed and looked away. He hadn't meant for his frustration at the circumstances to come out in his words like that.

His gaze drifted to the shelves of the corner cabinet, mostly bare save a few tins of beans, a bag of flour, and a jar of fruit. Was she short on money?

She caught him looking at her shelves as she closed the stove door. "I had hoped the storm would hold off long enough for me to visit Heyer's grocery this afternoon to stock up."

Outside the window, a thick veil of snow obscured the afternoon light. No one was going anywhere in this whiteout.

"There's enough flour to make biscuits. And canned beans

to hold us over. It won't be Christmas dinner, though." She crouched in front of the corner cabinet, opened the door, and pulled out her mixing bowl. She plucked a sagging flour bag and other things from the upper shelves and placed them in the bowl, then shuffled over to the table to set up shop.

She'd always liked to keep busy, but this near-frantic energy was . . . more. Was he making her uncomfortable? He stood, planning to retreat to the barn. And then coughed.

"Lilly, I think the room is filling with smoke," he choked out.

"It always gets a little smoky when I put a new log on." She didn't lift her eyes from the bowl where her hands remained buried, mixing the dough.

"It shouldn't." He inspected the stove. The coffee had just begun to boil.

"Maybe the stovepipe is cracked. I'll fix it when I have more time." He heard the firm note in her voice. The subject was closed.

He couldn't keep himself from watching her sift flour onto the table. He'd always thought her the prettiest girl in Calvin. But he saw the changes in her. The curve of her cheeks was sharper, and there were tired lines around her eyes. The girl he'd known had been open, freely sharing every thought that danced through her mind. The woman had become more reserved, holding her thoughts to herself. And even more self-reliant. He guessed she'd had to be since her pa passed away and her fiancé had abandoned her. How long had she been on her own? Nine months?

Longer? Guilt knotted in his stomach. He could see for himself the evidence of how alone she'd been.

"I should have come after your pa died—" he blurted out, then cut off mid-sentence. "It must have been hard. I am very sorry for your loss, Lilly."

He'd gone to the funeral at the church—stood in the back while her fiancé, Stephen Barclay, sat in the front pew beside her. As the preacher read a psalm, bittersweet memories of Angus Murdock washed through his mind, the tales he'd spun of his boyhood adventures, wandering among the red clay hills and Georgia pines, his southern roots threaded through his speech.

"Thank you, Jakob." Her words held a bit of stiffness, and she kept her focus on rolling out the biscuit dough. "You've got more than your share of work at the farm. I'm no one's responsibility but my own."

The words were a wall between them. He'd once known her every hurt, every secret. Even the ones she hadn't verbalized.

Now those thoughts were off limits.

The wind blasted against the outside wall, and the ceiling rafters groaned. He wanted to do the same when he thought about the heavy snow piled on the dilapidated roof. His eyes scanned her shabby, worn quarters again. Things were worse for her than he had imagined.

A cough tickled his throat again.

His attention shifted to the portrait of Lilly's mother hanging above the bed. The image of the dark-haired beauty had held that place of honor for as long as he had known her. Lilly resembled her mother except for the auburn hair she inherited from her father. His gaze caught on the white gloves draped over one corner of the portrait. Hazy gray wisps of smoke hovered in front of the delicate white gloves.

Pushing the coffeepot aside, he quickly pulled off the front iron burner with the lid lifter handle and inspected the stove's firebox. The log quarter she'd put in earlier crackled and burned orange, but the smoke wasn't traveling up the chimney. He reached to the back of the stove and fiddled with the damper lever. It was jammed. He closed his eyes for a moment against the stinging from the heat and smoke. Lilly rushed to the window and cracked it open, the howling wind clawing its way inside.

"I can fix it, Jakob." She put a floury hand on his arm. "It's been getting stuck lately. You have to . . ." She leaned sideways, her shoulder brushing his. He felt her warm breath near his ear. For a moment, his hand froze on the lever.

"I see it, Lilly." He held his space, not letting her push him out of the way. He fiddled with the handle, then turned it with a little more force and the vent opened.

Lilly sent him a narrow-eyed gaze.

He had just extended his arm over his head to tap the pipe when she surprised him by saying, "The Jakob I knew before would never argue with me."

He didn't look at her. "Maybe you don't know me anymore, Lilly."

He had grown up. Had his heart broken. Moved on. Or thought he had.

He thought he had buried the old crush, but being near her again, the feelings lingered like the smoke in the air.

Lilly watched from the corner of her eye as Jakob tapped the pipe again for good measure. There was a soft thud and hiss as snow and ice dropped from the pipe into the oven.

"The damper and the pipe need repair." He stood with hands on his hips, watching the pipe. Thinking.

A knot of nervous energy twisted Lilly's gut. His quiet presence filled the space. Why was she so acutely aware of him? She chanced a glance at him, his blond hair curled above his shirt collar, his beard neatly trimmed. He held himself differently than she remembered. Or had it simply been too long since she'd seen him?

He glanced over and caught her staring. Flustered, she dropped her gaze.

There had to be something she could do in the livery for the quarter hour the biscuits needed to bake. Watering? Yes. She could do that.

"I'm going to get some of the watering done while the biscuits bake," she said over her shoulder as she stepped into the livery. Bandit sprang up and bolted after her.

Jakob turned from the stove. "I'll help you."

She was aware of him following closely behind her as she left the too-small living quarters and went into the livery. She breathed a sigh of relief. This was her space. The place she loved the most.

She stopped near the large barrels she used to store water when it was too cold to visit the pump outside, all lined up against one wall.

"These will freeze over, won't they?"

She heard the note of concern in Jakob's voice. More when he followed up with, "Did your pa use a stove in here?"

She shook her head. "Not for years."

When she realized there was no talking Jakob out of his notion of being useful, she gave him a pail and sent him down the aisle to each stall—the opposite direction she took.

Jakob exited Ike's mule's stall carrying an empty tin bucket at the same time Lilly exited another stall. Their gazes locked. He averted his eyes, turning to shut the stall door. She had a strange sense of the past and the present colliding. Jakob had helped her with chores many times over the years. He'd always had a shy smile. Now Jakob did not smile. His expression was carefully neutral.

Maybe you don't know me anymore.

There was a part of her that ached. She'd always counted on Jakob's steadiness, even when he hadn't seemed to want to be her friend anymore.

People changed. She knew that well.

Fancy nickered from her stall nearby, the sound was followed by the thud of hooves pawing at the ground, restless and uneasy. The mare paced in tight circles, her agitation clear. Lilly slipped into the stall.

"Should you go in with her?" Jakob's voice came from close by—he must've followed Lilly in this direction.

"It's all right," she reassured him.

The mare calmed when Lilly stroked her neck.

The mare moved close and stuck her warm, wet nose

behind her ear between her neck and shoulder and nipped at her braid again. Jakob approached the stall; one hand gripped the top rail. Fancy gave her another wet horse kiss, this time right on her ear.

Jakob chuckled. "I remember her doing that when she was a foal. You said it was her way of giving you a hug."

Lilly was more concerned with the still-full feed trough than his words.

"Little Fancy, all grown up and going to be a mama herself. What's that?" Jakob pointed to the hash marks on the opposite wall.

"I've been keeping careful count. Doing what I can to be ready." *Worrying.* Lilly couldn't quite admit to it.

She righted Fancy's water bucket. She'd been trying not to think about the day Fancy was born. But the memories came like flashes of lightning before a downpour.

Arriving home to the livery from school to find Winnie lying on the stall floor in a bed of blood and hay, her breathing sporadic and harsh.

Running to their quarters to find Pa slumped over the table, passed out. An empty bottle of whiskey in front of him.

Back in the barn, the metallic smell of blood.

Lilly blinked against the onslaught of images. Steadied her trembling lips. "I don't want to lose her. Not like . . ." Winnie.

"A breech birth is difficult. Your pa did what he had to do to save Fancy." Years ago, Jakob had arrived at the very moment Lilly had stared at the foal standing on wobbly feet, not knowing what to do.

He was the only reason she hadn't fallen apart. She'd never told him the truth about how they'd lost their prize mare that day.

Jakob's gaze rested on the horse. Lilly turned away so he wouldn't see the old hurt. *She'd* tried to save Winnie. Failed.

Lilly nudged the stall door, Jakob stepped back, and she let herself out of Fancy's stall.

"I should've done more to save her." Lilly instantly wished she could take back the vulnerable words.

"How could you have?" he demanded softly. "Your father delivered . . ." Jakob's voice faltered. "He didn't, did he?" Realization was there in his voice.

"When I raced home from school, she was already almost gone." Lilly whispered the words. Bandit sat on her foot. "He'd passed out—"

"From the bottle," he finished for her.

She nodded, risked a glance at him. Jakob's expression was easy to read this time. No surprise or shock, just quiet compassion.

"You knew."

"I noticed things."

"Why didn't you ever say?" Lilly asked.

"It wasn't my place."

He was right. Pa and those old secrets had been Lilly's burden to bear. No one else's.

She lifted her chin. "The biscuits will be ready to come out of the oven." She skirted around Jakob, but he held out a hand. She paused.

"You were just a girl, Lilly. Not much older than Marta. You are not to blame for Winnie's death."

"I shouldn't have gone to school that day."

She caught his anger in the set of his jaw. "Should you have skipped every day? To keep bad things from happening? Your pa heaped a lot of responsibility on your shoulders. It wasn't yours to carry."

Maybe.

His words dusted her like snowflakes. Not quite sticking.

"This time I will be right here when Fancy goes into labor." She crossed her arms over her chest in determination.

Jakob watched her for a moment before he nodded slowly.

She grew uncomfortable under his scrutiny, and that made her words fall out in a rushed ramble. "I see signs that she is getting closer to foaling. Just today, her milk sack—" She broke off. Stephen's disapproving face popped into her mind. Heat traveled up her neck.

"I'm sorry. I don't know what I was thinking." She started walking toward her rooms, knowing the biscuits must be brown and hot by now. "I shouldn't speak so openly about birthing. It is improper for a woman to speak of such things."

Jakob fell in beside her. He made a scoffing noise in his throat. "Birth is a part of life." His words carried a sense of ease and confidence. They'd both grown up, but he was more at peace, settled in a way she couldn't seem to grasp.

"Stephen didn't like it when I discussed such things." She said over her shoulder. "A *lady* does not talk about such things. Let alone spend her days in the thick of it," she parroted Stephen's words. Why had she brought up Stephen? Their engagement had been over months ago.

Jakob came even with her as they arrived at the door.

"At the farm, we talk about our animals all the time—my sisters and my mother too, all of us." A boyish grin pulled at his lips. "We are happy to speak of such things. There is joy and excitement in waiting, and beauty when the Lord brings new life into the world."

Suddenly the tension that had squeezed at her middle like a saddle cinched too tight, loosened. How she had missed Jakob's plainspoken honesty. Where Jakob saw beauty in the simple rhythms of life, Stephen saw impropriety.

The two men were so different.

She'd thought Jakob was out of her life, like Stephen.

God had brought him to her doorstep. But why?

Three

J AKOB, YOU DO NOT NEED TO MAKE RE-
pairs for me."

Lilly hadn't meant for her voice to be so sharp. She'd just come in from the livery where she finished the last of the watering to find Jakob crouched in front of the corner cabinet, wiggling the leaning door. Since he'd devoured three biscuits and another cup of coffee, he'd filled the wood bin, replenished the water barrel, and tightened the loose slat on one of her chairs.

Maybe he felt as restless as she did, needed an outlet for this energy crackling between them since his expression of compassion outside Fancy's stall.

"I like fixing things," he said over his shoulder.

Her stomach knotted. He probably thought he needed to fix her too. Stephen had.

Bandit bounded through the doorway behind her.

As soon as he spotted Jakob crouched down, he assumed

it was a game and raced over, jumping up and placing his front paws on Jakob's shoulders. Jakob's balance wavered, but he quickly steadied himself and gently pushed the dog off with his elbow and a laugh.

"What? You want to help too?" he asked affectionately.

"Bandit, go lie down." The dog's attention shifted to Lilly. She pointed to the rug near the bed, and the dog obeyed with one more sweep of his tail.

Jakob finished tightening the screws on the old door hinges, pulling the door open and closed a couple of times. The door shut properly now. He stood and rolled his shoulders, his back muscles flexing under the fabric of his shirt. Lilly's eyes lingered longer than she intended. An unexpected rush of warmth spread through her face. She quickly looked away as Jakob turned. Heavens! What nonsense was this? This was Jakob. They were friends, had been since school.

Her eyes caught on the empty coffee cup on the table. She made a beeline to the table, swiped the cup up, and moved to the dry sink where her mixing bowl was still soaking.

"I'll add another log," Jakob said. He grabbed a split log from the bin and moved to the stove.

Wasn't it already too warm in the room? She spread a cloth to set the few dishes on it to dry, but Jakob, towel in hand, had sidled up beside her and reached to take the cup from her hand. For a moment, they held the cup between them.

"You don't have to—"

His brows lifted, and a new intensity flickered in his eyes.

"I know," he said, pulling the cup gently from her grip. His fingers brushed hers, a spark passing between them. She plunged her hands into the now-cool dishwater, clutched the dishrag, and began scrubbing the baking sheet.

She glanced up to see him standing near the bed, his gaze lingering on the satin gloves draped over the portrait's frame.

Pa had always praised Mama for being a great beauty. Lilly had never compared.

"The gloves were my mother's," she said quietly. "She wore them the day she married my father. I thought I would wear them when I married Stephen." Why hadn't she put them away?

Lilly caught the subtle shift in Jakob's posture.

"We don't have to talk about him," he said. "Unless you want to."

"I'm sure you heard the gossip." She scrubbed the dirty pan with more force.

"Some," he said carefully. "Mor taught me to ignore it. That most of it is nonsense."

She bared her teeth in a semblance of a smile. Stephen had broken things off in such a public way. There was no confusion in the words that had been spread around town.

How could it still hurt so badly? It was her pride. All these years spent trying to prove she belonged.

She put the clean pan on a towel laid on the tiny bit of counter space and looked at her hands before she plunged them back in the sudsy water. Imagine those delicate gloves on her work-hardened hands!

It didn't work.

But she'd once believed it could. Somehow. Pa had pushed her to consider Stephen. Called her first—and only—suitor a fine, hardworking businessman. She had to swallow a lump in her throat as she remembered the joy on her pa's face when she'd accepted Stephen's proposal.

Pa had wanted her to become a genteel woman like her mother had been. But Lilly wasn't that woman. And never would be.

"I'm glad we didn't marry," she said, not quite able to meet Jakob's gaze.

Jakob's chin jerked up. "I thought you wanted to marry him."

She'd never wanted anything but to run the livery with Pa. She'd thought she loved Stephen, but now she knew she'd loved the idea of being with someone who wanted her for herself.

"I was mistaken. About all of it. I couldn't be the woman he wanted."

Jakob shook his head. "Maybe the problem was with him. I think you would be a good helpmate to any man."

She caught the slight wince as he said the words.

Jakob was a good friend to say so. But her engagement to Stephen had exposed her flaws. She was not like other women.

"Did you know Stephen's parents saw an opportunity to expand their business? They bought another small hotel in Rock Springs. Stephen jumped at the chance to be out from under his father's watchful eyes."

It was the only saving grace for her now. Stephen no longer resided in Calvin. She didn't have to see him every day around town.

"He would have taken you away from your home here in Calvin and your horses?" Jakob chewed on that thought for a long moment. "The town would suffer. People depend on you here."

She took a deep, satisfying breath and let his words soothe her. Jakob understood intuitively what Stephen refused to see. Lilly needed the livery and to stay connected to the town of Calvin, the only place where she had roots.

"After Pa passed, Stephen wanted me to spend less time at the livery. He wanted me to be more of a partner to him. Someone who threw fancy dinner parties. Could hold a conversation with the mayor or other business owners."

He had wanted Lilly to trade her work clothes for fancy dresses and tea in a parlor that smelled of roses and polish. He couldn't fathom that she didn't want the same thing. *What kind of woman prefers horse manure and hay?*

"I can't see you like that." Jakob sounded genuinely stumped.

Agitated, she stalked to the stove, then pulled over a pot that rested on the right back burner and dumped the beans into it. Snatching a wooden spoon from a crock on the side shelf, she turned to Jakob, who'd side-stepped a few feet away from the stove to give her space.

"That night at the hotel, while we were eating, he issued an ultimatum. I had to give up the livery and go with him." *No wife of mine is going to smell like manure.* "I couldn't do it," she admitted.

Jakob frowned fiercely. "Barclay is a proud man."

She stiffened her shoulders and attacked the beans, scraping the spoon against the bottom of the pot. The sound grated.

She had hurt Stephen's pride, and he had publicly humiliated her by breaking off their engagement in a room full of diners. People at church still whispered. Conversations stopped abruptly when she passed by on the boardwalk. But she'd caught snippets. *Poor Lilly, she couldn't keep her man. A man wants a homemaker.* They were right. She wasn't wife material.

She dropped the spoon in the pot and whirled round. Brushing past Jakob, she marched to the bed, plucking the ornate gloves from the portrait frame. Her hands looked clumsy and too large just holding them.

She held the gloves out to Jakob.

"I'm never getting married. Give these to one of your sisters."

I'm never getting married.

The words circled around Jakob's brain and stuck in the pit of his stomach.

Lilly had put a plate of beans and leftover biscuits on the table before him, but Jakob couldn't lift the spoon to eat it. Not with his insides twisted up like they were.

She'd moved to sit on the edge of the bed, bent over an

old bridle. She leaned closer to the lamp beside her and cleaned the dirt and grime from the old leather.

He couldn't let her declaration pass.

"You cannot be serious," he said, his tone gruffer than he intended.

She looked up from her work. "I am." Her spine went as straight as the wooden stiles on the chair.

"Barclay was a fool. You are not." And so was he, with his tongue-tied shyness around her.

By keeping his distance from her even after Barclay had skipped town, he'd added to her feelings of inadequacy.

"There are plenty of men in Calvin who admire you and would be proud to take you as a wife." He looked at the wall as his face burned.

She lifted her brows, green eyes flashing in the lamplight.

"You mean like Ike Miller?" She meant it as a joke, he could see it in the curl of her lips, her smile too false to be real.

"I would have married you," he blurted.

Her eyes flew to his face.

He hadn't meant to say it. Didn't mean to look at her, but the vulnerable light in her eyes meant foolish words kept falling from his lips.

"I asked your pa if I could come courting. Before Barclay put that ring on your finger," he admitted.

Her fingers flexed on the bridle leather. "You did not!" He saw the flare of her nostrils, the pinch of her lips.

"I did," he said, his voice low. "I came to your father before Barclay." That morning was burned into his memories.

He'd gathered all his courage and come to see her pa when he knew Lilly would be gone.

"Pa never said anything."

"I figured as much."

Her pa hadn't said anything to *her*. He'd said plenty to Jakob. He closed his eyes, cheeks burning as he remembered Angus Murdock's words, the way he'd looked Jakob up and down. *You can't give her what Barclay can. I want more for her. More than a husband who can barely speak our language, a farmer who will struggle to eke out a living from the land. She's not the woman for you, Jakob. She wants a better life.*

Humiliation had washed over him. Humiliation and anger. How could Murdock know what she wanted when he could barely drag himself away from the bottle?

"I've only ever thought of you as a friend." Lilly's voice softened with the admission. She stood from the bed, leaving the bridle lying on the quilt. Paced to the window and back.

He looked down at the scarred wood of the table.

"I figured that too," he said with a chagrined laugh. Jakob had debated going against her father's wishes. Asking her to go courting with him.

He'd fought with himself for too long. She'd accepted Barclay's proposal before Jakob had worked up the courage to say anything to her about his own feelings.

"Jakob—" Lilly started to say something then broke off.

He cut his eyes from the table to the stove. He didn't want to see her pity.

The wind blasted snow against the windows hard enough

to rattle them. It'd been snowing all day, adding to what had already accumulated from the past week's weather.

A foreboding groan echoed through the silence. The hair at the back of his neck rose.

The stovepipe shifted. Wispy clouds of smoke seeped out of the top of the stovepipe. Urgency drove Jakob out of his chair toward the stove.

No, not the stovepipe—the ceiling.

He thought the groaning sound was just the wind, but it was coming from the wood.

"Lilly, get back."

"What is it?"

He was aware of her stepping toward him instead of away. He waved one arm, unable to look away from the splintering wood.

"The roof—"

The rafters keened.

"Lilly!" he shouted. "Run!"

The creaking sound intensified, filling his ears.

He turned and she was *right there*.

She must've seen the fear in his eyes. By the time he'd reached out to push her or grab her up and run—he hadn't decided which—she was already in motion.

The dog leaped from its place in the corner, tangling with Jakob's boots. Slowed him down a step, and by the time he'd righted his feet, Lilly and the dog were in the doorway.

Good—

A terrible sound roared, and the ceiling fell in.

Jakob tried to jump toward the door, but something huge crashed into his back, hot enough to burn through his shirt. He got knocked in the head and everything went black.

Four

L ILLY'S HOME WAS DESTROYED.
Jakob stood in the doorway of Lilly's quarters, an arm braced against the doorframe.

His head pounded and the adrenaline of dragging himself up and out of the debris of the collapsed roof was fading—as was the memory of Lilly's voice crying out—and without the distraction, he felt every forming bruise, every scrape, and the burn that seemed to stretch across his back from the top of his right shoulder almost to his waist. Every time he breathed, pain seared through him.

He peered through the smoke and dust at the damage. An entire corner of the roof had caved in. Planks and wood pieces and shingles covered nearly every surface, while two rafter beams hung precariously above. The stove pipe lay dented on the floor between the stove and the iron bed. Snow swirled inside and scattered in all directions.

"I need to make sure the fire is out," Lilly said from where she hovered beside him.

"Yes." He could see the swirls of smoke still rising from the stove, now partially covered with wood. Lilly would be worried that if a spark escaped, the entire structure could catch fire.

But she didn't move into the room, instead turned toward him, her face pale and eyes red and watery. "Are you sure you're all right?" Her voice held a waver that he hadn't heard in years.

"I just need to catch my breath." He would tell her about the burn soon enough. Right now, it was more important that they salvage what they could from her quarters and close off the room. At least the damage was contained in this one place. The barn itself wasn't affected.

Lilly backed into the barn, and when he saw her grabbing a bucket to pull water from the barrel in the middle of the stable, he followed and got one too. In moments, they were picking their way through the debris, edging carefully to the stove to douse whatever flames were left inside.

"It's my fault," Lilly said as she stepped over a broken board. "I kept putting it off. I should have kept the roof in better repair." He heard the self-recrimination in her voice.

"Don't, Lilly, there isn't time to—"

He jumped when a couple of shingles slipped off the hole in the roof and tumbled inside, followed by a pile of snow that plopped on the floor.

After both buckets of water were dumped on the fire, Lilly left him to stir the now-soaking ashes. She bent at the corner cabinet and began collecting the dry goods into a large mixing bowl and her empty water bucket.

Hurry, hurry. He tromped out of her quarters to get one more bucket of water.

By the time he'd returned, she'd tossed the foodstuffs and a couple of clothing items that had been hanging on the wall into the barn, just beyond the doorway. He skirted them and went back inside, picking his way carefully back to the stove.

She was rummaging beneath the corner of the bed.

"We have to hurry," he urged. More snow was piling on the roof and he couldn't tell whether it was the wind causing the creaking or the roof itself. Would more of it cave in? He didn't want her anywhere near if that happened.

The ashes hissed and sputtered as he poured the last of his water on. He secured the stove door, knowing that it was as wet as he could make it right now.

"I can't—can you fetch this trunk for me?"

She moved out of the way as he squatted next to the bed and felt for the handle. The trunk was good and stuck— because the fallen rafter and boards had plunged straight down into the bed. His memory flashed to the moments when Lilly had stood near the bed, explaining about her mother's gloves. The very spot the roof had caved in.

What if it had been the middle of the night when the roof had caved in? What if she'd been sleeping in that bed, been crushed by the weight of the rafters and boards?

She could have died.

He gave a great heave, and the trunk came free.

"It's time to go," he said, and if his voice was too sharp, it was because of the way his chest was pinched tight, thinking of what might have happened.

He lifted the trunk and made his way carefully to the door, meeting her there. She paused for a moment, her arms full of a mishmash of cups and plates. Her gaze scanned the room behind him, and he caught the flash of sorrow and frustration.

If he'd been a better friend and visited her in town more often, he would have already taken care of the build-up of snow on the roof. Not all the blame for this disaster was Lilly's to accept.

The aisle outside the lean-to was piled up with a line of chairs, crates, bowls, blankets, and sundry bits and pieces stacked alongside.

His shoulder ached as he followed Lilly down the center aisle, dragging the trunk behind him. Bandit appeared and took up the rear. They stopped in the large area in front of the barn door where he'd parked his wagon this morning. Was it only this morning? It was coming on evening now.

He set down the trunk away from the fragile cups and plates she'd rescued. When he straightened, his burned skin stretched, and fiery pain shot through his shoulder and back. He was grateful for the momentary reprieve, a chance to catch his breath. The aches and bruises were getting worse.

He didn't realize Lilly had been watching him until she blurted, "Jakob, your shirt—it's burned!" She hurried to his side, eyes narrowing as she got closer. "Is that blood?"

"It will keep. Let's make sure you have everything you need."

"There's nothing else." Her eyes flicked to the small pile—all her worldly possessions in a meager, messy stack on the barn floor. When her gaze bounced back to his face, her jaw was set with determination.

"You're not fine," she mumbled as she hurried toward the tack wall.

She returned carrying a small round tin of ointment and a rolled bandage in one hand, a bucket of clean water in the other, and a cloth draped over her shoulder.

"Sit. I'll have a look now," she ordered.

When he didn't move, she huffed in frustration, her brows lifting. "Stop being stubborn."

Now that the adrenaline was wearing off, the burning on his back had intensified. He sighed and stepped in front of the trunk, muttering, "I am not the stubborn one here."

As he lowered himself on the trunk, he saw the worry in her eyes.

"You'll have to remove your shirt," she said, ducking her eyes and setting the water and the ointment on the trunk and moving behind him. He unbuttoned his shirt and removed one arm. When he tried to remove the other, the shirt stuck to his back. The scorching pipe must have burned through his shirt and several layers of skin. The leaking wound had all but glued the shirt to his back. He yanked at it and felt his skin tear. Pain radiated down his arm.

"Oh, Jakob. Stop. Let me help you."

There was no time to brace himself for her touch. Her fingers, feather light, brushed his shoulder as she clasped the shirt. His breath hitched. He stiffened his muscles against a tremor.

"It's not the first time I've been burned. Don't fret, Lilly."

She exhaled on a huff. "I will fret, Jakob Anderson!" She placed a warm palm on his bare back and gently tugged the shirt loose with her other hand. The exposed burn felt like a dozen tiny fires along his back.

He heard a soft splash, then water dripping as she wrung out a cloth before dabbing at the wound.

He hunched his shoulders and stared at the stall door, homing in on the metal latch.

"Try to relax. I'm not going to hurt you," she said, her voice soft as she dabbed further down his back.

He sucked in a breath as goose bumps rose on his neck and shoulders.

Suddenly, she blurted, "I had heard you'd sent for a wife from one of your kinfolks in Minnesota."

When her words registered, his face burned hotter than his wound.

He placed his hands on his thighs, studying the soot and dirt that marked them.

"It's true," he said, working to keep his voice steady. "Mor decided it was time for her oldest son to marry and give her some grandchildren." His mother had worried about him after he'd lost Lilly's friendship.

"You always said you wanted a big family like yours," she ventured.

He did. But he'd always imagined he'd have a family with her.

Out of the corner of his eye, he saw her set aside the wet

cloth and open the tin of ointment, releasing a faint whiff of camphor.

He needed a distraction, so he kept talking. "Mor had written letters to her cousin in Minnesota since we moved to Wyoming. A cousin twice removed has a daughter. I wrote to her, we exchanged letters over the past year. My mor and I invited her to come and see our home and farm."

He inhaled deeply, holding his breath as he waited for her touch again.

"Did she come?" she asked, placing her left hand on his back, leaning down to get a closer look. He felt her warm breath on the back of his neck, a sensation that sent a wave of heat through him.

"She did." He flinched slightly when she dabbed on the ointment.

She stilled, her breath catching. For a moment, her hand lingered. Jakob's mind raced—*Are the burns worse than I thought?* But then he realized what had caught her attention, the old scar from when he'd been backed into barbed wire by an ornery cow. He had others. His gaze went to his hands again. Farmer's hands. He turned them over, taking in the thin white lines and thick calluses. Barclay wouldn't have rough hands like his.

"And?" she asked, her voice only a breath as her fingers spread more salve on the burned area.

He twisted around. Her green eyes were wide, and her cheeks had flushed deep pink.

"Since Gunnar was already in Chicago, he was tasked to accompany her from Minnesota."

He watched her spine go straight. Her brows furrowed,

and her eyes sparked fire. She had already put two and two together. Or in this case, one and one—Gunnar and Astrid. His shoulders slumped. Could he get any more pathetic? Two women who chose other men over him.

"Astrid was your intended?" she asked, her voice rising in disbelief.

He didn't reply, just nodded once and lowered his gaze.

"Why, that little fox! He was always a rascal." She gave a sharp, angry huff. "He knew more English than he let on at school. Used those big blue eyes and sad smile to wheedle the answers to our geography assignment out of Mary Hopkins. I am surprised he found his way back from Chicago!"

He snorted out a laugh that felt like a release. His chest eased, the weight of his disappointment easing with her taking up his cause.

"They fell in love." He shrugged, then grimaced through the pain.

"He stole your bride." Her voice bristled with indignation on his behalf. She snatched up a rolled bandage and moved to stand in front of him.

"What could I do in such circumstances? You cannot make people love you," he said.

"She would have loved you had your brother not intervened. How could she not?" His eyes locked with hers. Suddenly, the tension between them was tighter than the barbed wire fence that had cut him. As if any moment it might snap. She looked away. Still, her words were more of a balm to his wounded pride than the salve she had put on his burn.

Lilly made short work of applying a bandage to the burn. The tricky part was to keep talking as she leaned in close to wind a long piece of cotton around his torso. He breathed in the faint flowery scent of her, and sucked in his gut, every muscle tensing.

"When Gunnar and Astrid arrived back at home, I could see something was going on between them." He frowned, recalling the agony on his brother's face when he confessed his love for Astrid.

When Lilly finished the bandaging, he stood and faced her, the trunk between them. Her eyes caught on his exposed bare chest before she snatched up his shirt, shook it out, eyed the burn hole, then set it aside. She rummaged through the pile of items on the floor, found an old carpet bag, and pulled out a wrinkled but clean men's shirt, one of her father's.

"You didn't fight for her? No fisticuffs in the barn over the beautiful bride?" The teasing was back in her voice. He shook his head.

"I could see Astrid wanted him too. What was there to fight for?"

She held up the shirt, ready to help him into it, then stunned him by asking, "What about what you want, Jakob? You don't always have to play the martyr, you know."

As he slid his arm into the sleeve, her hands trembled, and her lashes fluttered against her flushed cheeks. The air felt as thick as honey, making it hard to breathe but undeniably sweet.

He stared at her as he fastened a button. He longed to say he had what he wanted standing right in front of him.

She released a heavy sigh, her gaze dropping for a moment, then sliding back to his.

"You didn't really love her. If you had, you would have fought for her."

"Are you certain you don't want me to drag the camping stove out here?" Jakob's voice carried from the cluttered annex at the back of the livery to where Lilly was forking hay into the small buckboard wagon she'd chosen to make her bed for the night.

"I'm sure it's not in working condition," she called back.

"It looks all right to me." His head popped out of the room.

She tipped her head toward the pile of hay cascading out of one of the stalls where she'd stored it. "I don't want to take any chances. There's too much flammable material inside this barn."

He wrinkled his nose and disappeared again.

An hour had passed since the roof had collapsed. Since she'd doctored Jakob's injury.

She was relieved when he'd broken away after that to pile hay in his own wagon and then wander into the annex.

She was less relieved that things wouldn't be as proper as she had planned before. Now she would be sleeping in the same room as Jakob.

It shouldn't matter.

She was never getting married. She'd told him so.

Now she called out, "It's always been warm enough for the horses. And we can bundle up in our coats if need be."

She lifted her gaze to the thick beams that held up the roof of the livery. The wind battered the walls, and snow still fell, but the structure of the livery was solid. Snow and wind wouldn't take them down. But fire? It was too big a risk. Pa might've had his faults, but he'd always cautioned her against the danger of fire in a barn like this.

Jakob left the annex, moved across the wide aisle to his own wagon, and began spreading an old quilt over the layer of hay.

He'd pushed aside the supplies he'd ridden into town for, several sacks and wooden crates were stacked to one side of his wagon. With his injuries, his movements had become stiff, and he favored his right side.

"The temperature will drop again. Even with the straw and extra blankets, it's going to get very cold by morning," he warned, genuine concern in his voice.

"I'm certain."

Jakob nodded his easy acceptance, climbed down from the wagon, his back and shoulders rigid. She noticed the slight wince as his boots hit the floor. Unlike Stephen, who would have argued or bullied her into submission, Jakob was not a bit patronizing—he trusted her judgment.

But she could tell he wanted to take care of her because he truly cared for her. This was the Jakob she had known growing up, so why did she feel so disconcerted by him?

She folded another quilt and set it at the foot of the small wagon they had pulled from the wing opposite the horse stalls and angled it with Jakob's parked in front of the stable door. A warm light from a lamp on the trunk stationed in front of both their wagons flickered, casting shadows on

Jakob's handsome form. She was aware of his closeness in a way she hadn't been earlier.

I asked your father to court you.

Something had changed between them after he'd admitted he had wanted to court her. She couldn't reconcile it.

He'd fancied her in that way a man fancied a woman. She'd only ever thought of him as a boy, but after she'd doctored him, one thing had been clear. Jakob was no longer a boy, but a handsome, virile man. And he had fancied her once.

Agitation drove her into the bed of hay and blankets before she was ready. She didn't know what to do with the jitters racing through her. After Stephen had broken their engagement so publicly, Lilly had thought the part of her that could fall in love again was gone forever.

But somehow, with Jakob, the flutters in her belly were back.

This would never do.

She heard Jakob's throaty chuckle and couldn't resist raising up on one elbow to peer over the wagon bed. Bandit had jumped onto Jakob's tailgate, and the man was scratching his chest while the dog fawned over the attention. Jakob was good with animals. Always had been.

He must've sensed her watching, even though he didn't turn his head.

"Do you miss being with your family? Won't Marta be angry with you for missing Christmas?" Lilly blurted the question so she wouldn't ask something more personal.

"Last year she didn't notice when I got trapped in the barn overnight in that bad storm."

"You did?"

He moved his hand to scratch Bandit's ear now. The dog was eating up the extra attention. "It was before Christmas, though. And I made it back to the house fine in the morning. What about you? Were you stranded with another traveler who planned badly?"

She smiled a little. Last December, there'd been a big storm that had trapped folks inside for three days straight.

"Pa and I spent the time together. I didn't realize at the time—" That it would be their last Christmas together. She'd been worried that Stephen would be angry that she'd missed a planned evening together. But those memories of that last Christmas together were irreplaceable.

Jakob's smile said he understood. He motioned for the dog to get down. "Go on, go sleep by Lilly."

Bandit jumped off his wagon and quickly crossed to hop into hers. He made a circle and then curled up on Lilly's feet.

She settled back into the nest of hay as Jakob's wagon creaked as he climbed inside.

It was strange to be here, in two separate wagons only a stone's throw apart.

He put out the lantern, and darkness descended.

Who could sleep with this invisible tension coiling between them in the dark?

She tried to distract herself with thoughts of the one Christmas she'd spent with Jakob's family, when she'd been about thirteen. Her pa had come down with a nasty case of the flu, and Jakob's mother had insisted Lilly come to stay.

She'd found a Christmas sock hung on the mantel for her

on Christmas morning. She'd forgotten about it. Hadn't thought about it in years.

Being with Jakob was bringing back many old memories.

"Good night, Lilly," Jakob called softly.

She released the breath she hadn't realized she was holding. It was the first time since Pa passed that someone wished her good night.

"Good night, Jakob," she returned.

One of the horses blew. Another stomped.

Her thoughts whirled until she was dizzy with them.

Her rooms were destroyed. Should she rent a room at one of the boarding houses? No, she needed the money to buy materials to fix the roof.

Jakob had asked her father to court her!

What would it be like to spend another Christmas with Jakob's family?

She rolled to her back, pulling the blankets up to her chin and staring into the black.

She needed to sleep. Tomorrow would be another day filled with hard work and worry.

Tomorrow was Christmas Eve! Her own words to Marshal O'Grady came back to her.

I think the lesson is about making room for the Savior.

God had seemed far away this past year. Was it because she had not made room for Him?

Had she shut Him out like the folks in Bethlehem?

Pa was gone.

Stephen had abandoned her.

But Jakob, her friend, was back.

And everything had changed.

Five

J AKOB CLUTCHED THE SATCHEL TO HIS chest as he slogged through the deep snow back to the livery from one of Lilly's closest neighbors, Jack and Merritt Easton. It was past daybreak, but with the thick cloud cover and snow, one couldn't tell.

The wind picked up again and blew snow into his face. He blinked it away, kept his eyes on the livery as he edged along the fence of the small pasture between the two places. He'd not slept well. Lilly's words played over and over in his mind with each knee-deep step. *You didn't love her. You didn't fight for her.* Each repetition dug deeper, like the sharp blade of a plow cutting into fallow ground. He hadn't fought for Astrid because he didn't love her. His heart had always belonged to Lilly. Why hadn't he fought for Lilly?

Because he was a coward. He was afraid what her pa said was true . . . that he wasn't enough—couldn't give her what she deserved. Afraid she wouldn't choose him over

Barclay. So, he'd just given up and gone home to the farm to lick his wounds and put his boyhood dreams away. And then he'd walked into the livery yesterday and everything had changed.

Or maybe he was the one who had changed. This time he would not let his fears win. This time he would be the kind of man who fought, patiently, with a plan. He was a farmer after all, he knew how to plant, nurture, and wait for the time of harvest.

He would help her repair the roof.

He would visit her often, renew their friendship.

He would find ways to tell her she was a woman he admired.

And then he would reveal his deepening feelings.

He slipped back into the livery, closing the door on the howling wind. The dim light inside the livery was a stark contrast to the blinding white of the snowstorm outside. He closed his eyes, breathed deeply. The warmer air was thick with the familiar smells of hay, leather, and horses. His back and shoulder protested slightly as he shifted the weight of his bag, the burn still a dull ache under his shirt.

Everything was quiet until Bandit greeted him with a happy woof, tail wagging. Pia nickered from her stall. Jakob stomped the snow from his boots as quietly as he could manage and crept toward the wagons. He set the satchel on the trunk and froze as he lifted his head and caught the movement from Lilly's wagon.

Lilly sat up in her pallet, pulling the quilt up to her chin. Her eyes caught on his face, and her expression went soft, pink lips curving into a gentle smile. Her hair, freed from the usual tight braid, spilled around her shoulders in loose waves. Her delicate eyelashes fluttered as she blinked away the sleep. A rush of tenderness washed over him. He'd always thought her beautiful, but this morning, his chest felt tight. Seeing her like this, so unguarded, made him ache with longing. What he wouldn't give to wake up with her like this every morning.

"Jakob?" Her voice was a husky whisper, but the moment she saw his snow-crusted coat and the satchel, she stiffened her spine. "You went out in the storm?" The sharp note of concern in her voice gave him hope.

He pulled off one stiff glove and then the other, placing them on the box board of the wagon to dry.

"Just crossed over to Jack and Merritt's." He lifted the satchel. "I wasn't sure what we could use for breakfast without a cookstove. I brought coffee," he said, pulling out a jar filled with dark brown liquid, still hot, and setting it on the trunk.

"Has the storm let up, then?" she asked, straightening her blouse and pulling down her sleeves. She looked up and caught his slight hesitation. Snow dropped to the floor as he unwrapped his scarf.

"It hasn't," she accused, lifting a boot and sliding a foot out from under the quilt. "You should not have risked it. What if you—"

"Lilly." He saw the worry in her eyes and cut her off. "I was careful. Stayed on the fence line, then tied a rope off from the fence to the woodshed at the back of Jack and Merrit's house." He kept his face averted as he said, "After all that happened yesterday, I wanted to do this small thing for you. There is coffee and some bread, and even a bit of ham."

He risked a glance at her. Something chased through her eyes before she dropped her gaze. He saw her shiver as she tossed back the blankets and pulled on a thick wool sweater. It was too cold in here. His mind went to the small stove in the annex again. The storm meant no repairs to the roof—maybe not until spring. She meant to stay in the livery indefinitely. She'd said so. She would need a way to stay warm.

He took her hand as she climbed down from the wagon. Her stomach gurgled, and she let out an embarrassed laugh.

Her hair hid her face as she pulled plates and cups from the crate and set them onto the trunk. He couldn't help but relish the touch of her fingers against his, her sweet blush.

As they finished the quiet meal, she shivered again. He figured now was as good a time as any to broach the subject. "If you are determined to stay here in the livery until the weather warms enough for the roof to get repaired, you're going to need a stove. I'll pull that old stove out here and clean it up."

She gazed toward the annex, her eyes distant. "That stove has to be at least twenty years old. Pa bought it thinking it would bring in extra income—there are probably some soldering irons stored back there too from when Pa repaired pots and pans and tools." She frowned at the memory. "Pa had lots of ideas. Only most of them never panned out." She hitched her chin stubbornly. Shook her head. "That stove hasn't been used in years. Since a camping trip he and I took when I was little."

She'd gone from an outright no yesterday to reminiscing about the stove. Was she changing her mind?

"I'll clean it up, check it over."

She sipped her coffee, peered at him over the rim of the cup, and relented with a nod.

He stuffed the last bit of bread in his mouth and rose from his chair while she stacked their plates. He reached for his cup before she could grab it and drained the last of the dark brew, then hurried to the annex before she could reconsider.

He heard her grumble something that ended with, "Stubborn man."

A grin tugged at his lips. She had given in, trusted him. It was a start. He paused in the annex doorway and turned to watch her.

She began the morning chores, starting with the mustang who was ready to bust out of his stall like a racehorse at the starting line.

"Can't let you outside, but let's take a walk about," he heard her say. Her calm but firm voice gentled the horse. She slipped on a halter and attached a lead rope. She walked the horse by their wagons, into the buggy storage area, and circled round ready to pass the annex.

He spun into the room, pushed aside a barrel, and rolled an old wheel aside, freeing a path to the small cast-iron camp stove. The top had a small cooking surface at the front and a stout chimney at the back. Pain stabbed at his shoulder as he dragged the short, stocky stove to the aisle where the light was better.

Ike's mule began braying. The stall door rattled when he kicked it as Lilly passed by, leading the mustang.

"That mule is as ornery as Ike," Jakob commented without looking up as she passed by him too. Everyone in town knew Ike and his reputation.

"Festus is determined to escape this stall and explore the world." She offered him a wry smile over her shoulder.

"You still name them all?" Jakob knew Ike wasn't the kind of man to give his mule a name.

"I can't seem to help myself." Her eyes held the familiar twinkle that had drawn him to her from the beginning.

He watched her carry the water down to the end of the aisle. She hesitated outside of Fancy's stall, concern furrowing her brow. She disappeared into another stall at the same moment that Festus appeared in the aisle. Jakob blinked. The mule was loose, stall door wide open.

"Lilly?" He pitched his voice so it would carry to her.

She stepped into the aisle and spotted Festus.

"Why, you wily creature. Did you loosen the latch again?" Lilly strode forward and pulled the mule back into his stall.

Jakob glanced at the latch. Was it broken?

As if she'd read his thoughts, Lilly said, "Festus figured out how to open the latch during his second week boarding here. If he starts to feel too cooped up"—she tipped her head to the window to indicate the howling wind and snow—"he makes it a game to escape his stall."

Jakob made a mental note to fix the latch later.

He squatted in front of the stove and opened the firebox door. Bandit was back, sidling so close his front paw covered Jakob's boot. He carried a stick in his mouth. Jakob scratched him behind the ears without thinking. Lilly approached, carrying an empty bucket in each hand.

"The stove's a little dusty, but the inside is clean and the grate is in good repair," Jakob said. Bandit moved in even closer, his shoulder pressing into Jakob's hip.

"You can push him away, you know," Lilly said.

Jakob peered down at Bandit from under his lashes. Something in the expression in the dog's almond-shaped eyes rooted out a memory. Jakob sitting on a grassy hill looking over the neat rows of newly plowed fields, Bjorn, a Lapphund, a common Swedish farm dog, warm and wiggling by his side. His inky black fur, dense and straight around his head, and his small triangular ears and pointed muzzle made him look like the bear he'd been named for. The dog had grown up with him and followed him everywhere.

Until his father had moved their family to America.

It had been a long time since he'd let himself think about Bjorn.

"He reminds me of a dog I had as a boy," he said, his voice sounding a bit rough to his ears.

He caught Lilly's curious expression as she scooped feed into the trough inside the nearest stall. "I didn't even know you liked dogs. Or should I say that dogs liked you so well? You've won Bandit's affection in less than a day. He looks like he's smitten every time he lays eyes on you. He whined for his owner for weeks after he was left here. Spent hours by the window near the door. Just waiting. It was rather heartbreaking to watch. Then he attached himself to me, wouldn't let me even a few yards out of his sight. Most of the time, he's right on my heels, tripping me up."

"Someone left him here?" Jakob stroked the dog, running his big hand over his head and down his neck. Bandit lifted his chin and closed his eyes in contentment.

Lilly nodded.

"Last roundup. Cowboy from Quade's ranch. Never returned."

Jakob's throat tightened. He knew what it was like to leave a dog behind. "Maybe he couldn't return," he said finally.

Lilly studied him, her expression softening. "Is that what happened to you?"

He turned his attention to the stove, straightened the grate inside the fire box.

He hadn't thought about Bjorn in a long time. It was easier to box up the old hurt and put it away. But maybe for Lilly, he could talk about it.

"He was our family dog. Bred to help on the farm in Sweden. But—he was my best friend. And when our family had to leave on the boat, we couldn't bring him with us."

He missed Bjorn. Still. Months after they had settled near Calvin, Jakob's father had tried to fill the gaping hole. The puppy he'd brought home to the farm had been cute and as friendly as Bandit was now. But all those years ago, Jakob hadn't wanted a *replacement*. Couldn't accept the new puppy. He hadn't had the courage to open his heart up to an animal like that again.

"Doesn't seem right that you had to leave your friend

behind," she said quietly as she moved down the aisle and filled another feed trough for a nickering horse.

He tried the stove door because it was easier than looking at her. When it squeaked badly, he reached for the oil can to put a drop on the hinge.

"I am the eldest, it was important to be brave for the others," he said. But on that ship, all those weeks, with the rough waves tossing them about, how he had longed for his best friend.

"You've always been brave for them. A good brother and son." Her gaze traveled down the row of stalls, then back to him. Her expression held a mix of empathy and affection.

When Jakob stood, Bandit sat on his feet. He couldn't help looking down at the dog and that silly, lolling tongue as Lilly's quiet words met his ears.

"Perhaps the brave thing to do now is to let yourself get attached."

She wasn't really hiding from Jakob, Lilly told herself even as she kept her head ducked and brushed Buttercup's thick winter coat for the second time inside his stall. She just needed a reprieve from Jakob's distracting presence.

Having him here hauling water, teasing about Ike . . . every time she caught Jakob's warm gaze from across the barn, something inside her lit up.

She had her friend back.

Over the past months, she hadn't realized just how lonely her life had become. When Jakob had teased that he was going to give her a new latch for Festus's stall for Christmas, she'd grown pensive. She hadn't planned on giving or receiving any Christmas gifts this year.

She didn't know what to do with the hope and anticipation that having Jakob back in her life was making her feel.

She took a deep, steadying breath and steeled herself to leave the stall. Jakob moved into the aisle and gestured for her to join him.

"Come, Lilly, I have the stove set up," he called out.

He'd positioned it in the space between the front door and the stable door, well away from the walls and the wagons. An oval metal bin with kindling and split logs sat ready a few feet away.

Jakob crouched in front of the stove and opened the firebox door as she joined him.

Inside, the kindling had been lit, and orange flames licked at thin branches, hungry for a larger split log. He took one from the bin and laid it on the fire, tiny sparks rose from the small pile. Still, a flutter of nerves washed over her.

"The fire is small and contained inside the stove, but it will give you enough heat to take the chill from the air."

"I don't know." Every time she walked past the door to her living quarters, she remembered the terror of the roof caving in on top of Jakob.

Lilly had known better than to let the piles of snow build up. Marshal O'Grady had reminded her of what she'd already known. But Lilly had put it off, ignored the danger.

She didn't know whether she could ignore having a fire inside the livery. All it would take was one spark to catch the dry hay on fire. Light up the entire structure like a tinderbox.

Jakob scraped a hand through his beard and dropped it to his side. Then lifted it again and motioned to the stove.

"It's several feet from anything that could catch fire," he reasoned. "Your water barrels are nearby."

He was right.

The cold in the barn had grown as the afternoon had worn on. She'd tossed and turned last night with the chilly air nipping at her exposed face. There were more months of winter to survive before spring arrived and she could rebuild.

He saw her vacillating and gently said, "Lilly, you cannot control everything—"

"It's better when I do." She instantly wished she could call back the revealing words. Warmth prickled over her neck and cheeks even as she shivered.

He watched her with an assessing gaze. "Your pa should've fixed the roof years ago."

"Pa hadn't been running the livery's operations for a long time," she said idly, watching one of the horses. "I was."

"I hadn't realized things had gotten so bad."

Blaze snorted and stomped from his stall nearby, reminding Lilly of the day of the almost tragedy. She shrugged, trying to release some of the tension from her shoulders. "Some days were better than others. I could never predict when the wound he'd suffered long ago would act up. Or his memories would eat at him.

"Then one day, a family came to rent a horse and buggy. They had a little boy, two or three years old. Pa didn't see him break away from his mother's hand. The boy wandered behind King, our big black Morgan, and startled him. Pa had been drinking, and in his drunken state, he lost his grip on the lead rope and King pranced backward." Lilly had seen it unfolding, knew the big horse would crush the child. "I stepped in just in time, scooping the boy up and out of the horse's path. I got stepped on."

"Was that when you limped around for two weeks?"

He remembered that?

When she glanced at him, she saw a muscle ticking in his jaw.

"You said you'd closed your foot in the barn door," he said tightly.

"No one knew," she explained. "Or I thought no one did."

The memory of the boy's father was so fresh, she could almost smell the fresh hay on that sunny day. Remember the boy's father coming to grab his son away from Pa, getting close enough to smell Pa's breath. And the whiskey on it.

The man's anger had been quickly banked. He'd stalked out, taking his family with him.

And the livery had lost a paying customer.

She'd been eleven. And she'd known that if they were to stay in business, she would need to make sure something like that never happened again. She would have to take charge of the livery stable. And try to take charge of her father.

Lilly wrapped her arms around her own waist. "How could I both love him and hate him?"

Jakob hesitated, but came close to her side, pressed one hand against her lower back.

"You were not much older than Marta. It wasn't right for you to bear the weight of such responsibility."

She leaned her head against his shoulder. She didn't know whether that was true. She'd simply done what had to be done.

"Would you ask Marta to run this place?" His words were a rumble beneath her cheek.

She hadn't seen Marta in eighteen months. Not since she'd accepted Stephen's proposal. Marta had a sweet, gentle spirit. She was lively. Loved to read.

She was a child.

And no, it wouldn't be fair to Marta to expect her to run the livery on her own.

Lilly had survived it. She loved the livery, and the animals.

It wasn't right. Jakob's words made her throat thick and her eyes sting.

She tipped her face upward, and his blue eyes locked with hers. He was so close.

His gaze dropped to her lips, and for a breathless moment, she wondered what it would be like to kiss him. Her pulse rushed in her ears.

One of the horses stomped and bumped the stall wall. The abrupt sound jolted Lilly. She whirled away, blurting, "Leave the stove for now."

Her face scalded with the realization of what she'd almost done.

She'd nearly kissed Jakob.

Six

THEY'D ALMOST KISSED! SHE AND JAKOB had almost kissed. Several moments had passed, but Lilly's heart still galloped as she replayed the moment. What was wrong with her?

She unlatched the door and entered Chestnut's stall, giving her hindquarters a wide berth.

"After the snow clears, you should come home with me. For Christmas," Jakob called the words out casually from where he knelt in the aisle, playing tug-of-war with Bandit.

What?

She watched Jakob playing with Bandit. He had tied a knot in an old piece of rope. The dog made soft growling noises while jerking his head from side to side, trying to wrench the rope from Jakob's hand.

"Oh, you are very fierce, are you not?" Jakob said, a mocking laugh rumbled through the livery. She paused at the unrestrained joy that spread across his face, making him look almost boyish again. Bandit fought harder, backing up, pulling. Then Jakob loosened his grip as the dog gave the rope a powerful jerk, yanking it from Jakob's hand and racing under her wagon. When Jakob caught her watching, she quickly turned away.

Lilly tried to keep her focus on the horse as Jakob's suggestion ricocheted in her mind.

Chestnut usually had an easygoing nature, but today she seemed nervous. Looking at her now, Lilly knew something was wrong. Chestnut was leaning slightly on her left side. Lilly stroked the horse's neck.

"Mor would love to see you. You know you always have a place at the farm," he said, as if she'd argued with him in the first place.

"Jakob, I . . ."

She wanted to. For a moment, as she bent to grip the mare's front right fetlock, thoughts of what it would be like to ride in Jakob's wagon, next to him, to be folded into the family's Christmas festivities filled her mind's eye.

And she wanted it. *Foolishness.* She closed her eyes against the wish she couldn't have.

"Just think about it," he said.

She forced her eyes open and began to examine the bottom of the hoof. Sure enough, it was packed with dirt around the shoe, and a small stone was lodged near the frog. How had she missed this yesterday? She was distracted and out of sorts, that's how.

She left the stall and hurried to the tack wall for her hoof pick, relieved that Jakob had gone into the annex.

"This room isn't so bad," he called out from inside. "With the little window."

He appeared in the doorway. "I could clear out some of the extra barrels and old junk. We could clean it up, make it a living space for you."

We?

She quickened her steps to retrieve her hoof pick from a slotted wooden box stored near the tack wall.

Thankfully, he'd ducked back inside the annex when she passed by on her way back to Chestnut's stall.

She hadn't spoken to Jakob in months. Now he was back in her life as determined to rekindle their friendship as he had been to light that stove and get it burning.

And she didn't quite know how it made her feel.

Back in Chestnut's stall, she held the horse's hoof in her left hand and used the pick hook to dig out the dirt at the front of the hoof. That was better.

If only Lilly could figure out what to do about this new Jakob in her life as easily.

She stepped out of the stall. The air held a hint of new warmth. She sighed deeply, her shoulders slumping under the weight of her feelings, a tangled mess of gratitude and guilt. Jakob was working hard to give her what she needed to keep the livery running until the roof could be repaired. Was it wrong to accept Jakob's kindness? She should focus on being a good friend in return, and keep her attraction reined in. Everything would go back to normal. She straightened her shoulders, trying to appear more composed.

Two steps into the aisle, she heard a sound that made the

skin on the back of her neck prickle. Before she could react, Festus was out of his stall and heading away from her. He bolted toward the wagons.

She saw Jakob emerge from the annex as she raced after the mule.

"Festus! Stop!" she commanded.

She got close enough to lunge for the mule's halter, but watched in horror as he reared back, his hind legs kicking out and knocking the stove from its knobby metal legs. The stove crashed to the dirt floor with a harsh clang, the door flying open and spilling out burning logs and embers.

For one frozen moment, she stood with her hand on the mule's halter.

"Fire!" Lilly croaked, panic tightening her throat like a noose.

Jakob was already there, swiftly stomping out the flames. He closed the stove door with one gloved hand.

His actions jolted her, she rushed to put Festus away in his stall.

Jakob was jogging toward the smoldering mess on the ground, a bucket of water from the barrel splashing on his boots in his hurry.

He poured it slowly on the embers, smoke and steam rising and finally dissipating.

She could only stand and stare at the black ash marks left behind. And the hay strewn out of the mule's stall from when he'd run out—only feet away from the now-soggy ashes.

"I'll rig the latch right now," Jakob said.

"We shouldn't have used that stove," she snapped.

"What?" he asked.

"I. Told. You." She enunciated each word, anger making her voice shake. "We should not have lit that stove."

The ashes were now a soggy mess, and she was reassured enough to let her eyes scan the horses.

The whole barn could have been destroyed. Her livelihood, gone.

"It was an accident," Jakob reasoned. "We won't let him get out again."

She whirled on him. "Put the stove away. It's too dangerous." She lifted trembling hands toward the stove. "Look how close I came to losing everything!"

"You'll freeze out here," he argued. "It'll be spring before the roof can be repaired."

"It's my job to decide," she said furiously. She'd let him talk her into using the stove. What a mistake that had been. She knew better.

Somewhere in the back of her mind, she knew her reaction was out of proportion. She knew it, but she couldn't stop herself from snapping.

"I would rather freeze than see my horses burned alive!"

Jakob's jaw tensed. "You need some source of heat. Or another place to stay."

The farm. Surely he was talking about the farm. Trying to get her to leave the livery, just like Stephen had.

"I don't need anything. I certainly don't need you." She spat the words, saw them hit when Jakob looked stricken.

Regret squeezed at her heart, but she couldn't seem to bridle the fear that had pushed the angry words out. She spun around and strode off.

She didn't need him.

Jakob squatted and stared at the soot marks on the floor. The stove had already cooled. The air was clear, not even a trace of smoke lingered. But her sharp words had nearly knocked the wind out of him. Had she meant them?

He closed his eyes and felt the weight of her rejection in each heavy thud of his heart. Since the snow had trapped him here, he'd believed it was Providence. That he was meant to be in Lilly's life again.

I can handle it.

Jakob, you do not need to make repairs for me.

I'm no one's responsibility but my own.

She had been trying to tell him. He just hadn't wanted to hear it.

Squatting down, he gripped the warm cast-iron barrel of the stove and put it back on its stubby legs. Because of their closeness, he had allowed his old one-sided feelings for her to reignite. He straightened the grate inside the stove and shut the door.

Lilly didn't want him.

He glanced around the tidy livery, taking in the bridles and harnesses hung with care on the tack wall. The buggy she rented out was parked beside the wagon, clean and ready for use. The water barrels and supplies were arranged along the wall near the barn door. And even though it was just packed dirt, the horse stalls and center aisle were swept clean. She certainly could and did handle the livery on her own.

His gaze went to the trunk and the wagons, all her supplies stacked neatly beside the wall. He could still be her friend.

He closed his eyes, seeing her again as he had this morning, with her hair down around her shoulders, cheeks flushed pink, and her eyes warm with a sleepy tenderness.

He shook his head. No. He couldn't stay in close proximity to her. Not when he'd fallen for her all over again.

But he wouldn't put his horses at risk while the storm still hung on. Sure, the wind had died down a little, but the snow was still falling heavily.

I don't need you.

Her pa had told him he wasn't enough. *She's not the woman for you.*

Jakob had to get out of here. Longed to be back at the farm, where he could lose himself in the work: milking and feeding the cows and cleaning his own stalls.

As he slid into his heavy canvas jacket, he felt a twinge of pain in his shoulder. He wrapped the thick knit scarf around his neck and shoved his hat on his head. The dog nipped and dodged around his feet as he made his way to the door. The shepherd's second nature kicking in, his sole purpose to prevent cattle—or people—from leaving the herd.

Jakob sat on his haunches, lifting a hand to pet the dog. Bandit leaned into his hand. A memory flashed of another dog and another farewell. Like a fool, he'd opened up and shared with Lilly, thinking it would bring them closer. Now the whole exchange just left him feeling raw.

A hot knot formed in his throat. "I wish . . ." He croaked, then cleared his throat. "I wish I could stay, but . . ." It hurt too much. Being here had only made things worse for Lilly, but leaving her was like leaving half of himself behind.

Bandit laid his chin on his knee.

"Sorry, buddy," he choked out. He gently stroked the dog's head, then stood.

"Do me a favor and go sit with Lilly."

Bandit sat watching him with pleading eyes.

Jakob sighed as he pulled on his worn leather gloves. He flung an arm in the direction Lilly had escaped to.

"Go on now," he ordered, making his voice more forceful.

Bandit turned and trotted down toward Fancy's stall. He swung around and sent Jakob a soulful whine.

Jakob stepped out the door into the biting cold.

Seven

JAKOB HAD BEEN OUTSIDE FOR OVER AN hour when he sensed eyes on him. Jack Easton stood on the little back porch, hands in his coat pockets, watching from where the roofline offered a bit of shelter.

Thwack!

Jakob swung the axe, and its blade bit through the log. The split pieces flew off the block, rolling into the white snow while the axe embedded into the block. He retrieved the split logs and stacked them on the growing pile nearby.

Jack stepped down from the porch and crossed to where the open lean-to and the back corner of the bungalow provided better cover. He said nothing, just stood there watching with an intensity that made Jakob's skin crawl.

Jakob hadn't come out here for company. He'd come to get away from the married couple inside—their calf-eyed gazes and tender smiles felt like salt in a raw wound.

Jakob paused after stacking two more logs.

"Still more logs to be split," he grunted as he grabbed another thick log and placed it on the block. Every time he raised the axe, fire licked along his back. Was he bleeding? It felt like it. Especially on the inside.

"You've been out here for hours. Your hands will have more than one blister." Jack rubbed his gloved hands together.

Jakob flexed his fingers inside the damp gloves. They were stiff from gripping the wooden axe handle and ached from the shuddering impact.

"Come in and warm up with some hot coffee. We've just made a fresh pot," Jack said.

Jakob put another log on the chopping block.

"I'd rather stay out here and finish the chopping," he mumbled through cold, numb lips and lifted the axe. A few snowflakes landed and clung to his beard and his eyelashes.

He paused to blink and met Jack's challenging gaze.

Jack heaved out a frustrated breath.

"Why are you punishing yourself?" Jack prodded.

Thwack!

The wood split, and the axe lodged into the chopping block.

Jakob let go of the axe and stepped back. Is that what he was doing? His hands were as stiff as boards, his shoulder was screaming now, and he could no longer feel the tip of his nose.

He was punishing himself.

Abusing his body in a way he would never allow someone he cared about to do. He rubbed a gloved hand over his face and beard, turning his back to Jack.

"I don't know what happened between you and our fine neighbor, but I do know that sometimes a woman just needs to hear you say you are sorry," Jack said, stamping his feet to keep warm. "Go back and apologize. She'll forgive you."

"It's not that simple," Jakob said. If an apology could make Lilly see him as a man worthy of her love, he would say he was sorry until the cows came home.

"What is it, then?" The man was shaking like an aspen in fall. He was hatless and his ears were turning red from the cold. But Jack was waiting for an answer, so Jakob had mercy on him.

"I've only loved one woman in my life." Jakob lifted a chin to point toward the livery. "She was my first friend in this new country. A fierce defender against the teasing and ridicule of the other kids because I was different, an outsider. We grew up and she was still my friend, but I thought . . ."

He paused, then blurted, "I wanted more." He looked down, flexing his cold, aching fingers and rubbing them together for warmth, but he felt the heat of humiliation on his neck and face.

He told Jack the story. Jack was a good listener.

"I know a thing or two about feeling unworthy of a good woman," Jack said with a self-mocking chuckle. "I almost lost Merritt because of my stubbornness. If a stranger on a train hadn't set me straight, I would have lost the best thing that ever happened to me. A man like me, with a past that—well, let's just say I had to accept the fact that my worthiness doesn't come from what I have done or what I can do, but from what He did on the cross a long time ago.

It's one thing to know that up here." Jack touched a finger to his head. "And another thing to let it sink down deep in here." His hand went to his chest. "We're gonna fall short, no matter how good we try to be. It's by grace we are saved. Even from ourselves."

Jakob let the words of the scripture he loved wash over him.

Of course, he knew he could never be good enough to earn salvation. Had he been trying to be worthy of God's grace like he'd been trying to be worthy of Lilly?

Jack's nose had turned red, and his eyes were watery from the cold.

"You should go back inside. I am grateful for your advice."

Jack nodded, taking a few steps toward the house before turning back to add, "That man on the train? He asked me another question that I'll put to you: Have you told her you love her?"

Jack didn't wait for an answer. Just turned and walked into the house. The door closed on their conversation, but his question echoed in Jakob's mind.

He hadn't told her he loved her because he didn't want to risk his heart again in that way.

You didn't fight for her.

Lilly had said the words about Astrid. He'd never felt for Astrid what he felt for Lilly.

Today, he'd let his hurt blind him and had run off to lick his wounds again. And yes, punish himself. His numb and tingling fingers inside his gloves and his sore back were proof of that.

His eyes drifted to the livery in the dimming light. Lilly was alone. She needed help, even if she wouldn't admit it.

Jack was right. He needed to apologize for dismissing her fears and trust God for his self-worth.

He didn't know if he had the courage to tell her everything that was in his heart yet, but he wanted to show her that she was worth fighting for.

She'd said she thought he was brave—a good brother and a good son. He would be a good friend too, help her, give her what she needed, even if she never returned his love.

Lilly lit the lamp on the trunk in front of the wagons. Bandit trotted over to her with the rope toy Jakob had made and dropped it at her feet. The dog had pined for the man all afternoon. She stood in the same spot where Jakob had been that morning, the image of him from when she first opened her eyes still vivid in her mind. Tall and strong, shoulders broader with his coat still on. His high cheekbones and full beard gave him a rugged appearance, and his blue eyes seemed to shine brighter against his flushed skin. But it was the look in those eyes that warmed her from the top of her head to the soles of her feet—as if he had found an unexpected treasure and couldn't believe his good fortune.

A loud knock startled her out of her daydream. She rushed to the door and pulled it open to find Marshal O'Grady. Disappointment settled over her like the storm clouds obscuring the setting sun. Somewhere deep inside of her, she had hoped it was Jakob coming back home. The livery had been somber and lonely without him.

She shook that thought off and stepped aside to allow the marshal inside.

"You all right?" Danna asked, her voice edged with concern. "I saw part of that roof has fallen in." She stalked in, bringing with her a light dusting of snow and a small basket. Lilly peered outside before she shut the door. The wind had blown itself out. A light snow fell softly in the quiet twilight.

"Caroline Wilson sent a few things from the bakery." She handed Lilly the basket. "What else can we do to help you?" Danna asked, her eyes slightly narrowed, taking in every detail of the space around them: the stove that sat cold and empty nearby, then the wagons in the space in front of the stable door and the trunk with two chairs, and a lamp burning brightly on top.

"I'm fine. Jakob was here to help me. The storm moved in so quickly that he had to board his horses and take shelter here," Lilly said, as she led Danna toward the trunk. "We pulled most of my things out of the lean-to and sealed off the door. It's probably going to have to wait until spring before I can begin the repairs."

Lilly placed the woven basket on the old trunk, its contents wrapped in a cotton towel. As she peeled back the cloth, the mouthwatering aroma of golden fried chicken and warm cornbread wafted from the basket. Another jar of coffee, still hot, was tucked in the corner of the basket.

"Oh, this is so kind of Caroline to send this." Her stomach rumbled, reminding her that she hadn't eaten since breakfast with Jakob that morning. As she pulled two plates and cups from the crate nearby, she wondered if he had eaten since this morning.

"There'll be plenty of folks round here wanting to pitch in and help you when the time comes. We could get it done in a day with a barn raising," Danna said.

Lilly set the plates and cups on the trunk and pulled back a chair for Danna. She forced a weak smile, unable to meet Danna's eyes.

"That's not necessary. I can handle it myself," she argued, taking a seat on the other side of the trunk.

It was her own neglect that landed her in this position. She couldn't ask for charity.

Danna narrowed her eyes and leveled a stern look at Lilly. "You don't need to handle everything by yourself."

Lilly's shoulders tensed, and her grip on the jar of coffee tightened. This seemed rather rich coming from the woman who kept law and order in the town of Calvin. A woman she admired and whose example had given her the courage to keep running the livery after her father died.

"You do," Lilly stated. "You're here right now watching over the town, even stopped in to check on me."

Danna removed her wet hat and held it in her lap. She leaned forward.

"The only reason I can be here is because Chas is at home with the children. He takes care of me. When I need help, he is a partner to me." Her lips twitched. "He practically orders me to go home and sleep. Believe me, there have been plenty of times when I might have worked myself to the bone had he not stepped in to save me from my stubborn self. God made us to need each other. Husbands and wives. And neighbors."

The words sank in. *A threefold cord is not quickly broken . . .* She'd read the verse once in Sunday school. Back when she'd felt so alone. Wished for someone . . . and Jakob had been there all along.

"You're right," she said. "I'll accept the help with rebuilding."

"Good. Lotta folks rely on you in this town." Danna shivered and huddled deeper in her coat, and her gaze went to the stove.

"It's cold in here," Danna commented while Lilly poured two cups of coffee from the jar. "Saw you pulled out that old tinker's stove of your pa's. Why don't you have it going?"

Lilly made herself look at the small cast-iron barrel standing like a squat soldier awaiting duty. Shame burned inside her while the cold stove mocked her. Why didn't she have the stove going? Because she was a foolish woman who let fear get in the way of common sense. Jakob was right, and she had treated him horribly.

"Where is Jakob, by the way?"

Lilly shivered, but not from the cold. The marshal had an uncanny way of reading her thoughts that gave her goosebumps.

"He left." Lilly pinched her lips together.

Danna's forehead wrinkled as she waited for an explanation.

"We had a disagreement. I was trying to control everything." She huffed out a breath in self-disgust. "Over the stove. I pushed him away—said things I didn't mean. And he left."

She had pushed Jakob away. The man who had been the most loyal and . . . loving . . . person in her life. Why had she pushed him away? Why did she push everyone away?

Because she had to be in control, keep a tight grasp on the reins of her life. She swallowed against the lump in her throat, the taste bitter. If she was in control, no one could let her down, like her pa. But no one could help her either. Not even the Lord.

Danna sipped her coffee, deep in thought. When her cup was empty, she stood and stretched. One side of her mouth kicked up in a half smile.

"Somehow, I don't think you could run him off for good. You just need a chance to apologize," she said.

Lilly pushed back her chair and stood. She looked down at her stained skirt, scuffed men's boots, and touched her loose braid.

"Jakob deserves more than an apology," Lilly blurted. "More than a woman like me."

The curious expression was back on Danna's face.

"Jakob's a grown man and knows his own mind. Shouldn't you allow him to make that choice himself?" Danna's gaze scanned the crates and supplies piled up near the wagons, and the now-tidy annex, and landed on the lone empty stall. "It's Christmas," Danna said, her tone a little wistful for the marshal. "Wasn't it you who said the manger was about making room for the Savior? Maybe you could make a little room for love too?"

Danna's brisk manner was back in place within seconds,

and less than five minutes later, she was out the door. Lilly heard Fancy call and walked to the trunk to retrieve the lantern. Her eyes went to the annex where Jakob had worked to make room for her.

There are plenty of men in Calvin who admire you and would be proud to take you as a wife.

Not true. But Jakob had seen her that way. A woman to be admired, to be proud of.

I would have married you.

Eight

C'MON, FANCY. YOU CAN DO IT." LILLY fought to keep her words soothing while terror clawed at her throat.

She stooped close to Fancy, palm resting on her belly. The mare was in active labor now, and her muscles rippled with the effort to push the foal out.

After her confrontation with Jakob, Lilly retreated to Fancy's stall. The mare had been restless, her breathing becoming heavy and erratic, as the afternoon waned. After Danna had taken her leave—was that just a few hours ago?—Fancy had begun to pace, pawing at the straw, sweat glistening on her coat despite the chill that hung in the air. Lilly remained close, murmuring soothing words, hoping the delivery would proceed without trouble. Each contraction brought a flicker of hope . . . then despair.

Lilly closed her eyes, tried to calm herself. Her heart was pounding in time with Fancy's labored breaths. Her mind raced, grasping for some way to help the mare. Why had she been so pigheaded and determined to do things on her own? If Jakob were here, he would know what to do.

She opened her eyes and glanced toward the window. The storm seemed to be losing its strength—just like Fancy. Fancy's agitation had faded to lying listless on the hay, eyes glassy.

A memory of Winnie with the same empty stare as the life drained from her flashed before Lilly. Terror seized her in a stranglehold, leaving her gasping for air.

Maybe if she could get Fancy to turn to the other side, it would shift the position of the foal.

Lilly scrambled to her feet, grabbed the halter, and pulled.

"Come on, Fancy. Get up. Just one more time," Lilly pleaded, heaving at the halter. But Fancy was exhausted, lying almost still through another contraction with no progress.

Bandit paced outside the stall.

Jakob had to be close by. He'd probably gone to Jack and Merritt's. Lilly would go and get him.

She let go of Fancy's halter. Bandit trailed her to the door.

"I'm going to get Jakob," she told the dog, who jumped up with tongue lolling, as if he understood her.

She threw on her old wool cloak that hung by the door. Her hand grasped the doorknob, surprised as the metal handle turned under her palm. The door opened, and Jakob's broad frame filled the doorway like a Christmas miracle.

Relief flooded her. A dam burst. And a love so powerful washed over her it nearly knocked her off her feet.

"Jakob!" Even her voice was rough and watery. Tears pooled in her eyes.

"Hey, what's wrong?" He reached out, his fingers wrapped around her upper arms to steady her.

"I need you!" she blurted out before she could stop herself. His eyes lit with surprise, and something she couldn't read. She turned her face toward Fancy's stall. "Fancy is in trouble. I was coming to get you. I need your help."

His jaw tightened, and a flash of something passed across his face. Pain? His face relaxed, settling into a calm but determined expression. He pulled off his hat.

"It is good that I am here, then."

Snow fell from his shoulders as he stalked toward Fancy's stall. He shrugged out of his jacket, tossing it over the wall as he entered the stall.

In the stall, he lowered his bulk near Fancy's head, stroking her along her neck and withers, then slid his big hand to her belly.

"You have been working very hard at this, Fancy. This foal is giving you trouble already, hmmm?"

"I think she started labor after—after you left. She was agitated and pacing." Lilly extended the lantern over the stall. "In the last hour, though, the pains have come faster and harder. And she won't get up anymore."

Jakob moved to the mare's hind quarters, making a cursory examination as Fancy strained through another contraction.

"But the foal—it must be lodged inside, and Fancy is losing strength."

Lilly stationed herself at the mare's back, holding the lantern over her rump.

"I can see the foal's nose and a hoof." Jakob sat up and met her eyes across Fancy's heaving body. "Something is keeping the foal from coming. There is only one way to find out and fix it. I'm going to help Fancy to her feet." He lifted his big hands, chapped and blistered. "My hands are too big. Your hands are smaller. You will have to do it."

She knew what he was asking. A cold sweat broke out on her forehead, and her legs felt too shaky to move.

"Come, Lilly, we will fix the problem. Then this baby will be born." His voice held a calm surety that bolstered her courage. His hand at her shoulder steadied her.

Somehow, Jakob was able to get Fancy to her feet, and Lilly moved to Fancy's hindquarters. Jakob slid his big body behind her and reached for her hand, covering it with his own. A memory surfaced, Jakob at her back, guiding her hand like this, teaching her to milk her first cow. The terror that had gripped her a moment ago released its hold.

"There." Jakob pushed her hand forward and removed his.

A vice grip tightened around her forearm. Her fingers found a knobby knee but not a hoof.

"Jakob," Lilly hissed, her arm aching from the pressure; her fingers and wrists began to tingle. "One of the foal's legs is bent back."

"Push the foal back, then straighten the leg."

Pain radiated up her arm, and the pressure around her wrist was almost too much to bear.

"I can't . . ." Lilly's fingers were growing numb.

"Wait." Jakob lowered his head, his cheek to her ear and whispered, "Breathe. Just breathe."

She inhaled deeply. Felt his heart beating against her back. Jakob was here. She could breathe.

Then suddenly, the clamping slackened. Lilly pushed the foal upward and unbent the leg.

Fancy raised her head and snorted. Lilly stepped back quickly, bumping hard into Jakob's chest. His arms closed around her and pulled her out of the way as nature took its course, and the foal slid out onto the hay.

Relief flooded Lilly's veins, blurring her vision with tears as she watched Jakob gently wipe the foal down with a clean rag. Fancy turned to nuzzle her newborn, licking him with interest. The foal blinked his dewy eyes and gave a snort—more of a sneeze than a breath.

She met Jakob's gaze and smiled, tasting the tears that traced her cheeks. The corners of his lips lifted as the two of them drew back from the mother and new baby.

He placed his hand on the small of her back and guided her to the corner of the stall, to the bucket of water and soap she had prepared earlier that afternoon. He crouched at the bucket, waiting for Lilly to go first. She leaned down, plunging her still trembling hands into the water. His hands slid into the water, their fingers brushing.

Their gazes met again, faces just inches apart. His lips curved into another smile.

"You did it," he said, his tone suffused with pride.

She shook her head, blinking away more tears.

"*We* did it," she said through tears of joy and overwhelming gratitude. "You. And me. And Fancy. Thank you, Jakob."

Jakob lifted his clean hand, using his thumb to wipe away another tear from her cheek.

"You're welcome."

Jakob stood with Lilly in front of Fancy's stall, the foal taking wobbly steps in front of them. He couldn't help but notice how close they were standing, their shoulders almost touching.

"He's adorable," Lilly said softly, her eyes fixed on the foal. "His legs are as fragile as spindles. He looks like he might tip over at any second."

Her grip on the top rail of the stall tightened, her knuckles turning white. Even with Fancy close by, he could see Lilly was fighting the urge to rush in and steady the foal. And he was waging his own battle. Fighting not to blurt out his pent-up feelings.

His heart had leaped in his chest when he had arrived back at the livery and she'd rushed to him, admitting she needed him. But with all that had happened since then, he didn't know how to talk to her. He didn't want to say the wrong thing. He stole a sidelong glance and saw her jaw tighten and her chin tilt stubbornly in that way it did when she was wanting to speak her mind. He instinctively turned to face her. Their eyes met. He felt her body tense, catching a flash of vulnerability behind the determination in her eyes.

"You came back," she said, breaking the silence that had grown tense between them.

His heart skipped a beat. Perhaps this was the moment. He steeled himself, taking a deep breath to gather his courage.

"Lilly." He began, his voice steady but soft. "I have some things to say to you. Words I should have said to you a long time ago." She inhaled, her lips parted, ready to interrupt. He shook his head slightly and raised a hand to cup her cheek. "Please, let me get the words out. I . . . I have loved you for a long time. The seed was planted on that first day at school. You offered me friendship and smoothed the path to this strange new life." His thumb caressed her cheek, a smile tugged at his lips as he recalled her first words to him in the schoolyard.

If you like horses, we can be friends.

"We became friends, and that seed budded and blossomed. I watched how hard you worked tending the horses. The fierce way you loved and protected your pa. How much you cared about the people here in town, and their animals. As time passed, my love for you grew stronger, like our tree out by the creek. Its branches reaching for the sky, and its roots growing deeper and wider each year."

He paused, watching surprise and hope flicker in her eyes, giving him courage to continue.

He slid his hand back, allowed himself to run his fingers through her soft hair. She trembled at his touch.

"You are so beautiful to me." He rested his hand on her shoulder and leaned down to look deeper into her eyes. "I shouldn't have left. I am sorry. I should have stayed so we could talk things out. I was afraid that you were not ready to know my feelings. I am just a farmer, with not much to offer."

Lilly looked down, hesitated, then glanced away. His stomach dropped—she didn't feel the same way. She drew in a deep breath. "I'm sorry too. For the stove. I shouldn't have said what I did—said those awful things. I was scared . . . of everything." The words seemed to spill out, and once the flow had started, she couldn't hold them back. "Ever since Stephen said all those things about me, I haven't believed that any man would want me." Her gaze shot back to him.

"You love me?" she asked, her tone held a bit of wonder and fear.

"I do." He lifted his other hand, turned her to him again, and squeezed her shoulders gently. "I told you. Stephen Barclay is a fool for leaving you, and every man in Calvin knows it. And I am the most fortunate man in the county, to have been stranded in a snowstorm with the prettiest livery owner in the world."

A twinkle appeared in her green eyes. She laughed. No, she giggled. Like when they were young, and her laughter spilled out, carefree.

"Oh, Jakob," she sighed after catching her breath. "I do love you."

Now it was he who found his breath hitching.

I do love you.

He let that settle over him, like a warm summer breeze gently wrapping around his heart.

He stepped even closer to her, his arms closing around

her waist. His mind spun with disbelief and elation. He searched her face, saw his love and desire mirrored in her eyes. He leaned down, she lifted her lips to him, and he met them, warm and wonderful. Her arms slid around his neck. He drew her in tighter and deepened the kiss. His heart pounded with the thrill of it, pure and tender, passionate and fervent.

He broke away, turning his head and brushing his lips over her soft cheek, then kissing it. "I love you, Hjärtat, my heart." Her arms tightened around his neck.

"I don't know what the future holds, but I want to be by your side," Jakob whispered like a vow. She rested her cheek on his chest. He could hear his heartbeats tick like the seconds on a watch in his ears.

"I want that too," she whispered.

The seconds became minutes as he held her. He finally had her in his arms and didn't want to let her go. But it was Christmas Eve, and his family would be worried, anxiously awaiting his return.

"I reckon you'll need to go home soon," Lilly said, reading his mind. "Your family will be worried about you."

"Hmmm."

"Astrid will be needing that flour and sugar. And your ma the gifts." Lilly lifted her head and stepped back.

He sighed, taking her hands in his.

"Yes, Mor and the rest of the family will be relieved and happy when I return safely home for Christmas with all the supplies and gifts."

"And you? Will you be happy to return home?"

She was watching him closely. He read the care and vulnerability in her words. He nodded. "But it would bring me more joy to return home with you." He released her hands and lifted his, brushing her hair back behind her ears, then cupping her cheeks. "Come home for Christmas, Lilly."

"You want me to come home with you for Christmas? You already have a full house."

"There is always room for you, Lilly."

A soft smile spread across her face.

"There is always room for you too, Jakob. In my home, and in my heart."

Epilogue

S HE'S DOING IT AGAIN." MARTA GIGGLED and put an arm around Fancy's neck.

"You know she's going to do that when you get close," Jakob's youngest brother, Peter, griped as he hurried over to Fancy's stall.

Lilly watched from an empty stall nearby as fifteen-year-old Peter, so like Jakob at the same age, rescued Marta's long, blond braid from the mare's playful nibbling.

They'd come this morning after their chores at the farm to help Lilly at the livery. It still surprised and amazed her how quickly her life had changed since that snowstorm had brought Jakob back to her like a Christmas gift. In less than six months, she had gone from orphan to sister, daughter, and wife . . .

"Hurry and finish the feeding," Peter ordered. "Jakob will be here any minute with the wagon to take us home."

Marta unlatched the stall, swinging the handle of the feed bucket.

"Jakob will help us finish. He doesn't want Lilly to lift the heavy things because of the baby."

. . . and soon-to-be mother. Warmth pooled in her belly. Her hand automatically went to the swell. Just last night, she and Jakob had felt the baby move. She couldn't stop the smile that pulled at her lips. Nothing compared to the exuberant joy that had lit up Jakob's face when he'd learned he would be a father.

"I know that!" Peter retorted, scowling. He refused to allow his sister to believe she was smarter than him.

A knock at the door interrupted the sibling argument.

"I will get it," Katerina, Jakob's oldest sister, called from the stall nearest the front and stepped to the business door.

Lilly exited the stall and strode down the aisle. Thank God for Jakob's family.

"I'll be needin' a horsh for a coupula days. Run along and get the owner," a male voice demanded. The hair on the back of Lilly's neck rose. She recognized the telltale slur of his words.

She hurried to the door, stepping in front of Katerina.

"You're looking at the owner," Lilly said in a calm but firm voice, lifting her chin.

The air reeked of sour whiskey and sweat. The disheveled cowboy in front of her had probably spent the afternoon at the saloon. Now he wanted to rent a horse and head out to who knew where! Not on one of her mounts.

"Kat, go help your brother and sister finish up." Katerina hesitated, then slipped away.

Harnesses jingled, and a wagon rattled up to the stable door.

"I'll be happy to provide a horse for you. *When you are sober.*"

Anger contorted the man's face. "I ain't drunk."

He certainly was. Lilly stood her ground.

"I ain't doing business with a woman." The cowboy looked at her swollen belly, and his lips twisted in disgust. "Git yer man."

Over the man's shoulder, Lilly saw Jakob climb down from the wagon and head toward them. He paused as their eyes met, sending a wave of tender reassurance through her.

The man followed her gaze and brightened when he saw Jakob.

"That yer man?" The cowboy's tone turned eager as Jakob neared. Her man towered over this cowboy. Not just in height, but in every way: his strength, his good looks, and his good character.

She nodded as Jakob came to stand next to her, gently placing his big hand at the small of her back.

She turned and met Jakob's blue gaze. "Yes, he's my man." *My husband. My heart.* She reined in her emotions before her eyes started leaking like they were apt to do since a baby began growing inside her. No need to raise Jakob's protective hackles.

"And he will tell you the same thing. Come back when you're sober."

When the foolish man opened his foul-smelling mouth, Jakob cut him off.

"You'll want to move along now, sir."

The man's mouth snapped shut, his lips turning down in a disgruntled frown. He spun around and slunk down the boardwalk, tripping on a loose board and almost falling into the street.

Lilly turned into Jakob, slid her arms around his neck. Rising on tiptoes, she kissed him, and he returned the favor. When the kiss ended, it was a good thing Jakob had tightened his hold on her, or she may have melted in a puddle on the ground. He laughed.

She pulled back. "What?"

He grinned, satisfaction glinting in his eyes.

"I came to claim my wife, take her home after a long day, and instead she claimed me."

Her Gingerbread Refuge

WENDY KLOPFENSTEIN

"HAST THOU ENTERED INTO THE TREASURES OF THE SNOW,
OR HAST THOU SEEN THE TREASURES OF THE HAIL,"

Job 38:22 KJV

This one is for my sister. Like the heroine, she always seems
to know how to help a child who is hurting.

One

WILL THE SNOW NEVER STOP?

Caroline Wilson glanced from the large picture window of the bakery shop to the pallet in the corner where her two-year-old Flora had finally settled down for a nap. With her still slumbering, she focused back out the front window. The snow swirled heavier than before. Heavier than the usual Wyoming snowstorm.

"Look! It's Billy." Caroline's nephew, Gilbert, left the chairs he'd been straightening to hurry toward the door. Even though he was only six, he enjoyed the good-natured teasing of the lanky teen who stopped to buy a sweet bread each afternoon after picking up the newspapers.

It was later than usual for him to stop by. Maybe he'd gotten a bonus for Christmas and would buy treats for his siblings too.

"Aunt Caroline?" Gilbert's brows shot up.

Her shoulders slumped as much as Gilbert's when Billy

pulled his collar higher and hurried past the door without making any sign of slowing. With the snow coming in blinding swirls, she couldn't blame him. No one had stopped in since noon. The display counter opposite the window was full of cinnamon rolls, gingerbread men, and frosted cookies. She'd been counting on those extra holiday sales of her sweet treats.

"The storm's getting worse." In the seven years she'd been in Wyoming, she'd never seen a snow this heavy. Caroline turned from the window to count the loaves still stacked on the bread rack along the wall next to the stairs. "I suppose the teacher was right in sending you children home early today."

Far too early for her to accomplish all the extra touches she had planned in order to make their Christmas special this year. Last year, after her sister Eliza passed, her nephew and two nieces had come to live with her. Drowning in her own sorrow, with Eliza's passing reminding her of the loss of her own husband the year before, Caroline hadn't been able to pull herself together to give anyone a proper holiday. Not her own two children, not Eliza's three, certainly not herself. She'd vowed to make up for it this year.

Christmas had to be perfect.

"Do you want me to start sweeping?" Lucy, Caroline's niece, was only nine, but she carried the weight of the world on her shoulders. Poor child never laughed. Always eager to help, how could Caroline disappoint her? Even if her attempts often left more of a mess than when she started.

"That would be wonderful." She tried to infuse energy into her voice, despite the weariness. If only she had a workshop full of elves to come finish her Christmas presents. None of her yarn had spun itself into mittens and scarves for the children while she slept. Not yet anyway.

At least she'd managed to put up a tree in the front of the bakery. The children and her customers alike enjoyed the lone hallmark of the holiday that stood in the corner.

Caroline sighed, then turned a smile on the children as she passed them on her way to the kitchen. She needed to check on the dough she'd left to rise. Little Davie trailed behind her, chanting his ABCs. At four. he wasn't old enough for school yet, but the older children had started teaching him, especially Lucy and her younger sister, Stella.

The warmth from the large cast-iron stove in the kitchen wrapped around her. They were blessed that she had wood stocked in the lean-to and a pantry of baking supplies. Maybe she ought to put on an extra loaf to rise, in case the weather got worse. Her stomach gurgled in agreement. She'd been too busy since the children burst through the door, home early from school, to stop and eat lunch.

"I want one. I want one." The chant coming from Davie registered in time for her to sweep him away from the large table in the center of the kitchen area. It was covered in cookies waiting to be frosted.

"Not until after dinner, little fella." She took to tickling him to ward off any protest. His green eyes, so like her own, sparkled with laughter. A boisterous laugh that filled the room as her late husband's always had. If only it'd reach down to soothe her aching heart.

A loud clatter echoed from the front of the bakery. Davie's eyes widened in surprise as she ceased her tickling to straighten. Flora's wail split the air, no doubt awakened by the crash. Davie grabbed her fingers, barely keeping up as she hurried past the doorway from the bakery's kitchen to the area out front where the tables and chairs were being cleaned and straightened for the night.

The three-layer chocolate cake that Caroline had hoped to sell for a pretty penny was splattered across the wooden floorboards. The glass pedestal display stand where it'd sat proudly on the counter was shattered among the mess of frosting and cake.

"She didn't mean to." Lucy worked with a fervor, trying to sweep fragments of glass, muddled with chocolate cake, from the floor. Her efforts merely swirled the gooey chocolate around, sticking it to the bristles of the broom.

Stella stood behind the sales counter, the cloth she'd been wiping the counter with frozen mid-motion. A lock of her light brown hair fell across those striking eyes of hers, the normally bright blue dulled by tears brimming on her lids. She ducked to avoid Caroline's gaze.

The stand lay in pieces all across the floor. Caroline worked to swallow back any sign of her disappointment as she crossed the room to Flora. The stand had been a gift from her husband on their third anniversary. God rest his soul.

A hiccupping sniffle replaced Flora's wail as Caroline bent to pick her up. She swiped the locks of blond curls that matched her own tresses from Flora's flushed face.

From the corner of her eye, she caught sight of Gilbert leading Davie up the stairs.

"Let's go before we get another chore. Or someone gets in trouble."

Caroline closed her eyes as she leaned her cheek against Flora's head. She inhaled a deep breath, then kissed her little one before settling her on the bottom stair.

Lord, help me extend love and patience to all the wee ones in my care.

She moved to place a reassuring hand on Stella's shoulder, pulling her in for a hug. Stella relinquished her frozen stance to lean in, hugging her back with hands gooey with frosting.

"I'm sorry." Stella's words were quiet, but enough to signal she'd rebounded.

Caroline offered a gentle smile of reassurance to her niece, garnering a shy smile back. "Lucy, do you and Stella mind taking Flora upstairs to play while I finish up down here?"

A crease lined Lucy's brow as Stella hurried to Flora's side.

"Let's sing a song." Stella had Flora's attention as a holiday melody of pear trees, partridges, and true love flowed out in her sweet soprano.

"What kind of Christmas is this going to be? So cold and blustery we can't go outside. A mess down here. No customers," Lucy mumbled as she brushed past Caroline, her braid of fair hair swinging as she followed Stella and Flora upstairs. "It's not like we have anyone sending us rings or birds."

"It's a song," Stella retorted, then went back to singing as they neared the top of the stairwell.

Caroline bit back a scolding. Her niece was right. There were no fancy gifts headed their way and no likelihood of customers in this storm. But she didn't want Lucy spoiling her attempts at giving them all a magical Christmas. Even if most of the gifts would be made with her own hands.

The broom in the middle of the room was too coated in chocolate cake to clean the mess, so she grabbed a stack of old rags from the kitchen. One more thing added to her list of things to do today. Back in the front area of the bakery, the outside ledges of the windows had a foot of snow built up along the edge where the wind blew it against the glass, with no sign of it stopping. If anything, the flakes were larger than they had been earlier. She could hardly make out the other storefronts across Calvin's main street.

The clock at the train station rang out six chimes. Closing time. She lifted her woolen skirt out of the way as she bent to clean the mess. In the distance, the train engine puffed at the station as if preparing to leave. Must be running late due to the storm.

The clomping of children's feet in the apartment above the bakery echoed off the walls. Her arms ached from exhaustion as she mopped the mess in a circular motion to bring all the bits of broken glass and cake into the center. Her favorite pedestal display stand. In splinters.

Ding. Ding.

The bell above the door jangled. Cold air filtered into the shop and wrapped around her.

"Be with you in a moment." Caroline swept the pieces closer, drawing the last of the glass, mingled with cake, up in her rag as she rose. She must have forgotten to lock the door, but she'd not turn away a paying customer. Not today.

As she spun, tucking the rag behind her back in one hand and a stray curl behind her ear with the other, her eyes riveted on the silent figure by the door.

A little girl she'd never seen before panted as if she'd run a long distance. Pretty blond curls tumbled out of her green hood to frame a face red with the cold. Her stare fixated on Caroline, as if pleading with her.

"Can I help you?" Caroline softened her voice, taking a tentative step forward. Where were the child's parents?

The girl opened her mouth to answer as the door jerked open behind her. She flinched as the space swirled with a flood of snow. Behind the girl, the doorway filled with a tall, well-dressed man, all covered in flakes.

What now?

Who in their right mind wrote this paragraph?
"I'm hungry. I'm hungry."
Jerome Barnett had tuned out the noise from the crowded passenger car, but couldn't tune out his half sister, Rose. The singsong words kept rhythm with her feet that swung in and out of his vision as he tried to concentrate on the latest contract, balanced on his lap.

He'd imagined the sweaty odor of the passengers pressing past them to exit would steal Rose's appetite. If she was really hungry. It'd only been two hours since they ate. But he was used to working through lunch. What had it been like when he was ten? As soon as he finished going over this contract, he'd see to getting her another meal.

"We'll visit the dining car once we're underway again."

"I'm still hungry." Each word went up an octave as she spoke, garnering a nasty stare from the man across the aisle.

One of the passenger train crew members shuffled past them, snowflakes clinging to his coat. Jerome strained to overhear his conversation about the track conditions.

"Are we going home?" Astonishing how such a young girl could mirror his father's facial expressions.

More astonishing how well Jerome remembered them. A pang hit his heart. Home? The solicitor had already sold the family home before locating Jerome. He hadn't stepped inside the old house since he left on his seventeenth birthday.

"We'll be living in my home in New York." He focused on his paper again.

"I don't want to live in New York." Her stubbornness must stem from her grief.

He'd been there. Losing his mother at eight, then attaching to a stepmother, only to have all the joy sucked from their home again at eleven. If his father and stepmother had comforted him, he might know how to comfort Rose. He rubbed the bridge of his nose, then shifted to focus on the next page of the contract.

"Can we get off the train?"

"Hmm." The wording on the top of page two had to be changed before the meeting.

A huge sigh erupted from where Rose sat on the red cushioned seat across from him. "Can we get off to dance in the snow?"

He jerked up his head to study Rose. Her fair hair and green eyes, such a stark contrast to his own dark hair and eyes, were a testament to their difference in mothers. As much a contrast as their view of the storm. "Why would we? It's cold and blustery."

Something like defiance glared back at him. Or hurt. His words may have been too sharp. This wasn't supposed to be so hard. He'd not thought how he'd handle her. Not thought past rescuing her from the Orphan Train after learning of her existence.

He returned his focus to the contract on his lap, the stark white of the paper glaring against his dark trousers. He propped his arm on his knee and leaned into it.

Fragments of legal jargon refused to register in his brain. Perhaps he'd have to hire a nanny when they returned to New York. Did the sentence on the bottom of page three need to be struck from the contract? Maybe he should try harder with Rose. He scanned page three again. She'd recently lost both her parents. If there was anything he understood, it was the pain of loss so young.

He sighed. He'd try again.

Without even looking up from the contract, he attempted to infuse his voice with interest. "What's your favorite subject to study?"

Silence greeted him.

"In school. Your favorite subject in school." Still no answer.

He tipped his head up.

The red cushion of the train seat sat empty. He hurried a glance past the seats, then turned to scan behind him.

Where had she gone to? He shoved his papers into his satchel. Panic threatened to seize him. He'd only just found her. He couldn't lose her. A flash of green outside the train window grabbed his attention.

Rose.

She spun in the snow, with her arms outstretched, catching snowflakes on her tongue. He waved his arms at her from the train. She lifted a hand to wave, then danced off down the boardwalk.

What was she thinking? He grabbed up their luggage as he stood, fighting against the slow movement of passengers disembarking from the locomotive. If he didn't get off now to grab her, they'd be separated. The muscles in his jaw worked. He had to get her back on this train if he wanted to arrive in New York on time.

He stepped from the train, spying her green hood a short distance away. "Rose!"

The flurrying snow all but swallowed his cry. In his rush, he bumped into another passenger.

"My apologies." He nodded to the man, then refocused his search. Where had she danced off to?

Jerome had left home before Rose was born, hadn't even known she existed until two weeks ago, when his father's attorney had finally located him. When he'd asked to meet her, he'd discovered she'd been sent west on the Orphan Train. He'd boarded a train, stopping to wire at each town along the way, trying to connect with the headmistress in charge of the orphans, and met up with Rose at the final stop.

She'd stood with a stubborn lift to her chin, tears in her

eyes. When he'd approached her, she'd been wary, but she'd come without protest. Apparently, she'd saved any protest for now. All he wanted to do was keep her safe.

"Rose!" He yelled against the wind. Unbalanced by the bags, he slipped on the snow-covered boardwalk. Confound it.

A blast from the train signaled the all-aboard.

Up ahead, he spied Rose entering a shop. In seven quick strides, he arrived, shifted the bags to one hand, then pulled on the door with the other. The scent of cinnamon and yeast filled his nostrils as he stepped inside.

"Why did you run off? The train is going to leave without us. Hurry, Rose." His voice came out in quick gasps after the exertion. As if to punctuate his statement, the train whistle sounded in the distance.

"I told you I was hungry." She crossed her arms, stamping her foot.

"You're my ward now. You must do as I say." Jerome worked to steady his voice.

"You *said* I was your sister."

He averted his eyes from Rose's face, only to find himself staring at the face of a woman. His ears heated with the pounding of his pulse. The woman stood staring at them with eyes as fine as the emeralds he'd once beheld in a museum. Her blond hair swept up into a softer version of the styles worn back east. Her cheeks were flushed in a lovely way. She was too beautiful to be real. None of this felt like reality. Had he drifted into a dream on the train?

The loud blare of the train whistle snapped him back to his senses.

He straightened. "I apologize for my sister's ill temper. It's been a difficult day." His eyes dropped to Rose. "Why did you leave the safety of the train?"

A chugging of gears sounded with a rumble as the train pulled out from the nearby station before Rose had a chance to answer. He flashed a look at the woman who'd moved closer to them.

"When will the next train come through?"

"It won't be until tomorrow. And that's if the snow stops." Her eyes widened to punctuate her doubt of a break in the storm.

"I need you." A young boy's voice sounded from somewhere above as a little girl's face peeked around from the end of a stairwell on the opposite side of the bakery.

The woman, half turned at the child's call, nodded to the young girl, signaling she'd be coming soon. Her hands made a motion for the girl to scurry back upstairs. As she turned her attention back to him, her eyes met his and his gut pinched. He'd been admiring a married woman.

"Where is the boarding house?"

Her brows crinkled in sympathy. "I delivered a batch of cinnamon rolls there this morning. I'm afraid it's full."

"It smells good in here," Rose interjected, stepping further into the bakery. She moved closer to the display cabinet on the wall that faced the window. "Are there any cinnamon rolls?"

"Is there a hotel? Surely it isn't full." He didn't have time to talk about cinnamon rolls.

"I'm hungry. Let's stay here." Rose singsonged her words again, running her hand along the fine wood cabinet.

He took a step closer to her. "We had a plan. To get home. Now, we'll get a room, then leave on the train tomorrow."

"I don't care about your plan. I'm hungry." She stamped her foot.

"The hotel is making repairs. That's why the boarding house is full." The woman offered an answer to his earlier question, as if Rose weren't making him appear inept with her antics.

Jerome scanned the bakery. All was neat. The walls were a soft shade. Every table and chair clean and polished. A rack with loaves of fresh bread stood along the wall next to the stairs.

He cleared his throat. "May I speak to your husband about lodging for the night?"

The woman's face paled. Her lips moved as if considering his proposal as her eyes focused on Rose with a pitying look.

"Tell him I'll gladly pay."

Her eyes shot to his. "Sir, my name is Caroline Wilson. I'm a widow. But under the circumstances, you and your sister are welcome to stay for the night."

His gut pinched. He'd not meant to cause her pain.

"I'm sure the children will enjoy getting to know you"—Caroline moved forward to wrap her arm around Rose's shoulder—"and your brother."

Rose turned to Caroline, tiptoeing up to whisper loudly in her ear. "He doesn't like children."

Caroline's eyes locked on his, an amused smile playing at her lips.

Two

THE THUMPING OF FEET ON WOOD echoed around Jerome, pulling his attention to the stairs on his left. Five faces peered down at him. He cast a glance at Rose, staring wide-eyed, then returned his attention to the descending children.

Caroline placed a hand on his sister's back.

"Before we get everyone something to eat, let me introduce you." Caroline nodded to the children. An aroma of meat and vegetables wafted from a room at the back of the bakery. Just past the door ahead of them.

Jerome fell in behind Rose. The thump of little feet bounded down the stairs. He side-stepped out of the way as a small hand touched his. Jerome hesitated to clasp his hand. The boy, with a lock of brown hair sticking out from his head, scrunched his frosting-smudged face up.

A girl with a neatly wound braid reached down to hold the boy's hand. She looked to be about Rose's age and wore as serious a face as his sister had the day he found her. "This is Davie. He's only four."

"Mr. Barnett, Rose, this is Lucy, and, as she said, Davie." Caroline placed her hand on the girl's shoulder as she introduced her, then moved to what must be a younger girl, with hair the color of maple syrup and a shy smile. "This is her younger sister, Stella."

He worked to commit the names to memory, using the same system he had for clients. Lucy's hair is golden, Stella's is like syrup, Davie's small and stocky. What about the other two? Did all these children belong to Caroline?

"This is Gilbert." Caroline had moved to stand behind him, gently patting his arm, even as Gilbert fidgeted from foot to foot. She then leaned down to pick up the smallest girl, the one with blond hair and eyes of blue. "Last, but not least, is Flora."

They all appeared well-mannered enough, although a few faces bore a smudge or two. Did children's faces need constant wiping? As the children filed past him, the boy named Gilbert broke into a skip. They continued to move around him as he passed through the doorway and toward a table in the middle of the little kitchen. Chairs scraped across the wooden floor as the older girls pulled them out to help the younger ones. Chatter and sniffles filtered around him in close proximity.

Cookies were strewn across the table, half of them frosted. A bowl of frosting rested in the middle, with a spatula balanced over the top. Popcorn littered the floor, and a string on the other end of the table waited for more popcorn to finish the decoration. Bowls of rising dough sat near the fire, their yeasty odor making his mouth water.

Rose skipped to take a seat by Stella. Maybe she enjoyed stringing popcorn. A rush of images from his childhood bombarded him, tightening his chest. He had to refocus. He had to get back to New York.

He eyed Caroline as she directed all the children like a fine, choreographed dance. She had Lucy and Davie frosting cookies, while Gilbert swept up spilled popcorn before joining the others. Jerome took a step forward, his bowler hat in his hand. "Do you know when the telegraph office opens tomorrow?"

Caroline whirled around from the table, almost bumping right into him. "I need to check the stew."

He stepped out of the way, turning to follow her over to the stove in the corner. The aroma as Caroline stirred set off a growl from his stomach. She dipped a large spoon in the pot. Her eyes met his, sending a jolt through him. No woman had done that in years. He'd avoided forming an attachment to anything but his work for so long.

"Have a taste." Caroline held up a spoonful for him.

In a flash, Flora leaned forward in Caroline's arms to slurp from the spoon. He held up his hand as Caroline held out the spoon to him. How many others might have tasted off that spoon already? He gave his head a quick shake to clear it. He had to focus. "The telegraph office?"

A chair scraped across the wooden floor as Gilbert rose with a bowl in his hands. "We ran out of frosting."

With a quick step, Jerome dodged being brushed by the bowl, as coated with frosting on the outside as the cookies.

What would it take to get a word in edgewise? He rubbed his forehead, a trick he'd learned to calm his nerves.

"There's enough left to finish what you have." Caroline smiled as she placed a hand on the boy's head, tussling his hair much like Jerome's father once had his. "Hurry, now. The stew is almost finished. We need to clear the table."

At the table, Rose leaned closer to Stella and giggled. A melodic sound he hadn't had the privilege to hear until now. Nothing this past week had brought as big a smile to Rose's face as a quarter of an hour spent in Caroline's kitchen.

"We didn't get any cookies on the awful train." Rose concentrated on the cookie she frosted while huddled close to Stella.

Caroline handed Jerome two bowls of stew, and he began placing them in front of the children, leaning close to hear his sister.

"Why did your dad take you on an awful train?" Cookie crumbs sprinkled from Gilbert's mouth as he spoke.

"He's not my dad. He didn't take me." Rose snatched a bite of cookie, but he refrained from scolding her for eating dessert before the stew.

With wide eyes, Davie leaned in. "Who is he?"

"Who took you?" That from Stella.

"He's my brother. People made me get on the train with other kids after my mom and dad died."

Jerome worked to steady the trembling of his hand as he lowered a bowl of stew in front of Stella. He'd not known. He would have stopped them from putting Rose on that train.

"Where are you going now?" Gilbert's words were muffled by cookie.

Lucy leveled a stare at her brother. "She's going home, silly."

"I don't have a home anymore. Not like I did." Silence stole over the table.

A knot formed in Jerome's gut. This pain. He knew it all too well. The knot twisted inside him as he placed a bowl in front of Rose. With the back of her hand, Rose swiped a tear away. All he could do was watch her, unsure of how to offer any comfort.

Caroline moved close with a plate of warm biscuits, her dark woolen skirt swaying with her graceful movements. She placed the biscuits on the table, then bent over to give Rose a hug before moving to place a bowl of stew in Jerome's hands. Caroline's eyes met his. Her hand rested on his forearm, giving it a gentle squeeze. As if she recognized his loss. His pain.

She let her hand fall from his arm. "Gilbert, will you ask the blessing?"

Jerome tried to follow the words, but memories of his own childhood prayers fought to transport him far into his past. What was it about being here with these people that kept bringing back memories he'd shut out for so long?

Gilbert elbowed him. "You can eat now that we've prayed."

He dipped a spoon of the steaming broth. It warmed his insides. Closing his eyes, he filtered out the surrounding chatter to pick apart the flavors. Garlic, pepper, a hint of parsley . . .

"What will Rose do while you are gone?"

His eyes flew open to find several faces waiting for his answer. "Gone?"

"When you work?" Lucy blinked at him.

"No worries." He wiped his mouth with the one clean napkin he'd managed to secure. "I'll write up an ad for a nanny."

Rose pulled a face, along with the other girls, but he didn't miss the tender look Caroline shot her in response. He'd thought a nanny the perfect answer. Perhaps he'd misjudged.

As they finished their stew, the children left the table in as much noisy chaos and stomping feet as they'd come. Rose waved at him, a pleased look on her face, as she exited with the others. He raised an eyebrow in question.

"Let her enjoy some time to play before bedtime." Caroline stood, picking up bowls as she did.

Jerome rose, taking his bowl to the sink. "If you show me where the bedding is, I can fix the pallets."

He turned to find her at his elbow. The warmth of her presence clutched at him. To garner space, he moved to pick up the rest of the dishes at the table while she began heating water to wash them.

"Do you have an extra dish cloth for me to wipe the table?" He held out his hand as she turned to study him.

Caroline wrung out another cloth, her brows arched in surprise. "Thank you."

He swiped at the table as water splashed into the sink from the pan where she'd heated it. He pushed in the chairs, wiping out the seats. Maybe Caroline could help him connect with Rose. The last chair scraped into place. Cupping the crumbs he'd scraped in one hand, he spun on his heel to face Caroline. Pans clanged as she dropped them into the rinse water.

"I need your help. You have managed to comfort Rose in a way that I haven't in the past week since I found her. Teach me how to be able to talk to Rose the way that you do. In exchange, I'm sure I can offer you ideas on how to run your business more efficiently."

She offered him a tight-lipped smile over her shoulder. Almost pitying. "I have no need of help running my bakery. Or my life. But I can see that Rose is a little girl in need of a soft touch. Especially this holiday season with her mom and dad gone."

Suds dripped from a bowl as she dunked it in the rinse water before handing it to him to dry.

"I'll help you out. Not for any sort of exchange." She held him with her clear eyes. "Simply out of Christian charity. If you stay a few days, it might help her to celebrate Christmas here with the other children."

"That's not possible." His body tensed. Getting home is how he met his deadlines for his job. The only means he had for caring for his sister. The only thing he knew. "We have to get home."

A rustling behind him stopped whatever Caroline was about to say. Rose stood in the doorway to the kitchen, weariness written on her face. He'd yet to make the pallet.

"I'll get some blankets." Caroline dried her hands, rushing from the room.

"Are you all ready for bed, then?" He didn't know what Rose did to prepare herself for bed.

A soft footstep told him Caroline had returned. She flurried past him, arranging a pallet on the floor in front of the fireplace at the far end of the room. Rose sat beside her, removing her shoes before slipping under the blankets. Caroline pulled a cover over her, tucking her in.

He ought to be the one doing those things for his sister. Rose was his flesh and blood. His responsibility now. Caroline's hand brushed his as she handed him another stack of quilts.

"Rose isn't the only one who needs comfort this holiday season." The warmth in Caroline's eyes unsettled him.

She turned to retreat from the kitchen, but not before he'd shot off his hasty reply.

"I have all I need."

I have all I need.

Caroline cast a glance over her shoulder as she picked up the lantern before reaching the stairs to the family rooms. Jerome stood watching her from the kitchen, a wisp of his chestnut hair falling across his forehead. For a moment, their eyes held. Then he shifted away.

She exhaled.

There hadn't been a man in her space since the passing of her husband, Paul. Her hand ran along the banister as she ascended the wooden stairs. There'd been moments during dinner that left her feeling discombobulated. Despite Jerome's formal exterior, she had discovered a softness underneath as he'd helped her clean up.

At the top stair, she stepped to the side, so as not to hit the board that squeaked. The children were likely already snuggled in their beds. By some miracle, she hoped a few of them had fallen asleep.

Turning to her left, she crossed the main family room and walked down the narrow hall to enter the room the boys shared. The space held a bed along one wall. Pegs jutted from the wall by the door, but the boys' clothes lay crumpled on the floor. Davie's mouth opened slightly as he dozed, leaning against Gilbert. One foot poked out of the covers, a hole in the toe of the sock. Three more that needed darning peeked out from the pile of dirty clothes.

Her chest tightened inside. There was always too much work to do. How could she give them all they needed?

Caroline tiptoed out of the room with her arms held close, and into the other bedroom that she shared with the three girls. Lucy and Stella peeked open their eyes as she tucked their quilt around them, fighting to hold back the emotions swelling inside her.

"Good night, girls. Don't stay up whispering." If only she could do more for them.

"We won't." The sluggishness of Lucy's voice reassured her more than her words.

A whimper rose from the crib, where Flora squirmed.

"Hush now." Caroline knelt near the wooden crib, almost too small for her two-year-old, but she hadn't the money to commission another bed from the local carpenter yet. Maybe next spring, she'd have the means to visit Ed

McGraw's shop and see about a new bed for Flora. Possibly even a few new wooden toys for the others.

"Hold me." Little Flora reached up her arms, her eyes still half closed, and Caroline pulled Flora onto her lap.

Caroline rocked her until she dozed again, then placed her near the other girls in the big bed. She paused a moment, watching them all slumber. Her heart warmed at the looks of contentment on their faces.

With all the children sleeping, she fished under the bed for her knitting needles and half-finished gloves for Stella. There were only two more days 'til Christmas. Her hands met bare boards. She must have left her knitting in the kitchen this morning.

Using careful steps, she descended the stairs. As she neared the doorway to the kitchen, she startled at the flickering candlelight. It danced with the firelight from the corner, casting shadows along the walls. The quilts by the fire were still. Rose must be sound asleep.

She caught sight of a slight movement by the kitchen table. Jerome's stocking feet were slowly shifting from where he'd propped them on the table to land on the floor. He rose from the chair with quiet intention, stoking the fire, then reaching to pull an extra blanket over Rose.

Jerome turned around, then startled.

Caroline moved forward, hating even to whisper into the beautiful stillness. "I'm only getting my knitting."

He stood in his stocking feet, hair tousled where he'd run his hands through it. "What are you working on so late?"

"Christmas gift." She fingered the yarn she'd retrieved from her earlier hiding place in the kitchen cabinet, averting her gaze from his feet, his rumpled hair, his untucked shirt. She pointed to his paperwork on the table for a distraction. "Some work never ends."

He ran his fingers through his hair and down his neck. "I have to put in my dues now while I'm studying law. In a few years, when I become a partner, I can turn it off more."

"That's a fine dream." She rubbed her finger along the yarn in her hands, her voice still low. "When I was married to my husband, I felt I was living my dream. How fast things changed."

"I'm afraid Rose feels the same." He eyed her with a softness in his expression. "It's hard when life forces change on us. We need our dreams more than ever then."

All of her dreams had faded with the death of Paul. Hadn't they?

He studied her. "What's your dream now, Mrs. Wilson?"

This man managed to get under her skin again. The room had felt so warm and safe as they spoke, a feeling she'd not known her heart longed for. She'd do well to check how fast she'd grown close to him.

"There's no time for dreams. Only time for the children. And survival." Caroline gripped the yarn with the knitting needles until it stung her hand.

Jerome held her gaze for a moment, as if searching her face for some indication of . . . what? He broke his stare to turn the intensity of his focus on Rose.

"I don't know if I can be everything she needs." His voice was a whisper, leaving her to wonder if she was meant to have heard the words.

"One day, she'll realize how much it means that you found her after she'd been sent on the Orphan Train."

"She never should have been sent away." The creases at the corners of his mouth grew more defined as he watched his sister.

"How did it happen?"

"She is actually my half sister. I was away when I got word about my father's estate. By then, she'd been shipped out on the Orphan Train."

The lines at his eyes, the weariness in his voice, all tugged at her. This man who'd set out to find Rose. How lost and alone Rose must have been. A flash of Lucy, so close to Rose's age, rolled through her mind. She'd be tied in knots with worry if her niece had been sent off like that. Lucy would've been lost, bewildered, and frightened beyond measure. No doubt Rose had been all those things when Jerome showed up to rescue her.

"May I ask? How long was it that you found out you had a sister before you left to find her?"

"I set out that day." He crossed his arms, a gravelly tone infiltrating his words.

When he pulled his gaze from Rose, his face held a haggard expression, as if he expected to meet her censure.

She held his eyes with hers until the lines of his face began to soften.

"No one was to blame," she said.

He scrubbed a weary hand over his face, letting his shoulders relax.

This man tugged at her heart in a way she hadn't felt in years.

"I'll help you all I can while you are here." Still gripping her knitting, she turned toward the kitchen door.

Three

J EROME PICKED UP HIS PEN TO MARK UP another contract by lamplight. He'd risen early. There'd been no reason to keep fighting a fitful sleep, disturbed by the cold, hard floor and the memory of Caroline's pretty features the evening before.

A soft rustling of skirts sounded behind him as the gentle fragrance of lilac soap reached him. Caroline moved across the kitchen toward the stove as a hint of light filtered through the window. He reread the line on the page again.

The clank of a cast-iron pan against the stove broke the stillness. He'd hoped to finish going over the last of his paperwork before Caroline came down, but the woman must never sleep. Up late, up early, she'd likely wear herself out. But that was none of his business. He'd best put her from his mind.

The aforementioned party, hereafter referred to as . . .

A sigh from where Caroline brushed past him to enter

the lean-to intruded on his study. Jerome dropped his pen, spilling a bit of ink across the document. This would never do. He hurried to shove papers and pen into his satchel as he rose to stand.

Jerome slipped his arm through one sleeve of his coat, then the other, as he moved to enter the lean-to. Caroline worked to stack firewood. He stepped to the other side of her, pulling the door to the outside open enough to see a pile of snow halfway up the doorframe. He'd not be taking this way to the train station after helping her with the wood.

He turned to Caroline, slipping his arms under her already half-laden ones. "Here. Let me take the wood. It will go faster if I hold it while you stack."

A soft smile of appreciation lifted her lips as she shifted the wood to his arms. "It's been a long time since we had this much snow."

"You've lived here long?"

"I moved here with my husband seven years ago. Right after we married. I was only eighteen." Her tone was hushed, no doubt not wanting to wake the rest of the household above or Rose on her pallet. She placed another stick of firewood on the growing stack in his arms, nodding toward the kitchen as she did.

"The children. They aren't all yours, then?" He followed her to the rack between the stove and the fireplace.

"The three oldest are my sister's. God rest her soul." She removed the pieces of wood from his arms to stack them.

Once one hand was free enough, he leaned in to help her

stack. "I'm sorry for your loss. Losing your sister and your husband so close must have been difficult."

"I managed." She swiped at a tear.

Her hands trembled as she snatched the last few pieces of wood from his hands, turning quickly to place them in the stove.

And it must have been difficult for her to take in three more children when she was still grieving. All while trying to run her bakery. How did she do it with them all underfoot? Of course, she couldn't let them go to an orphanage. That, he understood only too well.

"Your husband worked the bakery with you?" Jerome made his way back to get another stack of wood from the lean-to.

Caroline followed, helping load the wood onto his arms. "I started the bakery later. Paul died two years ago. He'd gone to get another load of supplies to add on to our house."

They moved back into the kitchen, where Rose stirred on her pallet.

"What happened?" Jerome stopped at the rack to unload, Caroline helping.

"It was storming. The wagon flipped on the way home. I never should have insisted he go to town that day." Her voice choked.

"It's not your fault. You couldn't have known. I'm sure he wanted to go." If the wood hadn't filled his arms, he'd find some way to comfort her. But how? He wasn't the best at comforting others. But he knew how badly he'd wished for comfort as a child.

Caroline sniffled, swiping her hand across her face. "If

I'd been satisfied with the house the way it was instead of wanting more for myself, he wouldn't have been on the road."

"I'm so sorry for your loss." What else should he say? What more had anyone offered him as a young boy? He wanted to give her more. To somehow ease a bit of the sting. "It must have been hard to manage."

"After Paul passed, I was so numb. Davie was only two. Flora was born a few weeks later. I'd never felt so alone, giving birth to my daughter without her father there. And Davie too young to really remember his father." Her face paled as if remembering the pain she'd endured. "I celebrated nothing that year. I barely held on. Farm chores were too much for a woman with a toddler and a baby, even with the help of neighbors. With Paul gone, I had to find a way to survive. I turned to the only thing I knew and opened the bakery."

He stood from where he'd been loading the woodpile. She'd endured so much. He wanted to reach out to her. Ease her pain somehow.

She swiped hard at her cheeks, setting her jaw as she did. "Now, I have to focus on giving the children the perfect Christmas."

Her emerald eyes held his, as if searching for something, then she ducked her head. Faint sniffles still filled the small space between them as she began to pull out bowls and supplies. He wanted nothing more than to bring back her lively smile. This woman had suffered immeasurably, yet she worked herself from dawn to dusk for those around her.

Footfalls echoed from above. No doubt the children

would be down soon. He grabbed up his satchel from the table, then moved it to rest next to his other bundle on the floor by Rose.

He needed to get to the train station to check the schedule. His fingers set to working the buttons on his coat. A hint of yeast permeated the air.

"If you are hoping to catch the train, I don't think it will be running today." Caroline punched down dough, her sleeves rolled up to reveal the soft curve of her forearms.

The snow drift against the kitchen window needled him as he pushed out a harrumph. "I can't afford to lose a day. I'm going to go see about the schedule."

In long strides, he hurried around her and into the front of the bakery. Out the window, he saw what she must already know. Snow drifts piled halfway up the front windowpane, no doubt blocking the front door as they had the back. Jerome shoved his hand through his hair. Too much hinged on returning to New York on time.

He returned to the kitchen in the back of the bakery, stopping next to where Caroline worked at the counter. "I think you may be right about the train. Can you give me directions to the telegraph office? I need to let my office know where I am."

A soft smirk played about her lips. She dusted the counter with a fresh coat of flour, then began tracing shapes in it. "You will need to cross the road here."

The scent of cinnamon and yeast swirled in his nostrils as he leaned closer to follow the movement of her slender finger through the white dusting. She glanced up at him, so close he could make out the flecks of gold in her pretty eyes. Her lashes fluttered as she glanced away, a hint of flour smudged above her brow.

"Continue to go this direction, then you will be able to see the train station from here." Her finger circled a spot on her impromptu map. "The telegraph office is just west of it."

"Thank you." He watched her swipe at the counter, erasing the map. "I think I can make it out the back window."

Caroline paused, a spatula in her hand. "If you go, I am sending a small loaf of bread with you for Mr. Jones and his wife, Margaret. They are most likely stranded there."

Her last words came with a pointed look in his direction, as if to warn of why he shouldn't go, even as she wrapped up a warm loaf of bread.

She held out the parcel as he worked to secure his scarf. She tipped her head toward the pallet where his sister had begun to stir. "Rose will wake up soon. She will be looking for you."

Jerome stopped tying the scarf for a split moment as he read concern in Caroline's face. Was it all on behalf of Rose? His gut pinched at the thought that she might be worried for him herself. Together, they pushed open the window.

"Pray I get back before she does." He offered her one last reassuring smile before sliding out the window onto the drift of snow.

Caroline moved close to where Rose sat at a table in the bakery staring out the large front window. She placed a hand on her shoulder, but the girl didn't even glance up.

"Your brother will be back soon."

Rose hadn't finished eating earlier, just sat there, fiddling with her spoon until Caroline began clearing the table. Poor child. Her brother was all she had left.

Pulling her shawl tighter, Caroline walked back to the kitchen and stepped into the lean-to. She gathered up the garland she'd been keeping there. The fresh picked greenery had been given to her in exchange for a box of cinnamon rolls the day before, but she'd stashed the decorations until they had time to put them up.

With the children's help, Caroline wound garland around the front windows of the bakery and across the front counter. As Caroline hummed, Stella began singing "Silent Night." Soon all the children, including Rose, had joined in as they transformed the front of the bakery into a holiday wonderland.

The window clanked in the kitchen.

"He's back." Rose whispered the words as she rushed to the kitchen.

Caroline followed with Flora in her arms. The other children trailed close on her heels. Jerome had returned, his feet sliding through the window.

"Stay clear," his voice muffled through the scarf as he wiggled himself inside, then pulled in a couple of bundles. Snow clung to his eyelashes. It shook off his pants and coat, drifting to the floor.

Rose crossed her arms, turning away with pursed lips. A flash of hurt crossed Jerome's face. If only he could have seen her before. He pulled down his scarf to reveal a nose red with cold.

Gilbert lunged to grab some of the fallen snow, chasing his sisters with it. The other children followed them into the other room, laughing. There was no sense in stopping them. She had to help Jerome warm up after being out in such cold for so long.

"Give me your gloves and scarf. I'll hang them by the fire." Noticing his stiff hands, Caroline reached out to help him unwind the scarf. A flush rose in his cheeks as their fingers brushed.

"I can get that." He leaned close to Caroline, the warmth of his breath tickling her cheek. His teeth chattered. "I brought back a ham. Gift from Margaret at the telegraph office. To thank you for the bread."

"A ham. I can't believe you hauled it all the way back here in all that snow." She turned it over in her hands with pure joy. The perfect piece for Christmas dinner. She'd serve it with potatoes and fresh bread. "Let me put it in the ice box."

"It was no trouble." He mumbled the words as she rushed to place the ham in the icebox where she kept the butter and fresh cream.

She'd noticed another bag in his hands too. A burlap sack. He'd tucked it behind him as if to hide it from the children. Finished with the ham, she turned to find him warming himself by the fire. The burlap sack sat in the corner with his other belongings.

"Should we go join the children in the front of the bakery? Sounds as if they are having fun." He stepped from the fire, rubbing his hands together.

"They have hung mistletoe over the door to the kitchen

and above the stairs." She'd caught the children whispering amongst themselves.

Jerome moved to stand in the kitchen's doorway despite her warning, oblivious to the plans of little matchmakers. "Looks like you've been busy decorating."

"One has to use all their creativity in order to keep six children busy while trapped indoors." She lifted her lips in a smile, then passed in front of him to the front room.

Gilbert darted a glance at Stella. Stella widened her eyes at him before she and Rose broke into a soft giggle. A blush crept up Caroline's neck.

If only Jerome knew what they must be plotting.

Rose patted the spot on the bottom step next to where she and Stella sat. Caroline crossed the floor in a few steps to sit by the girls.

"My family's servants used to decorate the house in a grand fashion." Jerome walked around the front of the bakery, past each counter. "I haven't enjoyed decorations like this in years. You've all done a beautiful job."

The children beamed at his praise. But Caroline couldn't help noticing the way he worked his jaw. When he turned to face them, his eyes held a sorrow that blended with his appreciation. Caroline met his eyes until Gilbert asked another question of him. Perhaps she could make the time to knit a gift for Jerome and Rose too.

She squeezed Rose's shoulder gently. "Tell me what your holidays were like."

Stella fidgeted beside them as Rose chattered on. "Father was at his office most of the time, but he'd have the biggest tree delivered. It'd be set up in the front foyer by the windows so that all mother's friends would say how they loved it when they came to her parties. She had lots of parties. I wasn't allowed to come, but I'd sneak out to watch from the stairwell landing above. The tree would glisten with the ornaments the servants had hung on it. With an angel on top. I begged my parents to let me decorate too. But it was always the servants' job. I just wanted us to do it as a family like other people I knew."

"There wasn't anything that you were allowed to do?" Caroline asked.

"Our cook would sneak me into the kitchen. Her name was Gretchen. She let me decorate the gingerbread houses she'd made."

"I remember Gretchen. She always made time for me when no one else would."

The room grew quieter as Jerome moved closer. The man's brows knit together as he stared at Rose.

Caroline stood, motioning for him to take her place on the stairs. "Did the cook ever let you do anything like that when you were small?"

"She did. She always had spice gumdrops to decorate the roof with." He made a motion with his hand in the air as if reenacting it.

"What was your favorite?" Rose looped her arm in his as she leaned closer.

"Cinnamon."

A broad smile filled Rose's face as she gazed up at her brother. "Me too."

"I was terrible at putting them on. They would slide off."

"Can we make some?" Gilbert interrupted, and all the other children stared at Caroline in anticipation.

"I think that's a wonderful idea." Caroline turned her attention from Gilbert to Jerome. "I'm sure I can find a substitute for gumdrops. You and Rose could teach us all how to decorate them."

Jerome's face clouded over. "We don't have time. I have to get back."

Rose hung her head.

With a small jerk of her chin in Rose's direction while still focusing on Jerome, Caroline lifted her brows. His forehead crinkled, then relaxed as his mouth formed an O.

"But since we are stuck inside, anyway. If you have molasses to make the gingerbread. Maybe we could." He spluttered out the words. "It sounds like a grand idea."

Gilbert let out a whoop, smacking Davie on the back in a friendly manner as Stella beamed. Flora bounced on her toes, clapping chubby hands, though she didn't know what they were so excited about.

"You're under the mistletoe." Lucy pointed above Rose as Caroline took a step backward.

In a swift movement, Rose bounced up from the stair. She planted a kiss right on Jerome's cheek. A loud, silly, smacking kiss. The room erupted in laughter again as Jerome blushed, smiling the biggest smile Caroline had seen him wear yet. His eyes met hers. The joy there told her he thought things with his sister could work.

But Caroline wouldn't always be there to help him.

Four

I'M NOT TIRED." ROSE DIDN'T EVEN LOOK up at Jerome. Just kept coloring on the paper Caroline had given her earlier.

Jerome checked himself before arguing that her yawn not five minutes ago said otherwise. Things had gone so well earlier. He'd hoped it would extend longer than this. Part of him wanted Caroline to watch his victory in this new connection he'd formed with Rose. But it hadn't even lasted to bedtime.

He glanced at Caroline. She'd returned to sit by the table after helping the other children get ready for bed. Her soft features were highlighted by the glow of the lamp as she sat in a chair, knitting a scarf. If he asked for her help, he'd pull her from finishing whatever gift she worked on. And Christmas was only a day away.

He tore his eyes from Caroline to focus on Rose. Telling

her what to do would only make things worse. Perhaps he could negotiate with her.

"If you go to bed, I'll read to you."

Her eyes lit up as a smile played at her lips, but she kept coloring.

Jerome caught a pleased glance from Caroline. She set aside her knitting as she rose from her chair. On the corner of the table sat a large family Bible. Caroline pushed it toward Rose, while her eyes held his. "I've been reading the story of Christ's birth to the children."

His sister grinned up at Caroline, putting down her pencil. Rose's grin widened as she got up from the table to go sit on her pallet. She scrambled to unloose the ties on her shoes, then slid into the covers by the warmth of the kitchen fire. Wide green eyes peered from her face with anticipation. "You'll read the Christmas story, won't you? From Luke."

Caroline's face glowed. He wanted to get lost in her smile. The memory of the way she'd looked at him earlier, sitting next to Rose under the mistletoe, filled him with warmth. He let his gaze wander over to the doorway. Another bunch of the greenery and berries hung there haphazardly. He blinked any thoughts of mistletoe and kisses from his sleep riddled brain. Caroline had scurried away from it earlier when he didn't even know it was there. Besides, tonight he wanted to prove he could connect with Rose without any help.

A feeling of comfort rested in his chest as he gathered the Bible in his hands, then crossed the room again to settle next to Rose. How he longed for the warmth of family again. He let the large book fall open on his lap before he ran his finger through the pages, stopping at Luke.

"And it came to pass in those days, that there went out a decree from Caesar Augustus that all the world should be taxed." He read the chapter through, fighting the swell of memories rolling over him as Rose's head nodded. Behind him, Caroline began washing clothes. The gentle sloshing of the fabric in the water no doubt helping lull Rose to sleep.

Jerome gently closed the Bible, laying it aside. He rose, turning to study Caroline. She'd begun rinsing out the clothes. He crossed the room to stand near her.

"It worked." Her hands sloshed a shirt back and forth in the rinse water.

"I haven't read that story in years." He kept his voice low, fiddling with the button on his shirt. "My father used to read it every Christmas Eve, but all of that stopped . . ."

After the horrible Christmas that changed it all. They'd stopped all remembrance of the holiday from that day forward. Yet Rose asked for this chapter. Knew it.

A wisp of Caroline's hair drifted to curl on her cheek as she shifted to look up at him. "It seemed a comfort to Rose for you to read it to her."

Perhaps his family had healed after Rose was born. A healing he'd not been there for. He should have gone home in the last ten years. Should have tried to connect with his father again. He swallowed hard as he caught sight of Rose's eyelids fluttering, but her breathing kept the steady rhythm of slumber.

He stepped up to the sink beside Caroline, fishing his

hands in the rinse water to pull out a shirt. Holding it in both hands, he twisted, letting the water fall to the sink below. "Do you ever sleep?"

Caroline side-eyed him as he placed the shirt in the basket with the other pieces of clothing, then moved on to wring out a pair of trousers. "I hadn't expected you to be good at this."

A light chuckle escaped him. "Who do you think does my laundry?"

"When you mentioned you'd hire a nanny, I supposed you had a maid." A blush stole into her cheeks, making her all the prettier in the soft light. A look of sympathy flashed across her features. "My husband and I married so young that I hadn't thought what it was like for a bachelor, with no one to do these things for you."

As he turned to place the trousers in the basket, his shoulder bumped hers, shooting an awareness through him. He needed a distraction. "It must be difficult running the bakery with so many children while still making time for them. Keeping up with your chores—like laundry. How have you managed?"

"Not as well as I would like at times." Water sloshed in the sink as she pulled out a petticoat. She twisted up the fabric as she twisted up her mouth. "I should have done this laundry up earlier, I know, but I couldn't resist decorating with the children. Last year, I hadn't taken the time for such things."

"That hardly sounds like you." He leaned against the sink, studying her features as she continued wringing out the well-worn fabric.

"In the middle of getting the bakery going, I received word about my sister. Last Christmas I was too numb, too selfish, to give any of the children the holiday they deserved."

This dug deep into him. She was pouring out of herself, trying to create perfection that wasn't possible in this broken world. While he'd only ever closed himself off when faced with pain like she'd known. How he wanted to reach out and envelope her in his arms.

"The children don't need a perfect Christmas. You're giving them what they need. Not only by meeting their physical needs but how you love them."

She twisted the white cotton one last time before tossing it into the basket. "I owe it to them to try."

A sigh left her as she reached in to pull out the last piece of clothing. Soft wisps of her hair brushed against his chin as he leaned close. The fragrance of lilac in her hair mingled with the yeasty aroma of the kitchen. Caroline had risen to the challenge of caring for five children, despite her own pain. She'd make a suitable partner for any man wanting a family, especially a blended one.

He reached out to take her hand, guiding her to sit in the chair she'd left earlier. "The laundry is washed. Stop for a cup of tea before hanging it."

"I couldn't possibly."

"It won't be the perfect Christmas if you work yourself until you collapse."

Her brows rose in surprise, but she conceded, almost as if she were relieved to sit a moment. Jerome shook the kettle on the stove. As he suspected, it still had water in it.

"What was your childhood like?" Grabbing two cups from the drying rack, he flipped them over, then filled the strainers with loose tea from the box at the back of the counter.

A wisp of a smile filled her face, then diminished. "I was about Rose's age when my family left the East."

Her words held the faint hint of an eastern accent. Why hadn't he picked up on it before? He began to pour the water over the strainers, then brought the cups to the table. The thanks in Caroline's eyes gave his tired frame renewed energy.

"I worked in a factory with Eliza, my sister. One day, I asked my mother if I could quit and go to school. It was selfish of me, I know, as we needed the income to afford our apartment. I was so tired. I figured there had to be more to life than the factory." She lifted the strainer from her cup to take a sip.

"What did your mother say?" A drop of tea sloshed over as he lifted his cup.

"To my surprise, my mother let me stay home." Her clear eyes met his, but her fingers worked at the handle of the teacup. She pulled her eyes away, lifting it to take another sip. "The next week, we left. Just like I'd wanted. Moved west, where we children didn't have to work anymore. We could go to school. But I never saw my grandparents or my friends again."

"That must have been hard for you."

She stared over her cup, past him, as if remembering them. "I hadn't imagined how deeply we'd miss the ones we left behind. My mother most of all. That Christmas she cried more than I'd ever seen her. Especially when Pa asked for the fig pudding. Ma burst into tears. Later I learned she didn't know how to make it. Grandma always did. My family hurt that holiday. All because I'd put myself above everyone else. My choice affected everyone."

Jerome settled his cup on the table to reach for her hands, the softness a pleasant surprise, given all her hard work. With a quick motion, she squeezed his hand before rising.

"So. You see why I have to give the children the perfect Christmas this year. Whatever it takes."

Caroline turned her face from him as she spun toward the basket of clothes. Before she could lift it, he'd hurried to her side.

"Let me lift that for you."

He moved closer to grab the basket. His hands covered hers on the handles. Her hair brushed across his cheek, the soft strands tickling his skin in a delightful way. She shifted to look up at him as she pulled her hands from his, her eyes wide amidst her pretty features. With her face so close, everything in him wanted to close the gap between his lips and hers. A pit formed in his stomach. He wanted to wrap Caroline in his arms and never let her go.

What was he thinking?

Jerome forced himself to step away. As soon as the snow cleared, he was leaving.

Caroline grabbed the lamp from the table and followed Jerome from the kitchen. The lamp wobbled in her hands at first, her sweaty palms slick against the metal. Her mind filled with the memory of Jerome so close to her as he leaned in for the basket. As he ducked under the mistletoe at the door to the kitchen, the giggles of the children from earlier in the day washed over her. They'd been playing matchmaker, trying to get her under that mistletoe with Jerome.

She passed under the sprigs, touching her lips as she did. Had Jerome almost kissed her at the sink? Her pulse accelerated, drumming in her ears. She'd not had an attraction to a man like this in years.

At the staircase, Jerome paused to let her pass in front of him. "Ladies first."

Caroline lifted the hem of her woolen skirt. She sucked in a breath as she angled to slip past Jerome onto the staircase. Even with the basket between them, they were so close. Once her foot took the steps that turned the stairs toward the second floor, she caught Jerome in her side vision before he fell in directly behind her. He grinned as she turned to look back at him. One strand of dark hair fell over his forehead, the basket balanced on his shoulder. She snapped her head back around to focus forward.

With quiet steps, she led him to the little sitting room. A clothesline was strung across one end of the room. Two worn settees with faded floral patterns faced each other, creating a space for her and all the children to sit and read or play games. Strewn across one cushion was a primer and slate. Flora's doll peeked out from under one end of the furniture. Things had been too hectic the last few days for her to tidy the place.

"The kitchen would be a better place to hang the laundry." Jerome spoke with his business voice, no doubt assessing the situation for productivity.

"I can't risk customers seeing petticoats and stockings hung to dry." A blush lit her cheeks as she settled the lamp on a small table, then grasped at her petticoat in the basket.

"Good point." His voice was low, not wanting to disturb the sleeping children. His hand reached out to take hold of the pins she'd dug out of her apron for him. A tingle spread through her hand as his fingers brushed her skin.

Caroline flung the petticoat over the line, clipping a wooden clothespin over the garment. Next to her, Jerome spread out a shirt, clipping it in place by the shoulders. The low light of the lamp left them practically working in the dark, side by side. It felt so natural, so comfortable. So did her growing attraction to him. She'd do well to remember he was leaving soon.

"Do you mind if I ask why you left home?"

He bent to retrieve another garment as she pulled out Lucy's dress. The sensation of his warm hand brushing hers set the butterflies to working in her stomach.

"My father wanted me to take over the family business, but he and I butted heads all the time. Mostly, I wanted to see more of the world beyond our little town." Jerome let his shoulders droop. "He called my plans foolish."

She stilled. "Were things always so difficult with your father?"

"Not always. Our home had been a happy one. After my mother passed away, things were hard, but my father remarried quickly. My stepmother was kind. She tried to bring the softness between my father and me. Like you've done with Rose. She helped us smooth out our differences, until she . . ." He halted, as if contemplating whether to finish. His voice grew raspy. "She lost a child on Christmas Eve."

Caroline let out a gasp. She couldn't imagine the pain of such a loss. "How awful for her."

"After that, things changed. Christmas joy stopped in our house. She didn't come out of her room for weeks. Father threw himself into his work and we only grew apart."

Her heart grieved for all his family had been through. Hurt for the boy he'd been, enduring so much heartache with no one to comfort him.

Her fingers tangled with his as they both grasped for the same clothespin. His brown eyes settled on her, making her want to get lost in their depths.

"I'm sorry you never had the chance to reconnect with your father."

Frown lines crinkled his forehead as his hands placed the last sock over the line. "If I'd been enough for them, maybe they wouldn't have descended into such despair. Maybe we never would have lost what little we had." His voice dropped so low she almost didn't hear him.

"He must have loved you. Rose knew about you, even if you didn't know about her. And now you have each other." She reached over to place a hand on his arm, aware of the closeness it brought between them.

Jerome shuffled slightly closer until he faced her. The lamplight caught the warmth in his eyes. Her breath came in slow gasps as she leaned in.

"Momma, I thirsty."

At the sleepy voice of Davie, Caroline dropped her hold

on Jerome's hand to spin and face him. "Shh, now. Let's not wake the others. You go back to bed and I'll be there in a minute."

Davie nodded his head, hair sticking out in all directions, before stumbling back to his room. Her hand flew to her chest as heat filled her cheeks. What had she been thinking?

"You see to Davie. I'll take the basket back downstairs." The earnestness in Jerome's voice shot a flash of shame through her.

She hurried toward the boys' room, determined to outrun the pull he had on her by simple physical distance.

"Goodnight, Caroline." His deep voice rumbled the words, then she heard his tread on the stairs.

After getting Davie settled back in bed and reassuring a sleepy Gilbert that everything was fine, Caroline made her way down the hall to her room. Flora slept soundly in her crib. Without even bothering to remove her outer clothing, Caroline slipped under the covers with Stella and Lucy.

Even with her body bone tired, no sleep came. Images of Jerome's hands hanging Gilbert's trousers, even as his fingers brushed against her own, taunted her. They mingled with the way he'd looked at her as he'd leaned close enough to kiss her.

An image of Paul flitted through her mind. Was she betraying her late husband? With all these thoughts of Jerome? But Paul was gone. He would never come back to her.

Caroline shifted her head on the pillow, working to find a comfortable spot. A foot kicked against her back. Stella always did toss to and fro in the bed. Sometimes Stella had nightmares or called out for her mother. Another reason Caroline couldn't put herself above the needs of the children in her care. She couldn't risk them getting attached to Jerome and Rose too. She had to do right by them.

Besides, Caroline had too many things to get done before Christmas. She couldn't afford to focus on Jerome. Couldn't want this. If she dared, everything would fall apart.

And he'd made it clear he was leaving as soon as the train was back on schedule.

Five

"THIS IS DUMB." THE SCISSORS CLATTERED to the table as Rose jerked her hand out of Jerome's.

Jerome scrubbed a hand over his face as he glanced out the front bakery window at the bit of setting sun peeking out to glimmer across the mounds of snow for Christmas Eve.

"I did everything like I was supposed to. But it's not right." Rose's clipped words took Jerome back to his own school days.

He'd been trying to guide her as she angled the scissors, but she'd clamped down too hard, snipping the folds of the paper snowflake. The other children worked at the table, all but Davie and Flora, who played with a ball under the table. Soon, they would add their snowflakes to the tree for decoration. It had been Caroline's idea. No doubt a means to entertain the children and help him connect with his sister.

As Caroline leaned in to place a reassuring hand on Rose's back, the familiar lilac scent filled his senses, taking him back to last night on the stairs. A giggle from Stella jolted him back. Gilbert and Stella whispered, eyeing him from one of the other round café tables. Lucy let out a small laugh too. What had them whispering behind their hands?

"Snowflakes are supposed to be a work of art. Unique." Caroline spoke to Rose, but her hand gently nudged him. Her eyes shifted with a nod of her head, just out of Rose's sight, as if she wanted him to take over comforting Rose.

"No two snowflakes are alike." The words came out of his mouth in a bit of a rush. "Why don't you try again?"

Caroline slid him another folded paper from the other side of the table. He fingered the paper, his eyes reading Caroline's. It was as if she were trying to force him to connect with Rose on his own. Which is what he'd wanted. But was it still what he wanted? He slid the paper over to his sister.

Rose shot him a scowl.

"Try again."

Holding the scissors in her hand, Rose took a tentative snip. Then another. Her looks morphed from begrudging to delight as she unfurled a string of snowflakes.

He placed his hand on her shoulder. "Good job."

Rose turned to offer him a smile. A vision filled his mind. One of him wend Rose, living a happy life together. A better situation than the one he'd had with his father and stepmother. Not as strained. With Caroline right in the middle of it.

He let his eyes slip over to where Caroline now folded

papers with Stella at the other table. If only it'd work. But Caroline had a bakery in the wilds of Wyoming and his office sat atop a plot of land in New York.

Funny, he hadn't thought of his office, or work, or contracts since last night.

Last night.

Remembrance of those moments with Caroline set his pulse to racing in a good way. Maybe work wasn't all he needed in his life.

A tap landed on his arm. Rose had handed him another paper to fold. This was Caroline's doing. He glanced her way as he creased the folds. Caroline lifted her mouth in a grin.

"You're good at this. Do you make snowflakes like this for your house?" Rose set about clipping the paper he'd slid her way.

"I've never needed them at my house."

"Never needed them? Don't you like them?" Her eyes begged an answer.

Stella paused her scissors, intent on their conversation.

"I don't decorate for Christmas," he said.

"Why not?"

He paused his folding. "I'm not in the habit of celebrating it."

"You don't celebrate Christmas!" Rose stood from her seat, eyes intent on him.

Stella and Lucy exchanged glances.

Jerome held out a hand, motioning for Rose to sit.

"I haven't had anyone to celebrate it with." The thought of celebrating alone always brought back memories of that long ago Christmas. The doctor coming late on Christmas Eve. The whispered words. The sight of the servants snuffing out the candles on the tree in hushed sadness. His father's abrupt dismissal when he asked if they were reading the Christmas story. Too many memories he didn't want invading his space.

But this year was different.

"Now you've got me to celebrate with so you won't be alone." The small hand of Rose touched his shoulder and he placed his hand over hers.

"You've got all of us this year," Stella pronounced. The others murmured their agreement.

God had given him more than he'd thought to ask for this Christmas. More than he deserved. He worked to push back the raw emotion swelling in his throat.

The sound of crackling and sizzling erupted from the kitchen.

"The cider." Caroline lifted her skirt to rush from the room as the fragrance of cinnamon and cloves barreled into the front of the bakery.

Jerome followed close behind Caroline, welcoming the change of subject.

"I caught it in time." Stirring the cider, Caroline pushed a loose tendril of hair from her forehead. A lovely flush filled her cheeks.

Joyful voices came from behind him as the children filtered into the room. The feeling of Christmas filled the kitchen, as if the scent of the cider had heralded it.

"Let's hang stockings." Gilbert sank into a chair at the

table to untie his shoe, then rose to hop on his right foot as he pulled off one of his socks.

"Gilbert!" Stella waved her hand in front of her nose, sending up a holler of laughter from the others.

Davie sat on the floor, pulling off his socks. Flora leaned over to tug on her own.

"I'll go get one of my spare ones." Lucy spun to race upstairs, no doubt wanting to avoid taking a sock from her foot.

In all the commotion, he hadn't noticed when Caroline produced a stocking, but an adult stocking now hung by the fire. Gilbert worked with a flurry to hang the others.

"One, two, three, four, five, six, seven . . . seven." Gilbert turned to study Jerome with a gleam in his eye. "One is missing."

Jerome splayed his hands. "I don't think it's nec—"

"Stock-ing. Stock-ing." Rose started the chant as she walked toward him.

The other children grouped together, their faces all aglow with the fun of it. "Stock-ing. Stock-ing. Stock-ing."

He backed toward the kitchen doorway, sending a pleading glance at Caroline. With the coming advance, he spun to bolt from the kitchen. Shouts and giggles and tiny hands grasping for his shirt pushed him forward, until he stumbled, settling himself on the bottom step of the staircase. He sat panting, his own hearty chuckle surprising his ears. He'd not let himself enjoy life like this in so long.

Jerome held up a hand in surrender as he bent over to loosen his shoe with the other. His fingers bungled his first attempt, sending the children in a swarm around him. Little hands grasped at his sock, the action tickling his toes.

"Help us." Gilbert shot a pleading look at Caroline, who shrugged and waded in.

As she approached, the older children backed off, sharing glances and stilling Davie and Flora. Caroline bent to grab hold of his sock, her soft laugh filling the space between them until Jerome could hardly think straight.

"Look!" At Gilbert's shout, they all tilted their heads to where he pointed to the mistletoe above.

The only face in Jerome's vision that didn't blur belonged to Caroline. So close to him as she bent over him, one hand still gripping his sock. A deep blush crept up her neck to cover her delicate features, as if she'd leaned too close to the fire. The children stared.

What should he do now, with all the children watching? Caroline's delicately curved mouth drew closer, then stopped.

In a quick motion, a rush of fabric scraped over his foot, leaving him with a cold draft around his toes. Caroline stepped back, holding his stocking with triumph. She led the children back to the fireplace to hang it.

Jerome bent forward, running his fingers through his hair. The sounds of their chatter near the hearth in the kitchen echoed out to him. He rose from the stairs to follow them, then halted. Needing space, he pivoted on his bare foot to face the front windows of the bakery. The snow drew him. He crossed the floor, passing the glittering Christmas tree as he did, to stand by the window, looking out on a silent town. Only a few flakes fell now. Yet he hadn't made it back to the telegraph office to check for a reply.

A soft tap lighted on his arm. He glanced over his shoulder. Caroline held out a pair of socks for his feet. Thick, warm ones made for the Wyoming weather, no doubt. She'd slipped upstairs to retrieve them when he wasn't looking. They must have belonged to her husband. He fingered the tight weave.

"Thank you."

Caroline didn't say a word, stepping backward. She held his gaze with tenderness, then spun to slip back over to the children.

Telegram or not, nothing in him wanted to leave the warmth of the bakery. A warmth that filled him inside and out. What if he could take all this back to New York with him? Caroline, the children, the happy home? Rose would love it.

He would love it.

For once in his life, he'd have everything—a family, laughter, security, his job. His job that was waiting for him. Waiting for him to leave here and return to attend his meeting. He scrubbed his hand over his face.

Flora's fussy cry echoed in Caroline's ears as she tried to calm her. The distraction was almost welcome after being caught under the mistletoe with Jerome. She swayed with Flora on her hip as she hummed "Silent Night." Jerome crossed the distance, as if hoping to be a help in settling Flora. The little one was no doubt in need of a nap.

"Jome, Jome." Flora wiggled, stretching her arms out to Jerome as he moved closer.

Raising her head from watching Flora, Caroline planned to let him off the hook, but when her gaze met his, a tenderness wrapped around her. Jerome, now standing beside her, leaned in to take Flora. His arms lifted her little one with tenderness. As soon as she settled in his arms, Flora rested her head against his chest.

A tightness pulled at Caroline. It'd been so long since Flora rested contentedly against someone besides her. Jerome was the first man to ever hold Flora like a father would. The sounds of Stella and Davie joining hands to spin across the floor in a little dance filtered around them.

Jerome leaned close. The sensation of his breath across her ear bringing a new awareness. "There's flour on your nose."

Jerome reached out to swipe Caroline's nose just as Stella bumped into her. Caroline stepped backward. Relief at creating a distance from Jerome mixed with disappointment inside her. Stella and Davie continued their spinning.

Before Caroline could stop them, the children moved the table where they'd been cutting snowflakes to clear a dance floor. Even if she no longer drowsed against Jerome, at least Flora was so taken by the activity that she hadn't resumed fussing.

"Let's sing 'Jingle Bells.'" Gilbert grabbed Rose's hand to dance as he started into the livelier tune.

A hand brushed Caroline's arm, and she turned her head to lock her gaze with Jerome.

"Would you like this dance?"

"Yes." One arm still held Flora close as his other hand trailed from her elbow down her arm to grasp her fingers. Goosebumps rose on her neck as he spun her around.

The air filled with laughter as theirs mingled with the children's. Boots stomped across the wooden floor. Gilbert slapped his knees, then did a little jig as the girls spun, sending their dresses whirling. Memories of the barn dances she used to attend stole into her mind.

Jerome's eyes never left hers until Flora squirmed, all drowsing put aside for the celebration. He lowered the little one to the floor where Lucy took her hand to spin her around. He straightened, his arm clasping Caroline's waist to draw her closer.

Already warm from the flurry of the dancing, his touch left her melting like the butter atop a freshly baked loaf of bread. With their hands intertwined, his arm around her waist, her heart beat out a lively tune in time with their dancing.

Jerome's head bent over hers, face-to-face, still holding her with his arm—breathless and dizzy. Those deep mocha eyes of his echoing every tingle of hope running through her. They stepped to the side to watch the children's antics.

"Would you ever want something different? Than what you have here?" His words were soft, almost pleading.

Her eyes never left his. Something different? What did he mean? A husband? Part of her longed to say yes. "I can't. I have to put the children first. Wanting something for myself would be wrong."

"Why would it be wrong?" He crinkled his brows together, his eyes searching hers.

Flora rushed between them, interrupting the moment. At least Caroline would be free from answering his probing question.

Flora's little arms reached for Jerome. "Up!"

He reached down to lift Flora. A sleepy grin filled her face. While Flora rested her chin against Jerome's shoulder, they crossed to the other side of the room where the children still danced. Cocking her head, she watched Jerome sway to the rest of the tune. Flora's eyes fluttered.

Caroline extended her arms, ready to take Flora. Instead of relinquishing the little one, who was tossing her head back and forth on his shoulder in an attempt to stay awake, he started into the soft strains of "Silent Night." The clomping of the other children's boots could still be heard on the wooden floor, but he simply held the index finger of his free hand to his lips, silencing them.

With Flora sleeping on his shoulder, Jerome stepped closer. Caroline reached out to wrap her arms around the little one, brushing against him as she did. Did she dare look up? When she tilted up her head to step back, the intensity of his gaze took her back to the moments he'd held her in his arms while they danced. Their fingers brushed when she leaned in to situate Flora against her chest. His lips pursed as if wanting to ask her again why it would be wrong for her to want this.

Caroline ducked her head as she turned toward the stairs. Once up in her room, she placed Flora in the crib, then settled herself on the edge of her bed. She'd only stay long enough to be sure Flora slept soundly. And give herself distance from Jerome.

With the soft snores of Flora keeping a steady rhythm, Caroline pushed up from the bed. Her steps slowed on the stairs. This connection with Jerome was so sudden. How had she let herself feel again? Want this? If she dared to take a chance on a relationship with him, it would change everything. Jerome in his fancy suit floated through her mind. No way did she imagine him enjoying this chaos forever.

Below her place on the steps, Jerome leaned over Rose and Stella. They worked together on a project at the table, now back in the middle of the room. At least he'd found the connection with Rose that he wanted. He'd need it.

The sweet aroma of apples mixed with cinnamon met her as the children sipped cups of cider.

"Mama is so much more fun now that you're here." Davie took another sip of cider. "Are you going to stay?"

"I have to go back to New York. I have an important job there. My home is there."

Rose's shoulders slumped. "I don't want to go."

"That's where I live. You'll live there too." Jerome's tone remained patient.

"You could move here."

"Remember the deal." He leaned over to place a hand on Rose's shoulder.

Caroline faded back against the side of the wall where she couldn't be spotted from the main area of the bakery. Her hand pushed against her aching heart as she tried to steady her emotions. How had she let herself forget? She'd no right to wish for them to stay. To wish for anything for herself.

Jerome and Rose were leaving.

Six

CAROLINE STARTED AWAKE AT THE CRY. The darkness of the room closed in on her as she fought through a sleepy fog. One of her knitting needles pressed into her hand as she rose, having fallen asleep on the rug in the room she shared with the girls. She must have dropped off while working on Gilbert's gift.

Another cry came from the crib where Flora slept, followed by a raspy wheezing.

In her rush to rise, Caroline let the unfinished hat for Gilbert fall from her lap. Once at the crib, she lifted Flora into her arms. The soft whimpers tugged at her heart. She smoothed back Flora's sweaty blond curls. Her heart squeezed at the heat emanating from her toddler's forehead.

Caroline rubbed Flora's back, trying to ease the wheezing, as she rocked her in her arms. Flora coughed, a deep, raspy cough. Rustling sounded from the bed where Stella and Lucy were sleeping. No doubt the noise was rousting them.

Stella rolled over in the bed, pulling her knees closer to her stomach. "My chest hurts."

With Flora in her arms, Caroline moved across the floor. She settled on the edge of the bed and ran a cool hand over Stella's brow. At least her forehead wasn't as warm as Flora's.

A cough racked Stella's delicate frame. With two of the children ill, the tug on Caroline's heart deepened, her pulse rushing through her.

"What's wrong?" A drowsy grumble rose from Lucy, now shifting to sit up in bed.

Caroline bent to slide Flora in between the other two girls, hoping not to alarm her. "Flora and Stella have a bit of a wheeze. If you are awake enough to keep an eye on them, I'm going to go boil water for some steam."

"If it'll get us all some sleep, I'll be happy to," Lucy mumbled as she put an arm around Flora.

Sleep. Caroline rubbed the back of her neck as she rose from the bed and turned to go downstairs. What she wouldn't give for a good night's sleep. Deciding to make the gifts for Rose and Jerome had put her behind on finishing the others. So had the dancing. A blush crept up her neck. She'd let herself get swept up in the fun. She'd lost sight of what was important and now the children were sick.

At the kitchen door, Caroline slowed. She didn't want to disturb Jerome or Rose. By the fire, Rose slept peacefully while Jerome worked at the kitchen table. It seemed his work was everything to him. He looked up at her as she passed the table.

Whatever happiness lit his face at seeing her, quickly morphed into concern. "What's wrong?"

"Stella and Flora aren't feeling well. I didn't mean to disturb you." She focused on filling the kettle and settling it on the stove, even as Jerome stepped closer.

"How can I help?"

If he was leaving, the best thing she could do was protect her heart. "No need. I've got it."

Caroline glanced over her shoulder to see him standing there, brows scrunched together. A pain filtered into his eyes as he caught her glance. As if he recognized the walls she put up around her heart.

The water began to boil. Her hands shook as she searched the cabinet for the bowl she wanted. It was as if she could feel him still staring at her, those eyes still questioning. She fumbled with the bowl, bringing it to rest on the counter near the kettle.

"Are you sure there's nothing I can do?" His soft voice was closer.

She worked to stuff down the tears burning behind her eyes while she lifted the whistling kettle. With her shaking hand, she sloshed the water too fast, spilling it over on her other arm.

"Ow!" The cry escaped her before she could stop it.

Jerome stepped so near to her, she could feel his breath on her face.

"Caroline?" He moved the bowl and kettle out of the way.

The sting of the burn gave her a reason to let the tears

she'd been holding back slide down her cheeks. Surely, if she'd had enough sleep, she wouldn't be so emotional.

"You're injured." He bent close to her, his dark lashes falling over his eyes as he examined her hand. "We need to put some—"

"I don't need your help." She tried to pull her hand from his. Licking her lips, she caught a salty tear.

Jerome reached across her to the butter dish, where she'd left it sitting on the work counter near the stove. He scooped out a small bit of the butter. As he leaned close to her, his hair gave off the scent of ink mingled with the oil from the lantern. His fingers gently spread the butter across her burn, even as his glances held more questions. Her insides quivered, more from the pain of having to protect her heart from him than from the burn.

His brows crinkled, even as his hands cradled hers. "At least let me carry the bowl upstairs for you. Let me help you with the children."

She slipped her hands free of his hold.

"You're not my husband. This isn't your job."

She saw the flash of hurt in his eyes.

With a quick movement, she brushed the back of her hand across her cheeks to swipe away the tears. Not wanting another spill, she poured the water back into the kettle, grabbing it by the handle. She'd take them upstairs and pour the water there. Why hadn't her muddled brain thought of it before? As she moved forward toward the stairs, she dared not look back.

She couldn't afford to open her heart to Jerome.

But she feared she already had.

You're not my husband. This isn't your job.

Hours later, Jerome stood in the stream of early morning sunlight coming through the front windows of the bakery. The words had played over and over again in his head last night. He'd lain awake, unable to sleep as he listened to Caroline's tread overhead.

He watched the men outside as they shoveled the snow, conscious of Rose fidgeting with her boots instead of lacing them up. Earlier, one of the men had knocked on the door to check on Caroline. He'd confirmed that the train would run today.

Jerome scrubbed a hand over his face, the shoulders of his white cotton shirt crinkling against the movement. He didn't understand what had happened to cause the breach with Caroline. With a slow pivot on his heel, he took in the bakery. How had this little shop become like home to him in three days' time? A series of memories swirled across his mind's eye. Helping the children cut snowflakes. Being chased for his stocking, which still hung by the fire in the kitchen. The dance he'd had with Caroline on this very floor. The almost kisses. He shook his head.

It was time for him and Rose to leave.

He'd stumbled into the bakery with Caroline and her children and being with them had made him start to forget why he'd stopped celebrating Christmas. Forget what it meant to be alone. But Caroline's words last night had left no doubt there was no room in her heart for him.

"Miss Caroline wants us to stay." Rose tugged at the scarf

he'd wrapped around her neck, just as her words tugged at his heart.

"No, she doesn't."

Rose dropped one of her mittens while pulling them on, no doubt to stall. Her teeth gritted. "Yes, she does. *Ask* her."

"She doesn't." He turned to gather up their bags, only to find Caroline behind him.

The hint of morning sun caught her hair to form a halo. She averted her gaze from him, fidgeting with the basket in her hands. Her lips parted as if to offer a greeting, but no words came out. The rush of emotions inside of him was no longer a surprise. Now it was just painful. He hadn't meant to, but somehow in these short days together, he'd begun to fall for her.

"The little ones? Are they feeling better?" He cast a glance toward the stairs, then back at her. If only she'd let him comfort her in some small way.

"Yes, thank you." She kept her red-rimmed eyes averted from him. "I'm letting them sleep as long as they wish this morning. None of us slept too well last night."

He hadn't slept well, either. His thoughts had been on her.

Caroline held out the basket of food for their journey. As she waited for him to take it, she kept her focus on the treats. "I've packed you a fresh loaf of bread. I put in a bit of cheese." She directed a weary smile at Rose. "And cookies, of course. I'm sorry we never got around to making the gingerbread house."

"I have to say goodbye to them." Rose wormed her way

between them, her voice pleading as she gripped his coat. "They will miss me terribly. I know they will."

"Rose, we have to think about what they need. Not what we want." As much as he wanted to say farewell to the children who'd snuck their way into his heart, he knew it'd be too hard on all of them.

As he took the basket from Caroline, Rose's grip on his coat grew tighter, her lower lip puckering in a pout as her breaths grew louder as if she were about to burst into tears.

Caroline lowered herself to place an arm around Rose's shoulder. "I'm sure they will miss you, Rose. We all will."

Rose turned to weave her arms around Caroline's neck. Caroline whispered something in her ear, shooting a pang through Jerome. She'd become such a big part of their lives in so short a time. How would they make do without her?

"You'll tell them for me. Tell them goodbye?" Tears streaked Rose's cheeks as her voice hiccupped out the words.

"I will." Caroline let her arms slip away from Rose, still not meeting Jerome's gaze.

Jerome took hold of Rose's hand. "Goodbye, Caroline. Merry Christmas."

She still didn't look at him. With a trembling lip, she kept her focus on Rose. He barely breathed, hoping for a sign.

Just say it. Ask us to stay. Ask me to stay.

The train whistle sounded in the distance. That was their sign to go. If he didn't hurry, they'd miss their opportunity to return to New York in time.

Rose's head drooped when she reached for the handle of

her bag only to drag it behind her as they made their way to the door. Jerome pushed hard against the bit of snow still lodged against it on the other side. Once he had it open, he motioned Rose out first. With one hand still on the door and the other on Rose's shoulder, he glanced back as he stepped out into the cold.

But Caroline didn't even say goodbye.

Seven

I'M HUNGRY. AND COLD." ROSE PRESSED her nose to the window as the train rumbled forward, half full of weary passengers longing to spend the rest of the holiday with their loved ones.

Jerome flipped a page of the contract over, turning to stare out the window as he did. He pinched the bridge of his nose, unable to focus on the contract another minute. They'd only been on the train a little while, yet it felt like forever as fields of white dotted with evergreens flashed past. The number of houses grew as they barreled toward the next town. By now, Calvin lay miles behind them.

"It wasn't cold in Caroline's kitchen." Sitting in the seat directly across from him, Rose's lips pursed into a pout as she crossed her arms. "I wasn't hungry there, either."

A sigh escaped him. Over the past days, he'd felt a growing closeness with Rose. He'd shared parts of himself with her that he hadn't talked about with anyone in decades.

They'd laughed together, had fun together. But ever since this morning, she'd been back to the little girl he'd met that first day on the train.

"We will visit the dining car in half an hour."

The wail of a disgruntled infant rose from the back of the car. A man with a dapper hat shuffled down the aisle to sit in the seat in front of them.

"They don't have cider. Or cinnamon rolls." Rose shifted forward, sending him a glare as she whispered in a hoarse voice. "Why did you make me come?"

"We have to go home."

Home.

The word hurt now, somehow. With a pit in his stomach, Jerome returned his attention to the last of his paperwork. The one he'd not finished last night in the bakery. Seemed he couldn't connect with his sister or his work.

A sniffle drew his gaze back to Rose. Her head hung low. Digging in his coat, he located his handkerchief. He dangled it in front of her, but she swatted it away.

He stuffed the hanky back in his pocket. He tried to focus on the contract. Every bit of paperwork had to be in order. His boss would have high expectations.

Jerome scanned his notes, mouthing the words to himself. His finger stuck to one of his papers. A smudge of frosting. He ran his finger over it, garnering a light dusting of flour as he did. He closed his eyes, and he was back in Caroline's kitchen frosting cookies, consoling the children, almost kissing Caroline . . .

He shook his head as he tried to refocus on the words on the page, but they blurred. He lifted his eyes to Rose.

She sat with her head rested against the train window. Her puffy eyes reflected back at him. He stuffed the contracts into his satchel. Rose needed him in this moment.

He pulled out the handkerchief again. When Rose wouldn't turn his way, he placed it on her knee, placing his other hand on her shoulder like Caroline always did.

His mind went to his earlier plan to take Caroline and the children back to New York with them. While it'd work for him, what about them? What about Rose? He'd always be busy with work, staying gone for long hours. The idea of a nanny for Rose grated on him now. It'd seemed like such a perfect plan to him at the time, but none of it had been perfect.

Rose turned her face to him. "Are you mad at me?"

"Why would you ask that?"

"I cause trouble a lot."

"I didn't know I needed a sister. But God knew. You are part of my life now."

In an instant, she scooted closer, leaning her head against the chest of his coat. With an awkward motion, he lifted his hand to pat her shoulder as her soft cries reached his ears. He'd never been good at comforting.

"I used to ask Momma about my naughtiness. She used to tell me that everyone sins and that's why Jesus came. It's why we celebrate Christmas." She rubbed a finger under her eyes.

"I've been worried that I don't know enough. That I won't be enough of a parent for you." He patted her back, hoping to offer some comfort. Her words had settled in his soul. He never would be enough. But through Christ, he'd been made whole. And that was enough. "But I'm going to trust God to help me be what I should be."

She reached one hand over to hold on to his.

A restless passenger bumped their seat as they moved up the aisle, and Rose pulled back, releasing his hand and blowing her nose in his hankie. Her eyes were swollen and red, tugging at his heart. If only he could fix it all for her, but he didn't know what to do. His work as a lawyer was the only thing he was good at. The only thing he knew.

"She liked you." After all her crying, Rose hiccupped out the words. She tilted her chin up, locking him in a stare.

"No, she didn't." A thousand images from the last few days flashed through his mind, reminding him of how much Caroline cared. Snowflakes and mistletoe and hot apple cider. She'd been the key to opening up his relationship with Rose.

The train lurched as it slowed.

Rose sniffled. After patting his pocket to find it empty, he turned to rummage in his satchel for another handkerchief. His hand landed on something soft. He pulled it out. A scarf and a pair of brown mittens.

"Miss Caroline!" His sister scooped up the scarf, holding it close to her.

The mittens fit his hands perfectly. He lifted his eyes, meeting Rose's beaming smile.

"You like her." As she spoke the words, a rush of tingles ran over him.

He closed his eyes only to see the image of Caroline's lovely face, her smile lighting the room. He knew. Right up until those last moments at the bakery, he'd been falling in love with her. He felt Rose's hand on his shoulder, patting him. His heart swelled inside him, knowing Caroline had helped create this connection. As if all roads led back to her.

Jerome opened his eyes when Rose moved close enough that he could feel her breath only to find her eyes roaming over his face. Then she stopped, squinting as she peered deep into him.

He cleared his throat, shifting under her scrutiny.

In an instant, her face glowed as her eyes widened. "You *love* her."

"It's too soon for love." Jerome shifted in his seat, the words ringing false to his own ears.

"No, it's not. It's Christmas." With a swipe of her hand, she cleared the last of her tears away. "Miss Caroline and her love are like . . . like a Christmas miracle. We have to go back."

At Rose's words, his heart leaped inside him. They had to go back. It was right.

The train whooshed to a stop.

Then he remembered Caroline, standing at the door, refusing to even look at him. All the air sucked out of him. No matter what he wanted. No matter how right it seemed. Caroline didn't want him.

He cradled his head in his hands in defeat. "I have to go back to New York."

"For work? Why can't you work in Wyoming?"

He'd been so bent on rushing back for a job that had defined his existence—until this moment. Caroline was what he really wanted. Why couldn't he find work in Calvin? Surely their town needed an attorney.

"I'm hungry." Rose bounced on her seat.

What was she saying in that singsong voice of hers? He lifted his head.

He'd spent so much time imagining Caroline and the children had to come with him. What if he offered to stay there? Where he lived in New York was no place for the children, anyway. She hadn't asked him to stay, but no doubt she'd been too scared. He had been. He'd not said the words he wanted to say.

"Can we get off the train?" Her eyes glowed as she pulled her lips into a grin.

Get off the train?

His heart pulsed faster as he started piecing her clues together. He and his sister's relationship was so much deeper than when they'd gotten off the train before. He'd formed this bond with Rose. And she wanted to be with him. He was no longer second best. He was enough. Caroline helped him see that.

Rose arched a brow, still grinning from ear to ear as she stood. "Can we get off to dance in the snow?"

He lifted the corner of his mouth. When they'd disembarked the train in Calvin three days ago, Caroline had taken them in. As if God had guided them to the perfect place on that fateful day. Was He guiding them now?

Rose was right. They did need to get off the train. Jerome stood, gathering up their luggage. He nodded to Rose, "Come on."

Rose beamed brighter than a lit Christmas tree.

He wrapped his free hand around Rose's little one. They moved to the aisle, filtering in with the other passengers exiting at the stop. His foot hit the last step as the conductor called out. With a guiding hand, he led Rose out of the rush of boarding passengers to stand at the edge of the platform.

"Promise me you won't run away again. I'm your big brother and I love you." His voice caught in his throat.

Rose leaned her head on his arm. "I love you too. I'm glad you came for me."

His mittened hand, so warm in the gift from Caroline, gave hers a little squeeze. "I want to be a real family with you."

The spark of joy beaming back at him filled his heart.

"What about Caroline and the children?" Rose blinked up at him. "They need to be part of our family too. I know they want to."

A flash of all the times he'd wanted to go home to make amends with his father ran across his mind. He hadn't taken the chance, and now his father was gone. He'd not let his fears hold him back from Caroline.

He winked at Rose. "Let's go back to Calvin and find out."

Caroline bent to place the final gift under the tree, weariness pushing against her every muscle. The gift tag had Stella's name on it, but the mittens inside the package weren't completed. She'd put a note in the box promising to finish them. Her heart sank.

The smell of burning food had her pushing herself up in a hurry from where she'd knelt on the floor. Disappointment swelled inside her, threatening to spill over in the tears she'd been fighting all morning.

As she rushed past the stairs, she caught sight of Davie and Gilbert peeking down at her.

"Can we come down yet?" Gilbert had already scooted down two stairs from the top.

"Not yet." She scurried through the kitchen door.

Caroline hadn't wanted the children waking each other up with their impatience to celebrate the holiday, especially since the girls were in need of a little more sleep this morning after last night's illness. Even though her cough had cleared, Flora was still running a little fever when she'd checked on her earlier. Part of her hadn't wanted them up to say goodbye to Jerome and Rose, either. She sighed. Her decision might have caused more hard feelings than having let them come down to say their farewells.

She pulled the ham from the oven. Smoke rose from the burned edges.

A cough rang out behind her as she swatted at the smoke. Caroline shot a look at Davie and Gilbert.

"We couldn't be for sure what you had said, so we came down." Gilbert shrugged his shoulders as he grinned at her. "I like burned ham."

"Good. I hope you like burned yams too." With a towel wrapped around her hand, she lifted out the pan of sweet potatoes. At least the rolls hadn't made it to the oven yet. She slid them in.

Davie moved closer and pointed. "You aren't going to burn them, are you?"

Caroline placed a hand on his head, smoothing his hair. "I hope not."

"Where's—"

"Gilbert, why don't you see if the girls are up?" Her eyes latched onto Gilbert's.

A realization crossed his face and then, he was off, with Davie running after him. She worked to stuff down her own reaction to his pain. If only things had turned out the way she'd planned. Instead of the perfect Christmas, the gifts weren't finished and half the meal was burned. The stockings still hung on the mantel. A reminder that Jerome and Rose were gone.

The sting of Jerome's absence needled her. She never should have wanted something for herself. If she hadn't been so selfish, maybe the holiday would be more of what she and the children had envisioned. Instead, she'd caused them all pain. Her body felt too numb to even produce a tear.

The sound of scuffling overhead told her the children would all be down soon. She rallied to pull the rolls from the oven, a golden-brown hue to their tops, and placed them on the table in time for the children to filter in.

"Merry Christmas, children!" Caroline worked to put on her cheeriest smile as she settled the platter of ham in the center of the table. The smile that didn't reach farther than her lips. No matter how she tried to appear as if all were perfect, nothing about today was.

When they'd finished their meal, Caroline caught the glances and whispers between the children. They'd been solemn at the news that Rose and Jerome were gone. The disappointment in their faces pushed against all her de-fenses. Unable to bear it any longer, she rushed from the room.

Despite her efforts to hide her tears from the children, she hadn't even made it out of the kitchen before several pairs of feet thudded on the floor behind her.

Caroline settled on the stairs, grasping the apron with her hands and bringing it up to cover her face. Quiet sobs racked her body. Whispers and jostling surrounded her as the children moved closer. Soon, little hands and arms were encircling her.

"If it's about the ham, I loved the crispy part." Gilbert's breath was warm against her cheek where he'd leaned close to place an arm around her shoulder.

Caroline dropped her hands, letting the apron fall. Working her face into a weak smile, she brushed at her tears. "Nothing is perfect like I planned for today."

Stella leaned in. "You are perfect. The most perfect aunt a girl could want for a mom."

"You should open our gift." This from Lucy. "It will make you happy."

Gilbert hurried to the tree with Davie following behind him. They returned with a package, faces aglow with an-ticipation. Caroline unwound the ribbon. With a careful hand, she peeled back the rough paper. Five sets of eyes watched with intensity as she pulled out a picture.

Caroline sucked in a breath.

"How wonderful." She ran her hand over the delicate pieces. Some of it had been drawn, while other pieces were cutouts made to look like snow, glued onto the top. "It's the bakery. All decorated for Christmas. With snow outside."

"I glued the snow." Gilbert grinned. "Mr. Barnett helped."

"I do this." Flora pointed to a scribble in the corner.

"I drew the cake on the counter. Rose drew the cookies." Stella leaned in as she spoke.

Nothing about this picture screamed perfect, but it was—exactly right. She worked to clear her throat. "Thank you all so much."

Lucy beamed. "I told them you'd like it."

"Can we go open our gifts?" Gilbert was halfway to the front of the bakery where the tree waited.

"Of course." The hem of Caroline's skirt swished across the floor as she followed the children to the other side of the room. Her hands clutched the handmade picture. Jerome had made this happen. Somehow in the midst of all the craziness in the last few days, he'd managed this with the children. For her.

She'd made such a huge mistake in sending Jerome and Rose away.

"Look at this!" Davie exclaimed over a wooden horse Jerome had left for him. No doubt pulled from the burlap bag Jerome had brought back from the telegraph office. The one he'd been so secretive about. "This is the best Christmas!"

The best Christmas? Maybe good things had been happening, even as she'd spent time with Jerome. Maybe she could have something for herself and others too.

The children don't need a perfect Christmas. You're giving them what they need. Not only meeting their physical needs, but how you love them.

Jerome's words echoed in her head.

With all the joy, the ache of a missing piece to their holiday throbbed in her chest.

Jerome.

Why hadn't she seen? It's the people that make Christmas what it is, not the perfection she was seeking.

Why hadn't she asked him to stay?

Lucy leaned over, putting a hand on her knee, the scarf Caroline had knitted her already around her neck. "We miss Mr. Jerome and Rose too."

"Why did he leave? Now I don't get a pa for Christmas." A whine accompanied Davie's words as he stuck out his lower lip.

"What? No, Davie, I—" She missed Jerome, but for Davie to have pinned such hopes on him sent a rush of heat up her neck. She had fallen for Jerome, yet it'd been so short a time.

"We know you loved him." Stella spoke the words softly as she leaned in close to rest her head on Caroline's shoulder.

Gilbert walked over to stand in front of her, placing his hand over Stella's. He wore such a serious expression for such a young boy.

A small hand tugged on Caroline's skirt as Flora tried to climb into her lap. She welcomed the distraction as she pulled her up into her arms. "What if I go get the plate of cookies?"

Her heart was full as she rose from the chair with Flora on her hip. The children exchanged happy glances amongst themselves. On the way to the kitchen, she spied the telegram that had been delivered at her door for Jerome early this morning.

Urgent STOP Meeting Rescheduled STOP Respond by 26th STOP

The memory of the words in the telegram caused a pinch in her gut. Maybe his leaving had been the best thing. At least he'd make it in time. Or would he? What if they decided to get off the train somewhere along the way? Or he didn't contact his office until the twenty-seventh? Rose might be tired. She might persuade him to stay at home for the holiday, to help her get acclimated.

She picked up the plate, giving Flora a cookie before walking back to join the others. This meeting was all Jerome could think about. Hands grasped for cookies as the children smiled and laughed. She'd let her worrying go for now. Tomorrow would be soon enough to figure out how to get the message to Jerome.

Eight

CAROLINE LOWERED FLORA INTO HER crib in the upstairs bedroom. The little one's fever had broken earlier. She swiped a hand across her daughter's forehead, letting out a sigh of relief. After letting go of trying to make the day into an unreal vision, she'd been able to enjoy the afternoon with the children.

But Jerome's face kept needling into her thoughts—anxious when he'd followed Rose into the bakery that first day, tender with Rose as he bonded with her, laughing with the children, close enough to kiss her under the mistletoe. Despite only knowing him for a short time, she missed him until her heart ached.

A shout burst from the sitting room. "I won!"

"Let's play again." Lucy must have lost this round of jacks.

At least the children were enjoying their holiday. Caroline pulled her shawl closer around her shoulders. With another peek at Flora, sleeping soundly, she slipped from the room. No matter that the dishes needed to be washed, she stopped to lean against the wall and watch the children's game unfold. Tidying up would wait.

Perfection wasn't what she'd imagined it to be. They had each other. With God in control, everything would be okay. The children. The bakery. Her heart.

Ding. Ding.

The bell from the bakery door clattered. The children stilled from their play, turning curious eyes toward her.

She pushed up from the wall. "Don't stop. I'll go see who it is."

Her steps quickened on the stairs. She must have forgotten to lock the door after Margaret delivered the telegram. Perhaps Margaret had returned, bringing more news for Jerome. Or about him. Who else would enter her bakery tonight?

"Coming." Caroline slid her hand along the rail as she hurried down the stairs.

At the bottom step, she squinted, trying to make out the forms standing outside the bakery door in the evening light. Had someone entered, then left? She crossed the floor, her boots clomping on the wood. A tall figure of a man stood outside. The closer she got, the wilder her heart raced. It couldn't be. Hope rose inside her, speeding her steps until she swung open the door with a hurried force to find Jerome standing there. Her fingers lifted to her lips. No words came as her heart swelled inside her.

He was as handsome as ever, twirling his hat in his hand, while snow fell around him from where Rose stood on a crate, bowl in her hands, tossing snow down on him. Caroline cupped her mouth with her hand as Jerome's eyes met hers. They locked in place, questioning yet hopeful. He shifted a little, his hands working the hat.

"What are you doing here?" Caroline's heart pounded wildly.

Rose had finished emptying the bowl of snow. She leaped off the crate, glowing with a smile wider than any Caroline had yet seen on the girl's face. Tears stung Caroline's eyes, and she worked to keep them at bay.

"You wouldn't happen to have a place we can stay, would you?" His voice sent a jolt through her.

Caroline chewed her bottom lip, trying to hold back from flinging herself at them both. A well of hope sprung to life inside her.

He'd come back.

Pulling her shawl tighter, she worked to hold back the joyful tears threatening to explode. "It's cold out here. Come inside."

Was she hoping for too much? Why had they come back? What about his work?

They followed her inside the bakery. Her hands worked the shawl she'd been clutching closed. They'd want to warm themselves by the fire. She halted by the counter near the kitchen door when she caught sight of the telegram, still there from early this morning.

Caroline fumbled to grab the message with shaking hands. "This came for you."

A look of confusion crossed his face as he reached out to take the paper.

Shuffling from above told her the children were busy

with their game. They didn't know it was Jerome. Once he saw the telegram, he'd leave again. It'd only be harder for them if they got their hopes up.

Jerome's gaze lifted to meet Caroline's as he fingered the paper in his hands.

Rustling sounded behind her, then Gilbert's whisper. "He came back. I knew it."

"Shhhh." Must be Lucy.

From the creak of the stairs, the little ones were no doubt sneaking down closer behind them until they could see and hear all.

Jerome glanced past her to the children. His eyes held a hint of questioning, as if wondering if they'd want him back. He slid his gaze back to her. "Rose and I are right where we want to be. With you and your family." He tucked the telegram in his front shirt pocket. "I know you are still grieving your husband, but is there any chance that you have enough room in your heart for me?"

Could it be? Did he mean it?

The settled look in the depth of his eyes and the warmth of his hands as they cradled hers told her he did.

"Yes." The word came out in a breathless whisper.

Their eyes locked. So much hope radiated back at her, as if reflecting all that must be shining from her. He took a step forward. Closer. A rush of warmth flooded her from the inside out as he leaned in. She felt herself getting lost in the depths of his brown eyes as he drew close enough to kiss.

Little arms flung around her waist, knocking her forward

into Jerome's chest. He caught her as several sets of feet thumped closer.

And suddenly Caroline was surrounded by arms and hands and shouts from tiny voices. A deep chuckle flowed from Jerome as she worked to right herself, pushing up from his chest to peer up at his face. His focus in that second was on the children. This big, wonderful family he'd stepped into. She couldn't miss the way his eyes misted over and she found herself sniffing back tears of her own.

Davie squeezed between them. "I didn't think my mostest wanted gift was gonna get here. But it's still Christmas, and it did."

Laughter erupted. Caroline reached out to wind her arm around Rose, kissing the top of her head as she did.

"I told you." Gilbert's whisper to Stella wasn't as quiet as he'd planned.

A wink passed between Stella and Rose. Lucy grinned big, elbowing her brother.

Caroline snuck a peak at Jerome's reaction to all the little matchmakers, but he was watching her, eyes warm, blissful. So caught up in the joy of all the love that it didn't matter how it happened. Indeed it didn't. Wanting something for herself hadn't ruined Christmas. It'd added to all their lives on this glorious holiday of all holidays.

With a step back, Jerome cupped her shoulder, then let his hand trail down to clasp hers. "I know it's late. Do you still have those pallets in the kitchen?"

"We do. Don't go anywhere else." Gilbert held his hands up as if to plead with him.

Another rumble of laughter filled the room.

"Mr. Barnett is right. It is late." Caroline's eyes lifted to meet his over the children's heads. "You should all be getting ready for bed."

"But it's Christmas." Davie tilted begging green eyes up at her, even as a yawn escaped him.

"It's past your bedtime already, young man." Her fingers wound into his dark brown tresses. "But if it helps any, I think Mr. Barnett would be willing to tuck everyone in."

Without another word, Davie grinned like an angel as he clasped Jerome's hand in his, then started for the stairs. Jerome lifted his shoulders in a helpless shrug. Caroline motioned for the others to make their way up to their rooms. She fell in behind Lucy.

"*Silent Night . . .*" Stella's soprano echoed off the walls.

"*Holy Night . . .*" Gilbert melded with Lucy's alto.

"*All is calm . . .*" The deep baritone of Jerome filtered down the hallway as everyone joined together to finish the stanza of the well-loved carol. "*All is bright.*"

The tune continued even as the boys led Jerome to their room while Caroline followed the girls down the hall to help them ready for bed. A warm contentment filled her amidst the beautiful refrain. Theirs was a calm night, brilliant and bright, even if not as silent as the hushed one so long ago in Bethlehem. But filled with so much love.

It took longer than she wanted, but everyone was finally settled. Rose and Jerome had gone back down to make their pallets in the kitchen. Caroline tiptoed down the stairs, not wanting to wake anyone. As she slipped into the kitchen, she could see that Rose was curled up, asleep already. Jerome bent over his sister, settling a kiss on her forehead, then rose to come meet Caroline by the light of the fire.

The firelight flickered across his face as he settled into the chair next to her. His nearness warmed her more than the fire ever had. He reached out to take her hand in his.

"I'm sorry I left." The huskiness of his voice betrayed how deep his emotions ran. "I was scared of how deep my feelings had grown for you. And . . ."

"I was too." She worked her thumb, rubbing along his hand that clutched hers, even as she studied his features. No doubt all that had happened to him in his past had taught him to expect rejection at every turn. Of course he'd been scared to give his heart away.

He gently squeezed her hand in his. She studied his face, less stressed, but not fully relaxed. As if he were as nervous and hopeful inside as she was. As she fished for how to word what she wanted to ask, she placed her other hand atop their intertwined ones.

"I know you have to return to finish the contract, but could you ever see yourself living in a small town in the West? Could you see yourself here?"

Jerome let her questions settle in his chest, trying to find the right words. "You're right. I do have to go back."

Caroline's lips trembled as her smile began to falter. How he wanted to pull her close, but he had to tell her everything first.

"I've guarded my heart for so long. You taught me how to open it again." He reached his finger out to tilt her chin up.

Her eyes jumped up to meet his, full of expectation.

"You've taught me the true meaning of Christmas." He tipped his head at the front of the bakery where the tree stood, decorations hanging from every limb.

"You've taught me that I don't have to have everything planned out. Sometimes the rulebook needs to go out the window. And, yes, I do have to finish this deal and take the exam. But Rose is happy here, and I'm happy here, and this is where we want to make our life, and I want to make our life together. We both want to stay, if there's a place here for us."

"Of course there's a place for you. There was a big hole missing all day when you weren't here." The light in her eyes made him want to dance on air.

He released her hand to slide his arm around her waist, pulling her close to him. His heart thrummed against his chest. She fit against him so perfectly. This was all he'd ever wanted. "I've fallen in love with Calvin, this shop, the children." His eyes darted around the room, toward the stairs, then back to her radiant face. "I've fallen in love with you. I know it's fast. We can take the time you need to really get to know each other deeply." He paused to take in the way her face glowed in the moment. "Are you willing to see where this leads? Take a chance on a future together?"

Her lips trembled with a smile as she worked to hold in her emotion. A tear slipped free to roll down her cheek. Joyous whimpers escaped her. "Yes. I am."

Caroline leaned closer, breaking into a full-blown smile. Jerome followed her quick glance up at the mistletoe the children had hung. Finally, he understood all the shared looks and smirks between them. They'd been playing matchmaker all along.

His gaze reverted back to Caroline. All the glitter and gifts and mess faded away when their eyes locked together again. With their hands intertwined, he pulled her in. Leaning down ever so slowly, he brushed her lips with his. The sweetness he found there made the cold ride back on the horse worth every minute.

He slipped his hand from hers to encircle her waist. When his lips met hers again, he deepened the kiss. Caroline let out a soft sigh. Fireworks erupted inside of him.

A stifled chuckle drifted in from the kitchen doorway. Caroline stepped back in sync with Jerome. Gilbert peeked inside sheepishly. "I wanted a glass of milk. I sort of heard you say you were staying."

Jerome shifted his gaze back to Caroline to find her watching him. She reached for his hand as they burst into chuckles themselves.

Relief passed over Gilbert's face as he spread his hands wide. "This is the bestest Christmas ever!"

In a quick motion, Caroline leaned forward and landed another kiss on Jerome's cheek. As she pulled back, he caught a twinkle in her eye.

And he knew. It truly was the best Christmas ever.

Epilogue

T HERE'S A CHURCH IN THE VALLEY BY *the…*" Caroline's humming filled the air as she concentrated on smoothing out the frosting on a chocolate swirl cake for Calvin's most talked about wedding. The wedding to be held this lovely Saturday afternoon on the first day of spring.

Her wedding.

"*Hummm . . . Come to the church in the vale . . .*"

Another swipe of the spatula spun the frosting into a swirl on top. She stepped back to survey her handiwork. Jerome was careful to only give her advice when she asked for it. He'd encouraged her to create items for the sheer joy of it rather than what she imagined to be expected. When she did, sales had soared. And so had her happiness.

Or maybe that had something to do with the groom attending this afternoon's wedding.

She smiled to herself, still humming. From across the room, she spied the lemon tarts that Lucy and Rose made last night. The two girls had become quite an asset to the bakery, whipping up their own treats for sale after school. After a little bit of time of everyone getting to know each other better, they'd all grown in helping each other more and more.

"Come, come, come to the church—"

"In the wildwood." Jerome's deep baritone filled in the words from the other side of the room. He snuck up close. Leaning in to sneak a kiss on her cheek. His arms encircled her waist from behind as he leaned in to place his chin on her shoulder. "Excited to be going to church today?"

Caroline angled the spatula of frosting toward the cake for the final flourish, but not before Jerome reached out to swipe a large glob. He darted back as she playfully swatted at his arm. How handsome he looked with that impish grin on his clean-shaven face. Handsome and free of the old worries. They'd worked through his fears of not being a fit parent for Rose. She knew how deeply he longed for a family. He'd told her only last night how excited he was to be the children's stepfather. As excited as they were to call him Pa.

The corners of her mouth tugged upward. "Wait to eat the frosting until after the wedding."

His finger darted at her nose. From the metal serving spoon, she caught her reflection. Proof he'd left a streak of chocolate goo.

Rose halted at the door that separated the front of the bakery from the kitchen. "You're not supposed to be here. Seeing the bride before the wedding. Tsk."

She fake-stomped into the room, with Stella trailing behind her. With bouquets of bluebonnets in their hands.

"Those are lovely, girls. Put them in a glass of water for me."

"What's all the fuss?" Gilbert rubbed his neck as he lagged behind them. "I'm the one who has to wear the scratchiest collar ever. It itches just thinking about it."

"You'll stand up there with me today, won't you?" Jerome winked at him.

"I'll even smile in my scratchy shirt."

Caroline watched the pride swell in Gilbert's eyes as he grinned from ear to ear. The children were no longer her family and Jerome's family. They were all simply theirs.

With the flowers arranged in a glass of water, Rose turned back to Jerome, a hand on her hip. He shrugged at his sister as he swiped another finger full of frosting.

"Go." Rose got behind him, pushing him toward the door of the kitchen with a hearty laugh.

Jerome flashed an approving gaze over his shoulder. Straight at Caroline. A gaze so full of love and anticipation it set off the jitters she'd been pushing down all morning. Just a few more hours until the church bells would ring to announce Mr. and Mrs. Jerome Barnett.

Ding. Ding.

The bell on the front door to the bakery announced a visitor.

"Watch the cake for me, girls." She swiped her hands on her apron. "I forgot to turn the sign."

Jerome fell into step behind her after she rushed past him.

"Haven't you learned to lock that door yet? You don't know who might wander in when you aren't expecting it." His tone was light and teasing.

She paused to smile at him, tilting her head as she did. In this moment, her heart was full in a way she'd never expected. "The best surprises are never the ones you plan."

When Caroline turned her gaze to the front door, she found Lucy. The girl had paused to close the door behind her with Davie and Flora both trying to push on it. What a help Lucy was, offering to occupy the two littlest ones while Caroline finished the preparations. Lucy and Rose would have to be the brave ones tonight too. They'd have to help the littler ones adjust to staying with the Nelsons for the night. But they all knew them. After all, the Nelsons sat next to them each Sunday in church and had a toddler of their own that the children enjoyed doting on.

Then they'd all settle into family life together, with Rose and Jerome leaving the boarding house to move into the bakery. He'd talked about adding on to the back of the kitchen. But tonight, the children being somewhere else . . .

"You needn't worry," Jerome whispered in her ear.

She jerked her eyes up to meet his. "How did you know?"

He rubbed a finger across her brow, then touched his forehead to hers.

"Up." Flora reached out her hands to Jerome. Her giggles filled the room as he bent to scoop her into his arms.

A smile filled his face—so big, the whole of Wyoming could fit inside. He caught her watching them and jerked his head toward the stairs. "Better go get ready. You have a wedding to attend."

Laughter and tears and joy and a nervous flipping of her stomach rolled around inside her as she let his words sink in. She did have a wedding to get ready for.

Theirs.

Caroline walked over to flip the sign and lock the front door of the bakery. She'd be far too busy the rest of the day for any more customers.

Acknowledgments

Many thanks to everyone who has supported me in so many different ways – praying for me, reading my books, leaving reviews, and any other ways that I may have missed. It warms my heart and keeps me writing.

Her Yuletide *Protector*

TRACI SUMMERIL

"Behold, God is my salvation; I will trust and will not be afraid; for the LORD GOD is my strength and my song, and he has become my salvation."

Isaiah 12:2 ESV

To my Heavenly Father

One

A HISS OF BRAKES AND MOVEMENT from the seat next to her jostled Lizzie Hamilton out of the half daze she'd fallen into with her head leaning against the sooty train car window.

Steam puffed from the engine pulling the train, obscuring the view ahead, but as they rounded a bend in the hilly landscape, wind drove the smoke away, and a small town came into view.

The train whistle seemed to call for a stop. At least, the passengers moving to stand and crowd into the aisle around the door seemed to think so.

What time was it? It couldn't be later than two in the afternoon. Or maybe three?

Lizzie had lost track as she'd zigzagged along train routes from Topeka, Kansas, to Denver, Colorado, to somewhere west of Denver, always looking over her shoulder.

A blast of arctic wind rocked the train, not helping her

already queasy stomach. A queasiness that hadn't left since spotting her fiancé's detective still on her trail in Denver just yesterday.

Had it been only yesterday? Her days were running together. She hadn't slept since then.

Nothing mattered until she reached the remote ranch in Wyoming. She'd be safe there.

Lizzie's stomach growled, a reminder that she hadn't eaten since last night. It was safer to stay on the train. But surely with so many passengers disembarking, she could blend in with the crowd.

If she kept to herself, she'd be all right.

At least, that's what she told herself as she joined the group of jostling people, some with gaily wrapped Christmas packages in their arms.

Lizzie clutched her violin case to her middle as the train lurched to a stop. Benson had wanted to take everything from her. But he couldn't take her music.

From the platform, the conductor's shout was whisked away by the wind. Outside, snow pelted into her. The cold sliced through her thin black coat, its emerald collar flapping in her face. Back in St. Louis, she'd always been bundled into a carriage before the cold truly touched her. But out here, with wild mountains all around, her coat wasn't holding up.

Its frills and lace lacked the substance she needed, kind of like the rest of her life.

"Gonna be a bad one, I feel it in my bones."

"...blizzard..."

The worrisome words chased her as she scurried across

the open platform and onto the muddy, boardwalk-lined street beyond. A group of passengers headed toward a small café just down the boardwalk, and Lizzie followed them, trying to keep her face averted from anyone who might be looking her way.

If the grizzled old man on the platform thought the storm was just getting started . . . A shiver passed down her spine. She had a difficult time imagining a worse snowfall than this.

A harsh shout from nearby brought Lizzie's head up with a gasp. Had it come from one of the men on the boardwalk in front of the saloon nearby? One of the men shoved the other one, and Lizzie quaked with fear. She raised her hand not carrying the violin and rubbed her upper arm where Benson had left bruises just last week.

You've escaped, she reminded herself.

But the memory of the cold look in Benson's eyes as he'd threatened her shook her inside and out.

Get something to eat. Get back on the train.

Lizzie tried to stay focused. Inside the café, she quickly ordered at the counter and then tucked her coin purse back inside her coat pocket. She attempted to slip back into the crowd to stand between two tall men as she waited for her food.

"That's a fine coat, miss."

Drat.

Manners had been ingrained in Lizzie from a young age, and she couldn't ignore the voice speaking directly to her. Lizzie glanced up to find a woman with wiry gray hair reaching for the sleeve of her coat.

She startled back. "Thank you."

The woman smiled, revealing crooked front teeth. "A mighty fine coat indeed. Would you give it to me?"

"It—it's not for sale," Lizzie said quickly. "I need it."

The woman's smile turned to a glower in an instant. "Shame on you."

Before Lizzie could move away, the woman had disappeared among the customers. A glance around revealed that no one else seemed to have noticed the exchange.

Strange.

A newspaper on the counter caught Lizzie's attention, and the stuffiness of the warm room and the press of bodies had her absently pulling off her coat. She held it over her arm, still clutching the violin case, and leaned closer to get a look at the paper.

A headline on the right side of the page shouted at her. *MISSING HEIRESS!*

Blood rushed into Lizzie's ears as she leaned over the paper.

. . . disappeared from her father's residence . . .

. . . physical description: brown hair, green eyes . . .

. . . presumed to be wearing a dark coat with emerald trim . . .

"Miss? Miss!"

An insistent young waitress shoved the roasted chicken and cornbread at Lizzie, who blinked to realize she was still in the café in this small town at the border of Wyoming and Colorado.

Not in St. Louis.

Her thoughts whirled.

The article described Lizzie's coat. A coat the older woman had noticed. Had anyone else noticed who may have also read this article?

Her stomach tightened, and she wasn't hungry anymore. How could Benson's reach extend this far?

The train whistle sounded two short blasts from the station as Lizzie was bumped from behind. Not bumped. Jostled.

Someone tugged at the handle of her violin case.

When panic slithered over Lizzie and she reached both hands for the handle, someone from behind snatched her coat off her arm.

"Stop!" Lizzie cried.

She got a glimpse of the old woman, but the crowd that was pressing toward the door, heading back to the train, blocked and jostled Lizzie for long enough that when she could see clearly again, the woman was gone.

No! That woman had stolen her coat!

Lizzie ran out into the street, only for icy wind to lash her. Her teeth began to chatter.

Her first instinct was to look for a marshal's sign among the storefronts—until she realized that the newspaper article she'd just read might mean that a lawman could identify her.

And Benson had ties to law enforcement. Maybe not all the way out in this rural town, but didn't the law work together in different jurisdictions?

The train whistled again. Longer. With more urgency.

There was no time to think.

Tears prickled her eyes as she turned in a circle.

Next door sat a mercantile. In the window, a sturdy coat stood on display. Lizzie ducked into the store, praying she had enough time to purchase it. The shop owner wasn't in sight, but voices floated from the back room.

She opened her mouth to call out. And snapped it closed when her hand went to her pocket—but this gown had no pockets.

She'd left her coin purse—with all her money, save the nickel she'd snuck into her violin case—in the pocket of her coat.

The thief had stolen both her coat and her money.

And Benson's men were coming. That thought was the only one that mattered.

She looked at the coat in the window, her breath coming in spurts.

Stealing was wrong. She knew it.

But desperation swamped her.

Once she found where she was going, and a job, she could wire money. She *would* wire money.

Lizzie pulled the coat off the mannequin's form and ran out the door, pulling the coat over her arms as she went, wrangling her violin by the handle.

"Hey!" an angry voice called behind her, but she didn't slow. The train platform was just ahead.

"Stop her! Thief!"

Her shoes clacked against the platform even as the train chugged and chugged, lurching into motion. There was the door, with the conductor beckoning her to jump on board—

With her last spurt of energy, she bounded onto the train

as it lurched forward. Her heart pounded as more angry shouts echoed from the platform, but the door had closed.

The train was moving.

She ducked her head and closed her eyes. Never had she imagined she would be so desperate as to steal.

When she glanced back up, the conductor was gone. There were a few empty seats at the back of the train car.

Knees trembling, she started toward the nearest one.

Until a large hand landed on her shoulder.

A man stepped into view. Any words she might've said stalled in her throat when her eyes fell on the tin star pinned to his coat.

Slate saw the crime unfolding through the smudged train window as he was finding his seat on the train.

The angry shouts drew his attention back toward the sleepy town he'd just vacated. The train whistle muted all other sound, but he clearly saw the young woman run across the street and up the steps to the train platform. She looked over her shoulder once at the man rushing out of a shop in chase.

"Stop her! Thief!"

Those words were enough to put Slate in motion.

The woman was heading for the passenger car adjacent to the one Slate was occupying, and it was the work of a few moments to stride through the car and meet her there as the train chugged out of the station.

She was struggling for both balance and breath and

didn't even see him as he came behind her and put his hand on her shoulder.

He moved to block her escape with his body as memories from the past clashed with the present. That's what he blamed for the disconcerting feeling that flooded him when he got a good look at the sweep of dark lashes surrounding her bright green eyes, the splash of freckles across her pert nose, and her brown hair swept into some fancy hairdo behind her head.

Her gaze fell to the badge on his chest, visible where his coat parted, and her eyes widened. "M-marshal," she stammered.

"Deputy," he corrected her. The disconcerting feeling remained and made his words sharper. "Deputy Simon Jackson."

He wouldn't give her the name his friends called him. Not when she was likely a common thief.

"What's your name?" he demanded.

She was clutching an awkwardly-shaped bag to her middle like a shield—some kind of instrument?—and he was sure he saw her hands trembling. A sign of guilt. She shook her head. Didn't want to tell him?

He waited with raised brows.

"Lizzie," she finally whispered.

He waited another beat, but she didn't offer her surname. Another mark against her.

"You steal that coat?" he asked bluntly.

She blanched and his gut kicked. She had.

"I-I'm just a passenger. G-going to Wyoming."

He might've mistaken the wobbly words for fear or

uncertainty—except he'd been fooled once too often by a pretty face. Guilt was the likely culprit for that wobble.

She was ducking her head, shifting from side to side. *No*, he realized. She was hiding behind him. He was taller and broader than her. A glance over his shoulder showed they were drawing looks from other passengers, standing half in the vestibule, not in their seats.

Was she embarrassed by the attention? Too bad.

He turned back to her with a frown. "Then why was the proprietor of that store chasin' after you?"

Her eyes cut away and to the side. She was thinking too hard. No doubt trying to find some way to twist an explanation so he'd feel sorry for her.

She'd picked the wrong train to hop on, that much was certain.

Slate didn't have any sympathy left, not for lying, thieving women.

"Please—" she whispered.

But he figured he had enough evidence. He dropped his hand so it was banded around her upper arm. "If I had a pair of manacles, I'd put you in 'em," he mumbled as he turned toward the two empty seats at the rear of the train compartment. "C'mon. Sit down."

He saw the flash of relief in her expression as she went to sit down. Until he crowded into the seat next to her.

She practically cowered next to the window, and he straightened on the edge of the seat, making sure he wasn't touching her. What exactly did she think he was going to do with her?

She was still holding that case in her lap, but her chin came up slightly. "I would prefer to sit by myself."

"Why? So no one'll notice you pickpocketing your way through this cabin?"

She looked shocked for a moment, and he let his gaze take her in. The dress beneath the coat was a complete mismatch. He'd grown up in the small town of Calvin, Wyoming, and with all the time spent working his father's store as he'd grown up, he could recognize a home-sewn dress versus a store-bought one.

This was neither. It was fine blue satin, not made to stand up to a harsh Wyoming winter, and looked like it was tailored just for her. The shoes peeping out beneath her skirt were impractical, with narrow heels and tiny buckles. Even the instrument case shouted *expensive* with its hand-tooling and fine leather.

The coat was wool and a simple style. It didn't match the rest of her.

So why steal it?

"I'm not a thief," she insisted in a voice so low he had to tip his head to hear her.

He raised one eyebrow.

"I'm not," she said. "I have . . ." She bit her lip. "I have been thrown into a difficult circumstance, and I fully intend to pay back the cost of this coat. As soon as I reach my destination."

"That so?" he scoffed.

She nodded, her eyes begging for his understanding. He ignored the way his stomach knotted at her look.

"That might be the most original excuse I've heard," he said. "But it's still an excuse. Stealing is stealing."

He watched the hope in her expression fade to be replaced by something else. Frustration. Outside the window behind her, the snowy landscape became more and more hilly as they headed into the mountain pass.

"I'm good for it—" she started.

"Then why didn't you pay for it?"

Her mouth pinched at his question.

"Here's what we're going to do," he said. "You're going to get off this train—with me—at the next station. We'll ride back to that town"—he jerked his thumb over his shoulder—"and return the coat to the shopkeeper. And we'll see if he believes your story. If he doesn't, it'll be a visit to the town marshal."

She looked like she was about to shout at him, until a fierce glance around the train car silenced her. Her expression was a mix of both fright and anger.

"I can't go back there."

"Too bad." He was hit with a sudden wave of exhaustion. He was supposed to be heading *home*. To enjoy Christmas with his friends. His boss, town marshal Danna O'Grady, and her husband Chas had invited him for Christmas dinner.

And now he was going to have to take a detour that would cost him precious hours. He didn't even know whether there was an eastbound train coming through later this evening, or whether he could catch another westbound train after he settled things with the shopkeeper and this thief.

She was looking out the window, and he watched as her thoughts chased across her expressive face. She seemed to settle on one and turned to him so quickly that he barely flicked his eyes away before she realized he had been watching her.

"What if you just forgot you saw me get on the train?" she whispered fiercely. "It's—it's important that I stay on this train. I can't go back there—"

He laughed.

"I'll never forget," he said. He gestured to her fine clothing, up and down. "Maybe you're too far from it to realize just how much a loss like this coat means to a shopkeeper in a rural town."

But Slate wasn't. He gritted his molars together as the old shame washed over him. He'd cost his father so much more than the price of a coat. Pa had forgiven him, but Slate would never forgive himself for trusting the wrong person.

"Every crime hurts someone," he told her, watching the blood drain from her face. "And you're not getting away with this one."

She looked ready to keep arguing. "Deputy, if you'd only listen—"

Before she could finish, the train jerked. The brakes engaged with a loud squeal as the unexpected change in momentum caused most of the passengers to reach for something to steady themselves.

Lizzie clutched the case tight to her body, her knuckles going white. "What's happening?"

He didn't know.

Outside, snow swirled as the train rolled to a complete stop.

In the middle of nowhere.

Two

T HE TRAIN HAD STOPPED.

Slate rose to his feet, instantly alert. Worst-case scenarios filtered through his head. A holdup? An emergency?

His eyes flitted between the doors at each end of the passenger car, waiting.

Passengers around him murmured. Some stood up. Several plastered their faces against windows.

The woman beside him had gone completely still. Over the top of her head, he could see only a landscape of white, with more snow falling.

Cold wind blasted through the door as the conductor entered. Blowing snow pelted the door as he slammed it closed. The man's eyes fell to Slate's deputy star, and he nodded before returning his attention to other passengers. "Folks, there's been an avalanche. The tracks ahead are covered in snow, dirt, and rocks."

After a beat of stunned silence, voices rang out.

"I've gotta get home!"

"What are we gonna do?"

Slate couldn't seem to look away from Lizzie and her white-knuckled grip on the leather case across her lap. Was she even breathing?

And when the conductor announced, "I've sent one of the brakemen back to the nearest town to wire for help. Right now it'd be best for you to sit tight and wait," the passengers grew even more agitated.

"You can't keep us on this train."

"What if an avalanche hits us?"

A boy several seats ahead started crying.

The conductor kept talking in a calm and matter-of-fact voice. "Folks, I've got two passenger cars to watch over and several cars of stock to keep from freezing. The dining car is open when you get hungry." He paused, then added, "Any able-bodied man who can do physical labor is needed outside."

Men started to gather in the aisle, crowding around the conductor.

Slate waited until they had dispersed before he approached the conductor. The man had lines bracketing his mouth and tightness around his eyes. He wasn't as collected as he'd pretended.

"Anything I should know?" Slate asked, voice low.

The conductor glanced over Slate's shoulder. Straight to Lizzie. "Anything I should be aware of?"

Lizzie had shrunk into her seat, her eyes glued on the window. She worried her bottom lip with her teeth.

"She stole from a shop back in the last town," Slate said, making sure his voice didn't carry. He shook his head slightly. "There's something more she's not saying. I'd like to keep an eye on her."

The conductor gestured to the nearest window. "Snow's a foot deep and falling hard. Even the tracks behind us will be covered soon enough."

He was right.

"I can take a shift helping dig out," Slate said. "How long will it take?"

The conductor glanced away. A sign that there was something he didn't want to say. "It's bad. Half the mountain came down over the tracks."

He'd mentioned the dining car. Surely they had provisions for a day or two. They couldn't be stuck out here past Christmas, could they?

"I'll be right there," Slate told the conductor. He strode back to where Lizzie sat, caught the flash of distress in her eyes when she glanced at him before she hid it behind a stoic mask. He wished he could ignore the sweep of lashes against her cheek.

"I'm going to help clear the tracks," he told her.

Her eyes darted to the window.

"There's nowhere to go," he added. "We've come a good ten miles from that last town. Don't cause any trouble."

Her chin came up, but she didn't answer him directly.

He had a responsibility to the other travelers too. He buttoned up his coat and pulled his gloves from his pocket as he left the train car and joined several other men on the westbound tracks.

Steep mountains rose on either side of the train. They'd entered this remote valley where large crags disappeared into the heavy clouds.

The snow was blowing so much that he didn't see the problem until they were right in front of it.

A mountain of snow and soil so high he couldn't see over it obscured the tracks. Overhead, a steep slope was marred by a jagged scar shaped like a teardrop. The avalanche.

A few feet to his left, two porters were handing out shovels and pickaxes. This was more than a couple of hours of work. There was no way the shovels and pickaxes were going to clear this mess. Why hadn't the conductor decided to reverse course and go back to the nearest town?

Unease swirled through Slate like the flakes dancing across his vision as he took one of the shovels and got to work just feet away from a man in a fancy suit. The *snick* of his shovel into the dirt and snow was echoed by the other men working alongside him.

But as the sun began disappearing and lanterns were brought out, Slate wondered whether they were wasting their time. The snow had grown thicker. Were the workers even making a dent, with snow and sleet falling fast?

He was grateful when a man with a bowler hat pulled low over his eyes and a scarf obscuring his face tapped him on the shoulder. "Shift change."

Slate didn't know how long he'd been out in the wind and biting cold, but he'd lost feeling in his toes a while back, and the exposed skin of his face burned. His frozen hands hurt as he uncurled his fingers from the staff of the shovel.

He felt battered as he trudged back toward the passenger car in the last of the waning sunlight. He massaged his cramping palms. At least he had a warm place to recoup. Let his toes thaw.

Hours of work, and he and the other men had barely made a cut in the drifts of snow and rocks.

They'd need more than mere shovels. Slate would talk to the conductor. The train couldn't stay here. They needed to go back down the mountain pass.

He neared his passenger car, the wind cutting a chill through his body. Near the back exit of the car, he halted. A large patch of disturbed snow sprawled beneath the stairs, as if someone had fallen from the platform and scrambled to gain their footing. Footprints led away from the passenger car toward the woods nearby.

The muted rumble of voices from inside reminded him how desperately he wanted to go into the train car and get warm.

Who would leave the train out here in the middle of nowhere?

The tracks were uneven, as if whoever had jumped the six-foot-plus drop had injured themselves.

He sent one longing glance at the warm light shining from the windows over his head. And ran an icy, gloved hand down his face.

There was nothing for it. He sighed and started following the tracks.

Halfway up the slope, he heard panting, as if someone was out of breath. He went still, but when he strained his ears, whoever was out there had gone silent. Was that a sob?

There. A darker shadow, a body huddled against the bottom boughs of a pine tree. A skirt that billowed out into the snow. Slate took two steps in that direction, and she went perfectly quiet.

Another two steps and he squinted through the growing darkness, caught a glimpse of her.

Lizzie.

Frustration made his words sharp. "Do you happen to know how quickly a body freezes to death out here?"

She startled, and snow that had gathered on the lower boughs of that tree dropped on her head and shoulders in clumps.

"Why'd you leave the train?" he demanded when she didn't answer him.

It was only when he stepped toward her that she forced herself to stand. She wobbled, and he saw how she refused to put weight on her left foot.

"You hurt yourself."

"I'm fine."

Sure, she was fine. He swung his arm out wide, indicating the snow-covered expanse of mountain. "Where were you going?"

She raised her chin stubbornly. He couldn't see her eyes in the shadows under that tree. "I can't stay on that train."

"In case you didn't notice, this is a whiteout. You've got no snowshoes. Not even a scarf. The only place you're going out here is to your grave."

Shivering, she shoved away a strand of hair with a gloved hand. She was more frightened than she tried to show. "S-someone has to live out here. I thought I could find a ranch or someone that could help get me to the next town."

She shifted, still with her left foot not touching the ground. Her words echoed with desperation. Maybe he was asking the wrong questions.

"What is so important in Wyoming that you'd risk your life to get there?"

The punishment she'd get for stealing from a store wasn't enough to make someone that desperate.

She gave him her profile. "Someplace safe."

Her words stirred some protective instinct within him. But something held him back.

Wind blew through the branches above her head, and a flicker of moonlight cut through the shadows enough that he saw the tears glistening on her cheeks. She whisked them away, turning her face further from his gaze.

He wanted to believe her. And that was dangerous. He couldn't trust her.

"There's nothing out here," he said again. "Come back to the train."

Her lips firmed in a line. She took a faltering step and inhaled sharply. It must've hurt.

But she didn't ask for help, not even when another step sent her stumbling.

If she was in trouble, why hadn't she asked for his help? Stubborn woman.

He came beside her and extended his elbow for her to hang on to. She gave him such a look—one that clearly said she didn't want to lean on him.

But she must be in pain, because she grabbed onto his arm as she took her next step.

She limped slowly beside him, even as he tried to focus

on her and not thoughts of the warm interior waiting for him in that passenger car.

Someone else might've played up her hurt to gain Slate's sympathy. Outlaw Bessie surely would've turned on the waterworks, twisting his emotions with her tears.

But not Lizzie. She was holding so tightly to her emotion that he couldn't tell if she was actually breathing. Maybe the lack of trust went both ways.

An icy blast of wind jolted him out of his thoughts as they neared the train car. Someone had left a crate under the small platform outside the door, but it was still a reach of four feet or so.

Lizzie would have a tough time pulling herself up onto the platform in skirts, even without an injured foot.

"I'll give you a boost," he gruffed.

Her shoulders dropped, as if resigned to his help. She turned to face him, and he stepped close, placed his hands on her waist, and lifted her so she was sitting on the platform.

She was so slight this blizzard could carry her away.

When she rolled to her knees and then attempted to stand, she couldn't contain a cry, quickly bitten off.

He boosted himself up behind her, but she was already limping through the door, sending a blast of warmth out into the cold night. Her violin case bumped against a seatback in her haste to get away from Slate.

He watched her go inside, a thorny knot of emotion twisted inside him. If she needed help, it was his duty to give it. But what if he was wrong? What if it was all an act?

Lizzie limped through the cabin, her ankle throbbing so hard that her vision blurred. Warmth from the coal heater at the other end of the car instantly flushed her cheeks. She didn't care where she sat, only knew she had to get off her feet.

She fumbled the violin case as she sat down heavily in an empty seat, trying to ignore the curious stares from the other passengers, who were probably wondering why she'd gone outside. Wonderful. She'd drawn more attention to herself.

She was aware of Deputy Jackson close behind her. Couldn't stop thinking of the look in his eyes just before he'd lifted her to the platform. Concern.

For only a moment, when the deputy's hands had rested on her hips, she'd wanted to blurt out everything. Beg for his help.

She knew better. The only person she could rely on was herself.

Leaving the train hadn't been the answer. She'd rolled her ankle and was now trapped on this train. She couldn't help the terrible foreboding that swamped her.

She tried to adjust her soaked, icy skirts, wondering whether she could put her cold foot on the seat beside her for some relief.

And then the deputy loomed over her, his expression stormy. He was shucking his gloves, and she saw how his fingers were splotched red and white. Had he been out in the cold all this time? "I'd like to have a look at your ankle."

"That isn't necessary." Her quick words didn't dissuade him.

"You can barely walk on it." He sounded reasonable and patient, but she caught the grimace that pulled at his lips.

When she began to shake her head, he made a show of glancing around the cabin. "If you don't want me to check on your injury, perhaps I can find a doctor among the passengers."

That was the last thing she needed. More attention drawn to her predicament.

"Fine," she mumbled.

He knelt at her feet and brushed away her skirts, just enough to reveal her ankle.

Her breath got stuck in her lungs. "I don't have a button hook."

Head ducked, his large fingers fumbled with the buttons. "I'll manage." With a gentleness that surprised her, he slid her boot off.

The change of pressure gave her ankle a beat of relief, but the warmth of his hand as it closed over her ice-cold heel brought on a full-body flush. Thank goodness he was focused on her foot. Maybe he wouldn't notice.

Without looking up, he asked, "Are you going to tell me what you're running from?"

Pesky tears blurred her vision. She'd been so alone for so long, carrying the fear, the stress, on her own shoulders without a soul to help. Now, after a smidge of kindness from Deputy Jackson, something inside her melted.

"My fiancé must've hired investigators to find me. I saw a man looking for me. On the platform in Denver." Her teeth began to chatter, and she was helpless to stop the words from bubbling out of her. Whether she could trust the deputy or not.

He did glance up then. "What?"

For a second, the memory became sharper than the throb of her ankle. She'd recognized the man looming over the ticket agent. Long dark hair beneath his bowler hat and a particular way of standing—she'd seen him in Benson's office once as she'd passed down the hallway.

On the platform in Denver, Lizzie had frozen. It was a good thing he'd been looking the other direction. Someone had bumped into her from behind, and she'd done the first thing she'd thought of and ducked onto the nearest train, not even sure of her destination.

Deputy Jackson didn't poke or prod her like she expected, only gently maneuvered her foot this way and that. When he spoke, his words were aimed at the floor. "You've sprained it pretty bad, but I don't think it's broken. It's turning purple."

Sprained it.

She thought the words were meant to be reassuring, but realization stole over her. It would be so much harder to walk on a sprained ankle. Limping might draw more attention to her. This was a disaster.

"Might be good to elevate it," he said, allowing her skirts to fall as he straightened to his full height. "Want to wedge that case underneath it?"

He must have registered her offense at the suggestion of using her violin for that purpose, because one side of his mouth twitched. Was he trying not to smile?

"Or you can turn to the side and put it on the seat," he

suggested. "There's enough empty seats for now that it'll work."

He was right. Several people must've gone to the dining car, because the crowd had thinned.

She used her hands and carefully lifted her leg onto the seat beside her, spreading her skirts to cover her stockinged foot as much as possible.

Deputy Jackson perched on the seat behind her and to the left so she wouldn't have to twist at an odd angle to speak to him. Or so he could keep an eye on her. Probably the latter.

"Why would your fiancé send someone after you? You steal something from him?"

It took a moment for his quiet words to cut through her. After the gentleness as he'd looked over her foot, the question was jarring.

Of course he'd be on Benson's side. He simply assumed her to be in the wrong.

"I don't suppose Benson was happy that I left." She folded her arms around her middle, glancing away from the deputy. "I never agreed to marry him. My father made some sort of business deal, and I'm the bargaining chip."

She wasn't looking at him, but heard the deputy shift in his seat. "Most women would just say no instead of running away halfway across the country. Did you have a disagreement?"

She swallowed hard. "No one says no to Benson. He's an attorney. A formidable opponent on the bench. I once saw someone run from his office in tears. He treats his staff horribly."

She snapped her mouth closed. She hadn't meant to blurt all of that out. It seemed once her words were unstopped, she couldn't contain herself.

"The one time I dared refuse him, he struck me—"

The deputy had gone still in his seat. If she stared hard enough at the wavy reflection in the window against the darkness outside, she could make out the fierce frown on his expression.

"Couldn't you talk to anyone?" he asked.

"I tried. I asked a friend for help. I even reached out to the clergy at my church, but they all encouraged me in the match, saying it was time I settled down." Benson had everyone fooled.

Then, "Surely your father would understand if you explained things to him. He's probably worried about you."

She might've laughed if her heart didn't feel so bruised. Deputy Jackson sounded as if he truly thought the solution would be so simple.

"You don't know my father."

Three

N O ONE SAYS NO TO BENSON. LIZZIE'S words bounced around inside Slate's skull.

Not long after she'd revealed what she had about her circumstances, their conversation had ended when the conductor had passed through the car, distributing a few woolen blankets from the stock car. Slate had gotten up to ask the man why they couldn't reverse the train and go back to town that way.

The conductor had been grave and serious when he'd told Slate that the terrain and the delicate braking system on the train made it dangerous to reverse course. The safest option was to wait for help digging out.

The waiting was making Slate antsy.

Lizzie had gone silent, one stockinged leg and foot still extended on the seat beside her. He'd been happy for the distance and the seatback between them. He could watch her from his seat on the aisle, but she wasn't going anywhere fast with her foot swollen and tender.

Slate couldn't stop thinking about the desperation she'd tried to hide.

She hadn't asked for his help. Had seemed reluctant to share.

And his protective instincts had fired because of it.

But could he believe her? Experience told him he shouldn't.

Night had fallen in earnest, and she had that stolen coat wrapped tightly around her and arms crossed, leaning her head against the window. Was she asleep? Her eyes were closed, brows drawn as if she were frightened, even when she tried to rest.

He hated this uncertainty. Hated that he couldn't trust his own instincts.

A blast of cool air on his feet had him blinking into awareness and sitting up straighter as a mother and her two children entered the compartment. The mother had her arms full with two bulging carpetbags, while a little girl who looked about eight lugged a suitcase, pulling it along the ground.

"Cain't you help?" the little girl whined at her brother, who must've been all of five.

He only clutched one of the railroad company's woolen blankets tighter and trailed behind her. He stuck out his tongue at her.

The trio bustled inside and moved to the empty row of seats in front of Lizzie. The mother struggled to push their bags beneath the seats as the children bickered quietly.

Lizzie stirred, brushing fine strands of hair out of her face and gingerly putting her foot on the floor. She didn't look at Slate at all. Was she embarrassed about what she'd revealed? Or trying to hide more information?

"—but we didn't get anything to eat," the little boy whined.

"Hush, Mikey," the boy's mother said. Her head was bent as she rifled through a smaller bag. Counting coins, Slate realized.

"We ain't got enough money to eat at that expensive dining car," the girl muttered. "Guess we're gonna eat snow iffen we get hungry enough."

Lizzie was staring at them, obviously listening.

And then she bent down, her head and shoulders blocking his view of what she might be doing on the floor. Or underneath the seat in front of her.

Where the family had stashed their belongings.

He'd risen from his seat and rounded hers before he'd thought it through.

She was digging through something down there—

He grasped her wrist and gave a hearty tug. Enough that she sat upright with a gasp, her eyes wide and surprised. Between her fingers was a silver nickel.

"You stealing again?" he growled. "Give it back to them."

He'd drawn the attention of the mother and two children. The three had turned in their seats, now staring.

And when Slate dropped his gaze to check the evidence that she'd been rummaging in their bags, he caught sight of the open violin case on the floor at her feet.

Lizzie's case.

The compartment door opened and closed behind him. Attention split, he barely registered an older couple entering. Not until they took the two seats behind Lizzie, where Slate had been sitting.

An uncomfortable flush washed over him as he registered the small family staring and the hurt in Lizzie's eyes.

She spoke with an icy voice. "My funds were stolen at the last stop. But I have this. And I was going to give it to this young man."

She jerked her hand out of Slate's grasp and thrust the coin at Mikey. He took it hesitantly.

The little girl was looking at Slate with narrowed eyes and pursed lips. "You ain't very nice, mister."

She was suspicious of *Slate*?

"Turn around, Rosie," the mother whispered.

Lizzie shifted and winced when she must've put weight on her injured foot. She slumped into the seat, only pausing for a moment to close her case and hide away the violin inside. And when Slate would've slunk back to his previous seat, he realized all over again that it'd been taken in the midst of his mistake.

He perched on the edge of the seat next to Lizzie. "I'm sorry," he mumbled after a hesitation.

She stared out the window, expressionless. "We don't need to speak."

"I think we do."

Lizzie sent him a glance that somehow both conveyed her hurt at his assumption and a glittering anger. "Obviously, you believe the worst of me."

"Can you blame me?" The words burst out before he

could think them through. "You stole a coat and lied to me."

"I didn't lie."

"And yet you did steal that coat. Why would I believe you?"

She flinched.

He lowered his voice. "I see a lot of the dark side of folks. Women have a particular way of lying and tricking."

Her brow crinkled. He shouldn't have found it endearing.

"I know men who lost their entire livelihood because of a woman's lies."

The memory of Bessie's shot firing, the rancher's wife screaming her husband's name in grief, flashed through his mind.

"The criminal I just delivered to authorities in Denver was a woman. Town marshal had me investigating a spate of missing cattle."

His hand flexed on his knee. He didn't owe her an explanation, but somehow the words continued to tumble from his lips. "I met Bessie, one of the ranchers in the area. She told me about her stolen cattle with tears in her eyes. One of the other ranchers and his wife suspected more cattle were going to be stolen. They invited me to keep watch overnight at their place. I was on the wrong side of the barn, too late to save the rancher who walked into her bullet."

He had to look away from the compassion in Lizzie's gaze.

Straightened his shoulders. "She lied to my face. She'd been rustling cattle from her neighbors for months."

Saying the words aloud had a way of steadying him. Letting the cold slip over him. It was necessary in his job. How many men had tried to wheedle their way out of a cell when they were drunk or just foolish and made a mistake? Bessie had taught him that a woman could be even more insidious with her lies.

"That's how you see me?"

Her quiet words turned his head in her direction. Lizzie was watching him now in a way he couldn't understand. There were shadows in her eyes.

Was she like Bessie? He'd come to see the real Bessie after the fact. There'd been a hardness to Bessie that Slate couldn't see in Lizzie. Life had dealt Bessie a difficult hand, and she'd grasped and taken everything she could. Even the language she'd used had been coarse.

Lizzie seemed lost. Desperate.

But her recent actions, giving away her last nickel, spoke of a kindness that Bessie wouldn't have recognized.

He looked away, letting his eyes skim over the passengers. "I never should've trusted Bessie was telling the truth."

"So you won't trust anyone?" Lizzie pressed. "Ever again?"

If her quiet question had been mocking, he wouldn't have answered. "I trust people. My boss. Close friends."

She went quiet, and when he glanced at her briefly, he saw the way her brow was wrinkled.

"What?" he said.

"I feel sorry for you," she said. "It seems a terrible way to go through life. Expecting the worst from everyone."

Then she looked out the window, a sure sign she didn't want to talk anymore.

Hours later, Lizzie hobbled down the train aisle after being in the powder room. It was late, completely dark outside. One of the porters had turned down the lanterns inside the train car so that only a hint of light shone from each.

Lizzie tried not to drag her injured foot as she passed by a dozing mother with a child curled on her lap. Most of the passengers were trying to sleep. An occasional snore or rustle sounded from various parts of the enclosed space.

Deputy Jackson wasn't sleeping. She saw the glitter of his eyes beneath his hat brim as he watched her make her way slowly toward him.

He had been agitated after he'd talked about the outlaw Bessie. Lizzie had been shocked when he'd disappeared for a few minutes—apparently to go to the dining car—and brought back food for Mikey and Rosie and their mother.

And offered a half sandwich to Lizzie.

It was a kind thing to do. Out of character, since the man seemed to think her a hardened criminal.

Lizzie had been thankful for the silence between them as she'd scarfed down the sandwich and turned her face to the window. She couldn't help the fear that swirled inside her with every passing minute.

Deputy Jackson wanted to take her back to the last town. Turn her over to the shopkeeper and the marshal. Going back meant being closer to Benson and the men he'd sent after her.

Something caught her eye on an empty aisle seat, and she paused. Glanced around. Everyone was asleep. Even the deputy had tipped his head back toward the ceiling.

She tried to be inconspicuous as she leaned over the seat to see better.

It was the same article she'd seen in the café, right there on the front page. This time, her gaze caught on a different line in the article.

Miss Hamilton is considered hysterical and a pathological liar.

Cold fear slithered through her.

Movement from where the deputy shifted in his seat pushed her feet to move toward the back of the car. Where she'd be trapped by the lawman next to her.

How had Benson managed to get the article published so quickly? How many men had he sent to look for her?

Her heart pounded in her ears so loudly, she was shocked that no one around her woke when they heard it. Her legs trembled as she made her way back to her seat.

When she was close, she saw that Deputy Jackson's hat was pushed back. Those eyes searched her face.

He was the law. And already suspicious of her. From what he'd shared earlier, he had wounds of his own. She couldn't count on him to help.

He moved his legs out into the aisle so she could slip past him into her seat. Her foot nudged the violin case as she sat down, and she tried not to tear up in relief at being off her foot.

The deputy didn't pull his hat back down over his eyes. It would've been a kindness to her if he'd gone back to sleep.

"What were you looking at?" he demanded in a near-whisper.

"Hmm?" He'd been watching her.

"Just now. You stopped to look at something."

Could the man not give her *one* break? She jutted her chin up. "Are you going to search me? Perhaps I stole a crumb off the empty seat." Saying the words brought an echo of the earlier hurt.

He frowned. Crossed his arms over his chest and leaned forward. "Look—"

"Hello." The girl sitting in front of them—Rosie?—popped up, turned around against the seatback, and watched them curiously.

Deputy Jackson glanced at the girl's sleeping mother and brother.

"What's your name?" Lizzie asked in a whisper.

"Rosie." The girl leaned over the back of the seat. "Why are you fighting?"

Lizzie held one finger over her lips to quiet the girl. "I'm Lizzie," she whispered.

The deputy frowned at both of them.

"What makes you think we're fighting?" Lizzie asked.

"Cuz that's what my pa looks like when he's arguin' with my ma. Like this." Rosie crossed her arms and twisted her expression into a caricature of Deputy Jackson's thunderous frown.

Lizzie pressed her lips together to keep from smiling.

The deputy dropped his arms to his sides. "We aren't fighting," he said quietly.

Rosie dropped her arm on Lizzie's side of the seat, swinging it back and forth. "Ya shouldn't be fighting at Christmas."

Lizzie shivered. Deputy Jackson's glance flicked to her, and she saw a slight softening around his mouth.

Rosie wasn't finished. "My ma says that the best way to stop fighting is to say sorry."

She was right. "I'm sorry for causing trouble, Deputy Jackson," Lizzie said softly.

She saw the flash of surprise in his eyes, quickly hidden. "Most people call me Slate."

Lizzie couldn't stop the smile at his small acceptance of her apology, even if he mumbled it so low she almost didn't hear.

Rosie looked pointedly at Slate. "Your turn, Deputy."

Slate's frown was back. "What do I need to apologize for?"

"I ain't seen you lookin' at her 'cept like this." Rosie imitated a fierce scowl.

Slate's frown grew even bigger, and Rosie dropped her scowl to nod vigorously. "Yep, just like that."

An unexpected laugh bubbled from Lizzie's lips. She tried to cover it by clearing her throat. Then had to press one hand over her lips as Slate's gaze cut to her.

"Rosie," came a sleepy murmur from the girl's mother. "Leave those folks alone."

The little boy shifted against his mother.

Rosie twisted to speak to her mother, head and shoulders still above the seatback. "But he needs to tell his wife—"

Slate bristled. "Hold on. She's not my wife."

Lizzie couldn't help the sting of reaction at his words. It was silly. She knew what he thought of her.

Rosie's attention had swung right back to Slate. "Do you got another wife?"

"No." A bite to the word.

"Don't you think she's purty?" Rosie pushed.

Slate's gaze locked on Lizzie. Was she imagining the color flooding his cheeks in the dim light?

Rosie's mother shifted to touch her daughter's shoulder. "Sit back down." This was a demand, not a request. "Let those folks go back to sleep. I apologize," came the quiet words from the seat in front.

Slate settled. Sort of. Both hands were fisted on his thighs.

And Lizzie couldn't help the strange new awareness that seemed to dance in the silence between them.

"Don't be angry," she whispered. "Children say whatever is on their mind."

He spoke without looking directly at her. "You like kids?"

"Yes." Why did her cheeks still feel warm? "Kids are funny. My favorite place to play my violin at the hospital is the children's ward. Sometimes I'd even go to an orphanage. Something about playing for children, seeing them light up, it makes me feel like what I do is, well, you know. Worthwhile." She paused. "My father thought it was a waste of time."

She sensed more than saw Slate's stillness beside her.

"Did you ever tell him?" his voice was quiet in the darkness. "About your fiancé?"

"Of course." Her chin came up even as hurt swelled inside her.

"And he didn't help you? Didn't think you should end the engagement?"

"He thought I must've pushed Benson to it. Made him angry. Caused the disagreement."

From the corner of her eye, she caught the way Slate's scowl returned.

She looked out the window. There was only darkness and the way the blowing snow pinged against the pane of glass.

She wished she could stop her mind from spinning. Find sleep.

She still had to figure out a way to reach Wyoming. Find Jessica, find refuge with her friend.

But there weren't any solutions to be had tonight.

Slate shifted, his knee brushing against her skirts in the small space. She was suddenly afraid he'd ask more questions—and her emotions were far too close to the surface.

"I'm awfully tired," she said quickly.

She heard his indrawn breath, like he was going to say something more. But only a quiet "Good night" came.

Four

KEEP THAT BRAT QUIET!"

The words exploded from someone several rows behind Lizzie and startled her into turning.

Several passengers were glaring at a young mother with a screaming toddler on her hip, standing in front of her seat.

The young woman looked like she was about to start crying.

"Shut her up!" a man's voice muttered.

Lizzie had noticed the young mother last night. She seemed to be traveling alone. And being stuck on a stopped train with a little one couldn't be easy.

"How come she can't get the baby quiet?" Mikey asked his mother.

By midmorning, most folks had shifted around in the train car, and now Mikey and Rosie and their mother were seated just behind Lizzie and Slate. Snow was still falling in a whiteout, and the train hadn't moved one inch.

The boy's question was innocent, but the mother shushed him. "She's only two. She doesn't understand why she can't get down and play."

Rosie leaned over the seatback, bumping Lizzie's arm that was draped there.

"I don't understand either. Why can't the train go?"

The children's mother explained in a low voice while the toddler kept wailing. Even louder, so that Mikey put his hands over his ears.

"Maybe she's hungry." Lizzie was ravenous. She hadn't eaten since last evening.

Slate was the only one who seemed to hear her.

He'd been gone when she'd woken up in the chilly train car. On his turn trying to help dig out. When he'd returned, he'd seemed not only cold but resigned.

Now he leaned slightly closer and spoke low. "The conductor told me they may have to ration the supplies in the dining car. I'll go see if there's anything to spare."

He was back a few moments later with two wrapped bundles in his hands. He passed one to the young mother. Stopped and leaned over to say something to the man who'd made the outburst. And then he was back in his seat, passing the cloth-wrapped bundle to Lizzie.

"Oh. I—I can't." She glanced around at all the worried, frustrated faces. "There could be someone who needs it more."

He stared at her for a moment as if perplexed. "Eat it. I can hear your stomach rumbling."

She did, trying to ignore the new awareness of him. She didn't know what to do with this kind version of Slate.

She was wiping her hands with the cloth when she realized someone was kicking the back of her seat. She suspected Mikey.

"I'm bored," his voice whined.

There was a rustling beneath the seat, and she saw a small hand peep through near the floorboards by her feet. "What is that? I never seen a suitcase shaped like that."

"It's my violin," Lizzie said.

A moment later, Rosie's head popped up from behind the seat. "A violin! Will you play us some music?"

Stop that infernal racket! Her father's words echoed in Lizzie's mind. "I'm not sure everyone would appreciate the noise."

Most of the other travelers were already frustrated. She didn't want to push them over the edge to angry.

"Oh please, oh please, oh please?"

"I . . . don't know."

A glance at Slate, who looked at her in consideration. "Couldn't hurt. If someone asks you to stop . . ."

She nodded.

Rosie and Mikey both started cheering as she pulled her bow out from the case and tightened the horsehair to the precise tension before she ran her rosin along its length.

Her elbow bumped Slate.

Who cleared his throat and then stood up, moving to the space a few rows back, near the vestibule.

She plucked the strings one at a time, twisting the tuning peg until it aligned with her inner pitch. She was never off. Then she ran the bow over her strings with a fast scale.

Lizzie sat at the edge of her seat as the first notes lifted. She began to play a familiar Christmas carol.

Everyone around her went quiet.

Mikey watched with wide eyes and open mouth as Rosie couldn't help wiggling and then dancing.

Lizzie braced for someone to tell her to be quiet, but it didn't happen.

She was aware of Slate watching from his place near the door, but as always, the music enveloped her, and she closed her eyes as she lost herself to the carol. And then another one. And another.

Music always had that magic. Its power to change the mood always astonished her.

When she opened her eyes again, her gaze clashed with Slate's at the front of the car.

The corner of his mouth had tipped up, even though his arms were crossed in front of him. A sparkle reflected in his eyes. And it sent a hiccup to her heartbeat.

She registered Rosie singing along.

And when her repertoire of carols ran out, she began to fiddle a lively tune. Rosie cheered. Some other children among the passengers did too.

The melody wrapped around her and sealed away her fear, her pain, transporting her to a place where she wasn't running from an arranged marriage. Back to when she didn't have to pretend.

She kept playing until her energy flagged. Finally, the song came to an end, and she trailed the bow over the last note, basking in its resonance.

She hadn't heard Slate approach, but he stood there as

she packed away her violin. Her heart was thrumming, sending music through her veins. What would he think?

She slowly turned to face Slate, afraid his approval had turned to annoyance.

She found no annoyance when she dared to look at him. Instead, his eyes filled with a softness that stole her breath away.

Did her playing really give him pleasure?

Rosie and Mikey sat quietly in their seats, content. The other passengers were calm, most talking in low voices.

She had done that. Taken an unruly crowd and brought them peace.

When she finished tucking away her violin case safely underneath her feet, she sat up to see an enigmatic expression on his face.

"When you said you played, I imagined hymns and more serious music."

She couldn't help smiling at that.

"My uncle taught me," she explained. "I learned to fiddle . . . later."

He raised one questioning eyebrow.

"From . . . a friend."

She hadn't thought about Cal in a very long time. The memories crashed in, bringing heat to her face that had nothing to do with the exertion of the music she'd just played.

"Cal—my friend—was a stable boy. He worked for my father."

Somehow, Slate must've heard an inflection in her voice, because his eyes narrowed slightly. "Was this stable more boy than a friend? I thought you were engaged to Mr. High and Mighty."

She bit her lip. She'd never told anyone what had happened when she was sixteen.

"We were friends—my father controlled my friendships. Chose which parties I attended. I was often stuck at home."

She could remember the first time she'd heard Cal playing in the barn. His fiddling was magic. Or so she'd thought.

"Our friendship grew into something more." She placed trembling hands on her lap. "I thought we would marry."

Slate's expression had grown shuttered, and she plucked at a fold on her skirt nervously.

"I believed I was in love, but I also knew he would never live up to my father's expectations, so we met in secret. I'd take my violin and we would play music together in the barn. Other than my uncle, I'd never known someone who loved music as much as I did."

Cal had listened to her when she'd told him the dreams of her heart. Dreams of having a real family. Of music. She'd shared the grief of losing her uncle.

She'd been ready to run away with Cal.

"Servants talk," she said and was ashamed that her words trembled slightly. "My father found out."

Slate's brows knit together. "What did he do?"

A fresh wave of hurt constricted her lungs. "My father paid Cal to leave."

You can't understand how this money will change my future.

Those had been Cal's parting words to her. She had only understood that she hadn't been worthy of his love.

She shrugged and tried to smile, but it fell flat. "I guess the money was more valuable than me."

Slate considered her for a moment, then said, "I don't know. I was raised to believe that God not only created us but died for us. If true, how could you not be valuable?"

Lizzie studied his face. He seemed sincere, and it stirred something warm and deep within.

"You deserve someone who'll fight for you, Lizzie."

His words soaked into the cracks of her heart. If only she could believe it.

The outer door opened, and Lizzie startled.

The conductor came inside, looking around until his gaze landed on Slate.

Slate gave the conductor a nod, then, "I have to . . . it's my turn . . ."

For a second, Slate's apologetic gaze met her eyes, and the warmth in his expression stole her breath.

He was gone a moment later, leaving her to question whether she'd imagined it.

Slate had made no secret that he didn't trust her.

But fool that she was, she was starting to care about him.

As the hours had passed, Slate had watched Lizzie become more antsy.

He stared out the window at the walls of snowy white and couldn't stop thinking about what she'd looked like while she'd played her instrument.

Joy had spilled through her fingertips and wound a spell around everyone within hearing distance. Including Slate.

She'd ended one song and grinned at the children, and he'd felt a bolt of deep attraction in his core.

And then she'd told him about her past. He couldn't imagine having a father who would act in such a cruel way, manipulating her stable boy to leave her. She truly was on her own, in a desperate situation.

She wasn't a criminal, even if she'd made a bad decision to steal that coat. So what was he going to do with her?

He didn't know.

Rosie leaned her chin onto the seatback. "Can you play some more, Miss Lizzie?"

Lizzie jumped. Had she been lost in her thoughts? She'd grown quieter and more agitated as the afternoon wore on.

"Not now," Lizzie murmured.

Rosie sat back in her seat, disappointed.

Lizzie went back to watching out the window. What was she watching for? It'd be madness for someone to ride out in the blizzard, but she seemed to think someone was coming after her in this storm.

And a part of him wanted to distract her. "I had someone in my life," he blurted.

Why had he said that?

Heat flushed into his face. She looked as surprised as he felt.

"We were friends. Emma and I. And Joseph. We would meet up at socials. Sit together in Sunday service."

Her expression softened as she listened.

He glanced down at the worn carpet in the aisle so he could get the words out. "Emma used me to get close to

Joseph—her parents didn't approve of him. They ended up marrying."

He had to swallow hard. He hadn't talked about Emma or Joseph in a long time. "She lied about her intentions the entire time we were together."

Lizzie's hand closed over his, and he let his surprised gaze fall on their joined hands.

"I'm sorry," she said quietly.

"I asked her to come courting." It seemed he couldn't stop the flow of words now that he'd started speaking. "Escorted her to socials, Sunday service. I was falling for her. And after a while, I noticed she was gravitating toward Joseph." Bitterness crept into his voice. "It turned out she was using me. Her father didn't approve of him, and if she wanted to see Joseph, she needed a way to arrive at the events where her father wouldn't know."

Slate had made promises to her. Hadn't thought much of it when her own promises had been an echo of his. Had she ever outright said she loved him?

When he looked back up, a deep V had formed along Lizzie's delicate brow. Was she really so concerned about him?

"That's awful."

"I never should've believed she was falling for me. I wanted—" He swallowed hard against the memories crashing into him. How badly he'd wanted the connection.

"There hasn't been anyone since then?" she asked softly.

He shook his head. He'd closed himself off to the idea of finding romance again. "I'm not sure I can trust anyone. I can't afford to let my guard down."

She was quiet for a long moment, leaving him to stare at her hand, lying on top of his. She was warm and soft . . .

"Is it possible to have love without vulnerability?" Her voice was contemplative. "I mean, take Jesus's disciples. Judas betrayed him. Peter denied him. But Jesus didn't shut his disciples out. He died on the cross in the greatest act of love and then entrusted his disciples with sharing that love—Peter included. If you never trust anyone, you might protect yourself—but at what cost? Don't give up on everyone."

He couldn't help it. He let himself gaze into her eyes. Fell into the beautiful depths there, where her kindness and compassion shone through. Something swelled in the air between them.

Until a baby crying out broke the tension of the moment.

Lizzie blushed and turned back to stare out the window.

He'd need to take another turn digging at the snow and ice soon. But for now, he stared at her reflection in the glass, his thoughts swirling.

If you never trust anyone, you might protect yourself—but at what cost?

He hadn't thought about Emma and Joseph in a long time. Preferred to keep the past locked away. Because it couldn't hurt him if he didn't let it?

He thought he'd loved Emma, but maybe he'd never known what love truly was. His pride had certainly been bruised when she'd told him she'd never had feelings for him, that she wanted Joseph in her life. But had he loved her?

He'd wanted a family to belong to. Someone who loved

him, who couldn't wait to see him when he came in from a long day of work. Who kept his secrets and listened to his hurts.

His eyes focused on Lizzie's reflection, the way she'd tipped her cheek into her bent elbow.

He still wanted all that.

The realization hit him almost as hard as her statement had.

At what cost?

He jerked his gaze away, staring at one of the benches ahead and across the aisle. What was happening to him? He couldn't be attracted to her. She was making him doubt his first impression of her. Maybe she had stolen that coat, but she was desperate. She meant to pay it back.

No. Even if she was innocent, they came from two different worlds. She was wealthy. Probably born with a silver spoon in her mouth. And he most certainly wasn't of that station.

He needed to focus on what to do next.

Should he really take Lizzie back to the little town and let the town marshal there deal with her? It felt a little like abandoning her.

What if this Benson really was coming after her? Maybe the local marshal would protect her. Yet there were no guarantees. Especially if this Benson was as conniving as Lizzie seemed to think.

She'd confused him. That was for sure. Somewhere along the way, he'd stopped thinking of her as a criminal.

Slate was getting too mixed up in Lizzie's circumstances.

Doing the very thing he promised himself he would never do.

He needed to put distance between them. Find a place to wrangle his thoughts back into submission.

But on the crowded train car, how was he supposed to do that?

Five

S LATE CAME AWAKE SLOWLY.

Eyes still closed, he realized that one side of his body was cool—and remembered that he was stuck on this northbound train. His other side was warm.

It must be the middle of the night. Even in his half-asleep state, his worries—about the lack of food, how restless the passengers were growing, whether they'd be able to dig out—crawled over him like a swarm of ants.

He heard soft snores from nearby. A weight shifted slightly against him.

What had wakened him?

His eyes flew open, but he didn't move.

Lizzie was nestled into his side, sleeping. He barely moved, tipping his chin to see her head against his chest, her dark eyelashes fanning across her fair cheeks.

For once, the tension she carried seemed to have eased.

She was so beautiful.

He held his breath through the bolt of attraction that blasted him, an echo of what he'd felt earlier when he'd watched her playing.

More than the attraction, he was beginning to admire her. Her kindness, even in moments of frustration. Her joy spending time with the children. Her resilience.

That's how you see me? She'd asked him the question yesterday, whether he thought she was a criminal. He hadn't been able to formulate an answer.

His emotions were getting involved. Was that a mistake?

As he watched, her brows drew together. A gentle moan escaped her lips. Her eyelids fluttered.

He froze, air stuck in his lungs. He didn't want her to know he'd been staring, so he forced his eyes to the window.

Her breathing changed as she came awake, and she went still, tucked beside him. In the reflection of the glass, he watched as her eyes opened. He saw the vulnerability in her expression, and then the realization of how closely they were tucked together.

She inhaled sharply, and it was like watching a mask fall across her expressive features. All the vulnerability was shuttered away as she straightened.

Cool air replaced the warmth that her body had left behind, and for a moment, he ached to draw her back close. The way her shoulders were turned slightly away from him disabused that notion.

Her eyes flashed at him. "I'm sorry for leaning so close. I must've been cold."

Even her whispered words had a coolness to them.

"Why do you do that?" he kept his voice low, aware of the passengers sleeping all around them.

A momentary falter in her manner. "I'm not sure what you mean."

"You hide your true feelings. Your true self."

Shadows chased through her eyes before she averted her gaze. "I guess I've been expected to portray a certain role all my life. It's easier. To show people what they expect to see."

"What people? Your father?"

The way her lips firmed told him he'd guessed right.

"Why wouldn't he want to know the real you?"

That glint of vulnerability was back in her eyes before she cast them down to her lap. "I am actually a twin."

She studied her clenched hands in her lap, as if it was easier not to look at him.

Her sigh shuddered. "Mother died when we were babies. My sister Eleanor and I were mostly raised by nannies while Father worked. We were . . . close. She was always the quiet one, the one who followed along with my antics. She was more reserved. Shy, even. But she had such a sense of humor . . ." Her voice trailed off for a moment. Her expression had gone distant as if she were lost in remembering. She seemed to shake herself. "My father would always say, 'Why can't you be more like your sister?'"

A pause. She went on, "At night, when we'd been tucked away in our bedroom, Eleanor would tell me that I should be myself. That she wanted to be like me."

A silver tear slipped down her cheek, and she quickly whisked it away, looking surprised to see it glistening on her fingertips before she clasped her hands in her lap.

"When I was nine, Eleanor got sick. I remember a lot of doctors. I was kept out of the sickroom."

Curious that she didn't mention her father now. Had the man drawn away when his daughter needed him the most?

"One morning, I snuck into the bedroom. It was dark and cool. And when I tapped her hand, Eleanor didn't wake up."

Slate's heart ached for the little girl who had lost so much. But she wasn't finished.

"I was inconsolable. Finally put to bed."

His hand flexed with the urge to reach for her. The same way she'd reached for him yesterday. How had she had the courage to reach out when he couldn't make himself do it?

"I woke up late in the evening. My father's light was still on and I snuck into his room. He was kneeling by the side of the bed—I don't know. Saying a prayer? He didn't see me."

Slate's heart thudded with foreboding.

Lizzie stared at her hands in her lap as if they held the answers to the world's problems. "He said, 'Why did you take the good daughter?'"

Her whispered words came in a matter-of-fact manner, but Slate watched as her face crumpled. She turned toward the window. Hiding.

Before he could stop himself, his hand moved to cover hers. She froze, her head still bowed.

He'd deserve it if she rebuffed his attempt at comfort. But she didn't.

They stayed like that for a prolonged moment while he

tried to figure out the right thing to say. Maybe there was no right thing.

"Was there no one who could've comforted you? Been there for you?"

"Uncle Carter came the next morning, from out of town. He hugged me for the longest time."

It wasn't the same as her father's hug. Slate heard it in her voice. But he felt a fierce gladness for a man he'd never met, all the same.

"Good. You deserve to be loved, Lizzie." Maybe some of that fierceness leaked out in his voice, because she glanced up at him. More tears had clumped her eyelashes together.

And he stopped fighting against himself and tugged her to him. "Come here."

She folded into him as he wrapped his arm around her shoulder.

He was careful not to jostle her ankle.

She cried quietly as he held her steadily.

His overcoat had fallen open, and in the reflection from the window, the low lantern light glinted off his badge.

He'd let bitterness cloud his judgment. Especially where Lizzie was concerned. When he'd put on the badge seven years ago, he'd spoken vows to uphold the law, protect the innocent.

But now everything was topsy-turvy.

From the first moment he'd met Lizzie, he'd been the judge and the jury. He had noticed the fear she'd tried to hide. He'd seen her desperation when she jumped off the train, injuring her ankle. He'd questioned why she'd steal a coat of all things. And still, he'd put her in a box. Liar. Thief. Suspect.

She heaved a sigh, and he smoothed a hand over her shoulder.

If you never trust anyone, you might protect yourself—but at what cost?

Her words from yesterday echoed in his mind.

Somehow, he'd let his bitterness distract him from his job of helping someone in need. And she needed help.

When the snow cleared, he wouldn't leave her on her own.

He still wasn't sure he trusted his judgment. The people he did trust were his bosses, Danna and Chas O'Grady. They'd know how to resolve her crime and what to do about the fiancé who was tracking Lizzie.

Lizzie was undone by Slate's kindness, his closeness. If he'd kept his indifferent attitude, she'd have been fine.

But now, grief swamped her.

Mikey rustled in his sleep, accidentally kicking her seat from behind. It was the impetus that she needed to pull away from Slate and straighten.

Her face flared with heat as she brushed the damp spot on his coat. "I'm sorry. I got your coat wet."

He hesitated, then lifted away his arm, leaving a chill down her arm. "I don't mind."

She should go to the powder room and straighten up. But a part of her wanted to lean into his warmth all over again. And when his arm came back around her, she let herself lean in. Only for this moment. Only for tonight.

The compartment was silent around them. No one else was stirring. Tiny snowflakes pinged against the window. How could it still be snowing?

His voice rumbled in his chest beneath her cheek. "I lost my mother when I was six. After that, my pa and I, we became a team. Pa ran the mercantile. He taught me to count change, sell ribbon to ladies buying fabric. Stock the shelves." There was clear affection in his voice.

And her heart skipped a beat. Oh, no wonder he'd taken her stealing from that shopkeeper so personally.

Her tears had dried, and she moved slightly, but his arm remained around her shoulders. She sensed that maybe it was easier for him to say what he needed to without looking into her face.

He tipped his chin down, and it brushed her hair. "I knew how much he missed my ma. He met my step-ma, Vera, at a church social when I was about twelve. She was pretty and young. Much younger than my pa, but he was taken with her. I didn't want him to be lonely anymore. They got married."

Lizzie held her breath until he began talking again.

"I didn't realize until she was there how much I had missed having a ma. Someone to cook breakfast. Set out my clean shirt. Sneak me a peppermint candy from the counter jar and have Pa pretend he didn't see."

He paused for so long that she thought he might not continue. When he spoke again, his voice was rough.

"Pa hit a rough patch. Money started coming up missing

from the till. I liked having a mother so much that I never told my pa that I saw her opening the cash drawer when no one was around. Then one day Vera just disappeared with a take of two weeks' worth of cash."

Lizzie sat up, barely suppressing a gasp.

There was banked anger in Slate's expression, a muscle ticking in his jaw.

"Pa put everything together after she left. She'd been stealing since the beginning. He couldn't make rent. He had to close the store. We moved away."

Shame tinged his words.

Lizzie's throat constricted, hurting for the little boy who had lost so much.

He leaned his head back against the seat, staring at the ceiling as if the memory had stolen his strength. "Vera played her part well. My pa never had any suspicion." His gaze turned inward. "I should've told him, even if I didn't want to believe it."

"You were only a boy."

His lips turned down, and it was her turn to reach for him, to touch his hand. He looked surprised at their hands linked on the seat.

"It's not wrong to want a mother's love," she said. "To want connection."

He looked from their hands up into her eyes. She couldn't read what she was seeing in his gaze, but suddenly her chest was cinched tight.

"There's something about you," he whispered.

Her stomach did a slow flip.

"You make me think about things in a way I never have before."

Snowflakes danced through her stomach.

His breath changed slightly as his gaze searched hers. Something stretched between them. An invisible cord that seemed to be pulling tighter . . .

He swallowed and his eyes dropped down to her lips.

Was he thinking of kissing her?

She wanted him to lean in. Brush his lips to hers.

A sharp snore erupted behind them, and Slate sat back, the moment broken.

Slate's eyes cut away with a sharp inhale, and Lizzie pulled her hand back into her lap. He ran a hand down his face, looking everywhere but at her.

"Lizzie, I—" He blew out a strong exhale. "I think we should both get some rest."

He crossed his arms over his chest and leaned his head back again, eyes fixed somewhere above their heads. "Things are getting muddled."

Shaken, confused by his withdrawal, she blurted, "Is everything black and white for you?" She shouldn't have asked, but she couldn't help herself.

He pulled his hat to cover his face. "Yes."

But the word sounded almost like he was trying to convince himself.

Six

S LATE STARTLED AWAKE. EARLY-MORN-
ing light cast its glow through the windows. The first
thing he noticed was that the snow had stopped and
the sun was shining outside. The second, that the air in their
compartment was chilly.

Or maybe he noticed more because Lizzie was leaning
against the window. Definitely not snuggled up to him
this morning.

And it was his fault entirely.

He sat up straight and took stock of his surroundings.

Most of the passengers appeared to be still dozing. Except for a couple murmuring in whispers behind him and
the man at the front of the car reading a newspaper. He
glanced over his shoulder and saw Mikey rustling with
something in his seat. Rosie and the children's mother were
still resting.

He allowed his gaze to drift over to Lizzie sleeping

against the window, the morning rays dancing across her face. She was curled away from him, the space between them as wide as she could manage.

Part of him wanted to claim her hand again. Pull her close. He'd almost kissed her last night.

But this wasn't the time for that. He was going to take her home to Calvin with him. There was trust to be built between both of them.

More folks were slowly coming awake. If the train didn't start moving soon, people would get even hungrier. Angry. Desperate.

It was Christmas. Folks wanted to get home to their families.

A shout from outside the train pierced the quiet. Slate was instantly alert, leaning toward the window as Lizzie startled awake.

What was that?

The entire compartment bumped and rattled with a blast from outside.

Another muffled explosion rumbled through the passenger car. The windows rattled and the remaining travelers roused with a fresh excitement.

Not Lizzie. She'd gone pale, eyes fixed outside the window.

Come to Wyoming with me.

The words to ask her were trapped in his throat, his heartbeat pumping in his ears. Would she say yes?

Just then, the conductor strode through the compartment door with a man Slate didn't recognize on his heels.

The stranger wore a glower on his wind-burned cheeks,

and ice clung to the rim of his black hat. He exuded an air of exhaustion, like he'd been riding all night. Something about the way the man scanned his surroundings flared a warning in Slate's gut.

Lizzie sucked in a breath. In his peripheral vision, Slate noticed her face had washed of all color. She shrank toward the window.

The conductor looked harried and impatient. "Deputy, this man rode two days to catch up with our train. He's been asking about a woman matching the description of your charge."

Slate stood to meet the stranger, aware of Lizzie's stillness in her seat.

My fiancé must've hired investigators to find me.

The stranger flashed a badge from the palm of one gloved hand. "I'm U.S. Marshal Rykers. I'm glad the storm held you up."

U.S. Marshal?

Lizzie had said her fiancé would hire investigators. A U.S. Marshal wouldn't be called in unless a crime had been committed. A big one.

The conductor waved a hand. "I'll leave you to it. We'll pull out soon enough." He quickly disappeared back through the door.

Slate's mind scrambled to make sense of the situation.

"I've been chasing Miss Hamilton across the country for a week now," Rykers said. He sounded both angry and tired. His coat and boots were caked with ice.

"What do the Marshals want with her?" Slate asked.

Behind Slate, Lizzie barely seemed to be breathing.

"She stole a priceless heirloom brooch from Benson Charles White III Esq. back in St. Louis. Along with two hundred dollars cash."

She'd stolen more than a coat?

Slate heard the slight sound from Lizzie, turned his head enough to see her watching Rykers with terrified eyes.

She turned her gaze on Slate. A quiet plea filled her expression, hopeful and a little afraid. "I didn't steal any money," she whispered. "And the brooch was a gift."

The marshal's voice sounded cold and lethal. "A gift Mr. White only gave because you'd promised to marry him." To Slate, he said, "The conniving girl convinced him it was love—and then it was too late. It was all a confidence scheme."

Anger sparked inside Slate. What had she said when he'd confronted her about the coat? Something about "a difficult circumstance" and paying it back? And now this. The brooch was "a gift." All excuses she could easily blurt out.

She was watching his face. Must've seen the doubt crossing his expression, because a cold mask slipped over her features.

She gave Slate her profile, looking straight ahead.

He'd seen her different masks before, hadn't he? *It's easier. To show people what they expect to see.*

He was such a fool.

He'd given her exactly the ammunition she needed to play on his sympathies, get past his defenses.

"I'd like to take her into custody," Rykers said.

Slate looked at the other man. Saw someone as jaded as he was. A recognition passed between them.

Slate nodded and began to move out of the way.

Rykers shucked his gloves and pulled a piece of rope out of one coat pocket. Did he mean to tie her up?

"She's not going anywhere with that foot," Slate said.

But Rykers was already shouldering him out of the way. "She's a slippery one. Charmed Mr. White. And another fella back in the city."

Lizzie stared at Slate with her heart in her eyes. "Please listen," she said quickly.

"Why?" he demanded. "So you can lie to me some more?"

He hardened his heart against the tremble of her lips. "No, thanks."

He turned and left the compartment. Better to find a seat somewhere else.

Turn around. Come back.

Heart pounding, Lizzie stared at the door Slate had walked through. The door remained closed.

She tried to rally her thoughts. She needed to figure a way out.

She'd witnessed the moment her captor's words had hit Slate. The muscle in his jaw had ticked, followed by a hardening of his eyes. And it had rendered her heart numb.

The brooch really had been a gift. She'd sold it to a goldsmith in a seedy part of the city before she'd boarded that first train.

She was willing to bet Mr. Rykers wasn't a lawman. Or had been once but wasn't any longer. Benson liked to hire men who'd retired from being sheriff or town marshal. Men who didn't mind bending the law to their whims for a paycheck. As long as it was big enough.

Another blast startled her and shook the train. She glanced out the window but couldn't see far enough ahead of the train to tell whether the avalanche had been cleared.

Rykers loomed over her, the rope in his fingers the threat she most wanted to avoid.

He seemed to recognize it, because his eyes sharpened on her.

"I been riding through that storm, and I'm done chasing you. I almost froze to death. We're gonna git off at the next station and head back to St. Louis, where I hand you over to Mr. White."

"I won't marry him." She hated the quaver in her voice.

"I don't care." Rykers grabbed one wrist roughly and then the other. She struggled against his hold, but he was bigger and stronger. It was the work of a moment for him to lash her wrists together.

"I don't care if your ankle is hurt, the conductor said you tried to run before. Not gonna happen again."

As if to reinforce his words, he cinched the rope tighter. Enough to make her wince.

"Please loosen this," she demanded.

His gritty mustache twitched. The way his eyes flashed, it almost looked like he enjoyed her discomfort. "My directions are just to return you. In what condition, doesn't matter. Those were Mr. White's exact words."

Was this her future? Tied to a life she didn't want. Bending to Benson's will.

She refused to do it.

She glanced over her shoulder, sent a wide-eyed plea to Mrs. Russell, Rosie and Mikey's mother.

Rykers flicked his coat open, giving her a clear view of the gun holstered to his belt.

He sat heavily in the seat next to her. "No theatrics," he said. "Bullets flying, someone could get hurt."

"You'd shoot me?" Now her voice really wobbled, but she pitched it loud enough to carry.

He glared at her and made his words even louder. "You're a wanted criminal."

There was a quick gasp from behind her. Mrs. Russell got up, juggling suitcases as she ushered Rosie and Mikey into the aisle and toward the door.

She shot one glance over her shoulder. A withering glance that seemed to scald Lizzie.

Rykers took something out of his inside coat pocket. A paper of some kind. It rattled.

He waved it in front of Lizzie. "This where you were headed?"

She recognized her own handwriting. It was the letter she'd mailed to Jessica—but how had Rykers gotten it?

It hit her with the same power as if she'd been bludgeoned in the stomach. Lizzie had hidden the letter amidst her father's business mail. She'd thought no one would notice.

But perhaps one of the servants had gone through the mail before it had been picked up by the postal carrier.

It didn't really matter how Rykers had it. If Rykers knew

her destination, Benson would've had the information too. He'd have told all of the men he'd hired.

All this time, she'd only thought she was escaping. He'd known her plan the entire time.

"Maybe you're thinking about running again," Rykers said, voice low. "You won't get that far."

She'd known that Benson cared about his reputation. Having his fiancée run away rather than marry him would surely be gossip not easily dispelled. Especially after the wedding announcements in the papers.

But to go to these lengths . . .

Her heart fell. She truly had no way out.

Lizzie scanned the rest of the passengers, her breath coming in huffs. Most of them averted their gazes, acting like they hadn't heard a thing, while the remaining few gave her a cold stare.

Not one of them would help her.

Maybe—

"I want to talk to Deputy Jackson."

Rykers smirked coldly. "It won't help. He don't believe a word you say."

The truth of his words sank in.

She'd revealed the real Lizzie to Slate. Trusted him with the wounds of her past.

But at Rykers's false accusation, Slate had believed the worst of her.

The train lurched, and the passengers seemed to collectively hold their breath. Then the whistle pierced the air, the sound rebounding off the jagged crags surrounding them.

With steam hissing in the air, the train inched forward, and the passengers started cheering, excited to be finally moving forward.

Everyone but Lizzie. Forward motion only carried her to a prison.

Her eyes scanned the landscape. And then she saw it. The avalanche that had blocked the tracks and allowed Rykers to catch up.

Her stomach curled at the sight of the debris pile, jagged and rough. The train crept by the section blown away by dynamite, the snow walls towering along both sides of the train. Twisted tree roots stuck up out of the hardened snow like a graveyard.

She began to shiver. Was there any point to even trying?

She had no one.

No way out.

Seven

I 'M HUNGRY!"

"It won't be long now."

The voices of a mother and son rang out from somewhere in the cabin behind Lizzie. Mrs. Russell and the children hadn't come back. They'd believed Rykers, just like Slate had.

After two restless days of waiting, the energy on the train was high. Passengers excitedly shared what they would do when they arrived just in time for Christmas supper.

But not Lizzie.

While Rykers had thawed out, dripping ice and melting snow all over the floor and seat, Lizzie had reviewed every option, every possibility on how to escape.

She shifted her hands in her lap and winced as the bonds sliced into her raw wrists.

How could she ever escape with her hands bound? And running on her throbbing ankle would slow her down.

Even if she could somehow evade Benson's thug, he'd only catch her again. Besides, where could she go?

She couldn't go to Jessica's ranch. Not when Benson and his men knew to look for her there.

Tears she refused to let fall burned her eyes. No one believed her. The newspaper article had painted her as a hysterical female. Surely if she asked for help, no one would give it.

Rykers shifted his weight, as if tired of sitting. He stretched one leg out into the aisle. "Once at the station, we will wait for the compartment to clear out first. Can't have you getting lost in the crowd."

The motion of the train shifted, and the rolling hills out the window began to slow.

"Look, there!" one of the kids called behind her. "Is that our house?"

The patter of another kid's feet scurried to that side of the train as if trying to catch their first glimpse of civilization.

The adults seemed to restrain their excitement, but they stirred with restlessness just the same. Their eagerness grated against Lizzie's skin.

Not yet. She hadn't been able to formulate a plan to get away.

The other passengers started to stand, moving into the aisle as if they wanted to be the first off the train, then crowding around the door, juggling their luggage and coats. She thought she saw Mikey's face peeping through the tangle of elbows and coats. Thinking of Mikey brought her thoughts right back to Slate and the way the two had played a game of jacks on the floor.

Lizzie felt frozen, each breath stinging.

She'd prayed for God's deliverance. She'd believed Jessica's letter was providential.

But maybe God had abandoned her too.

Rykers slanted her a scowling look. He patted one hand on his coat where it covered his gun. A threat. One that meant he didn't have any compunction about shooting her.

If he shot her with witnesses to see, he might go to prison.

But she couldn't risk someone on this train or the platform getting hurt.

Benson's man stood up in the aisle, blocking her in her seat.

Someone bumped her chair from behind. She'd gotten used to it over the course of the journey, but this time, Mikey popped his face out from beneath her seat.

She angled her legs to hide Mikey from Rykers's view behind her skirts. "Go away," she whispered. Where was Mrs. Russell?

He shook his head. "I sneaked away. Where's Mr. Slate?"

Tears stung Lizzie's eyes.

"I know you ain't a bad guy, Miss Lizzie. You have to get away."

The child's words landed in the raw place of her heart, and she offered him a defeated smile. "There is no use. I'm all alone."

"No, you're not. Pastor Reuben says that God never leaves us alone."

This sweet child was trying to help her in the only way he could.

She smiled a teary smile at him. "I heard your mama reading Bible stories. Do you remember Paul?"

Mikey nodded so vigorously that Lizzie glanced at Rykers to make sure he hadn't seen. He was squinting at something ahead.

"Paul was shipwrecked," she whispered. "Bit by a snake. Imprisoned."

The words brought more tears to burn her eyes.

"But God was always with him."

The words slammed into her as Rykers shifted beside her and glanced in her direction. She lifted her chin stubbornly. Maybe this wasn't over.

When the henchman wasn't paying attention anymore, she whispered to Mikey, "I'll be all right. I promise. Go back to your mama."

Mikey nodded solemnly. "Here. I brung ya this."

He pressed something cool into her hand, still tied.

Rykers glanced at her sharply, and Lizzie rested both hands in her lap.

She felt the motion of Mikey crawling beneath the seat as her skirt nudged against her leg. Thank goodness Rykers hadn't noticed the boy.

"We're getting off here," Rykers said. "You try anything and I'll make you regret it."

Lizzie didn't answer. She glanced out the window.

The realization that had washed over her still made her heart pound.

Her father had abandoned her. Benson wanted to control her. Slate had left her to fend for herself.

But God had never abandoned her. He'd been the one

to bring comfort from Uncle Carter. Given her a love of music. God had given His Son.

She blinked back tears.

If she had no one else, she could rest on God's promises.

Rykers shifted a step into the aisle, and the distance gave her the chance to open her hand.

She looked down on Mikey's gift, resting in her palm.

A pocketknife.

No, this was definitely not over.

Just forget about her.

Slate sat in the second passenger car, a carbon copy of the one in which he'd spent two days with Lizzie, trying to talk himself into not turning around.

He had done the right thing. Walking away. It didn't matter that the memory of Lizzie's tearful, pleading gaze settled low in his gut like a slab of granite.

After he'd turned Bessie in, he'd felt a flow of righteous anger for days.

Right now, all he felt was . . . numb.

He'd let himself be fooled. Again.

He'd listened to Lizzie's tall tales of a life of loneliness and abandonment. Started to develop feelings for her. His heart had gotten involved.

He knew better. If he felt hurt and betrayed right now . . . well, it was his own fault.

The memory of her stark fear when the train had become stuck because of the avalanche hit him square in the chest. Her joy when she'd played her violin for the kids. The wistful look he'd caught when she'd watched the mother with her toddler and hadn't known Slate was looking.

He couldn't stop himself from looking over his shoulder toward the door.

Steeled himself against the desire to go back and check on Lizzie.

Here again was his emotion getting in the way.

The train started to slow, and passengers' voices grew louder and more excited as they gathered their things to leave the train and crowded into the aisle.

Slate joined them.

At what cost? Don't give up on everyone.

Lizzie's words might just chase him home to Wyoming.

The brakes gave one last screech as the train stopped at the platform.

A draft of cold air flooded in from the opening of the car's back door.

Mrs. Russell and her two kids were standing close by.

Rosie tugged on her ma's coat. "But what about Lizzie?"

Mrs. Russell frowned fiercely. "We're not getting involved."

Lizzie had told him her friends had been too afraid to help her.

Mikey chimed in. "We can't just leave her. I don't like the looks of that guy. He's mean."

"You don't know that," Mrs. Russell said.

Slate did.

He'd met lawmen like Rykers before. They had a certain manner, a coldness to them. They were tough—sometimes used methods to get information that Slate never would.

His chest cinched tight.

"Mr. Deputy, ya gotta do something!" Rosie turned a tearful gaze on Slate.

"Rosie—" Mrs. Russell started.

"What about what Jesus says?" Rosie interrupted, her gaze swinging between both of them. "What about forgiving seventy times seven?"

"It doesn't work like that," Mrs. Russell said, voice urgent and low. "Not for a criminal. Now come along."

Her words hit Slate hard, and he froze as the trio filed off the train. Someone bumped into him, and he moved out of the way as others got off. He couldn't stop the ache in his chest while he stood staring out the window without seeing the platform beyond.

Don't give up on everyone.

Lizzie's words from yesterday blasted him. Did he really want to go through life assuming the worst about people?

Pa had never been the same after Vera had stolen from them. He'd grieved like she'd died. But Pa hadn't lost his trusting nature. He'd still loaned to other families in need.

God had forgiven Slate for a whole heap of sins. Lizzie had stolen the coat—but she was alone and desperate. Trying to survive. And he suspected she was serious about intending to pay back the cost of the coat.

Did Slate want to end up bitter and alone?

Or take a risk and open his heart?

Maybe it was the risk that had scared him off in the first place.

When Rykers had made those accusations against Lizzie, Slate had seen confirmation that he couldn't trust anyone.

But if the marshal had been looking for a different criminal, Slate would've asked more questions. Would've asked to see the warrant.

Why hadn't he at least done that?

He needed to talk to Lizzie. Even if the accusations were true, she'd need a friend to stand by her. And if she'd been telling the truth, she needed someone to protect her.

His feet snapped into action. Slate pushed through the crowd between the doors and into the other compartment.

Impatience turned to frustration as he squeezed through the people moving entirely too slowly.

He would stand by Lizzie's side. Even if that meant going to St. Louis first before continuing to Calvin.

He exited the back of the train and hopped to the other passenger car door.

He opened the door, scanning the crowd, looking for her. But Lizzie and the marshal were already gone.

Eight

LIZZIE MUST'VE GOTTEN OFF THE TRAIN. The crowd clearing, Slate pushed through the door, instincts blaring that something was wrong.

Outside, he shielded his eyes against the afternoon sun and tried to scan the crowded platform. Some folks were practically running toward the nearby café, while others were embracing family.

Someone pushed Slate from behind, and he was forced to move down the step to the platform.

Where was Lizzie? She couldn't be moving fast on that foot . . .

There.

Lizzie elbowed her way through the crowd. She was limping heavily, her skirts gathered in front of her. Something dangled off one wrist. Was that a strip of rope?

How had she gotten away from Rykers?

She glanced over her shoulder, a flash of fear in her wide eyes.

Slate followed her line of sight and saw Rykers running after her. The marshal's back was to Slate, but he glanced over his shoulder, and Slate saw his cheeks were flushed red with anger.

Panic seized Slate's gut. Rykers might become violent.

He couldn't let that happen.

Slate made a beeline for Lizzie—and Rykers, who was rapidly gaining on her. He knocked into a man, didn't bother to say "excuse me" as he ran.

He was closing in on them when Rykers grabbed Lizzie's arm. She cried out.

Slate shouldered between the two, aware of Rykers still holding her wrist.

"Let her go." Slate gave the order in a low voice.

He heard the small gasp from Lizzie, just behind him.

Rykers finally let go of her, but didn't back away from Slate.

"I should've asked before." Slate worked to keep his voice level. "Show me the warrant for Miss Hamilton's arrest."

The man's gaze narrowed to a lethal slit. "I thought we'd already settled the transfer of this prisoner."

The word *prisoner* dropped like a stone in Slate's gut. With a little press of his arm, Slate moved Lizzie further behind him. She clutched at his sleeve.

Slate straightened, folding his fingers into a fist. "I will not release her without a warrant." He swallowed, regret nipping at his stomach. Why hadn't he made that declaration earlier? "She is under my protection."

Behind him, Lizzie's breath caught.

He swung his gaze to meet Lizzie's, trying to communicate his apology. He'd failed to do his job well.

But he didn't find accusation in her expression.

Instead, her lips whispered, "Thank you."

He turned back to the marshal, whose scowl deepened.

Passengers continued to mill around them, unaware of the exchange.

The marshal reached up to his chest pocket, his eyes not straying from Slate's. "Of course I have a warrant."

Slate hesitated before accepting the folded-up paper, crinkled from being in the man's pocket.

It wasn't a warrant. It was a newspaper clipping. He glanced down and caught the words *Missing Heiress*, but no article would change his mind.

Rykers tried to shoulder past Slate. "She's coming with me—"

Slate gave a closed-fisted shove against the other man's chest, the paper crumpling in his hand. Rykers was knocked a couple of steps back. His eyes glittered dangerously.

The people on the platform nearby were suddenly quiet, staring even as they kept walking.

"Out here in the West, you can't take people against their will without a warrant. That's called kidnapping."

For the first time, Slate felt Lizzie straighten behind him, like she'd finally gained confidence that he would protect her.

Seething, Rykers shot a hard glare toward Lizzie. "Her father will find her. Or Mr. White."

Slate straightened, his fists tight. "And if one of them does, he'll have to go through me to get to her."

As if shocked by Slate's statement, the man leaned backward, his jaw slamming shut into a hard line.

The marshal scanned the crowd, a wildness to his eyes that made the muscles in Slate's arms twitch.

After one more feral glare toward Lizzie, he sauntered away, his back rigid.

Behind him, Lizzie sniffled, reminding him of the apology he needed to make. He only hoped she'd forgive him.

Lizzie stared at Rykers's back as he skulked away, rage in the stiffness of his spine, but she almost couldn't believe it.

Her body trembled. She couldn't stop.

She clung to Slate's coat sleeve, not quite ready to let go. Slate, too, stared after the retreating figure, the muscles in his arm remaining tense.

Was it really over? What if he comes back?

Slate huffed a soft, scornful sound. "It usually only takes one person willing to stand up to a bully."

Had she spoken out loud?

Heat burned the backs of her eyes. He'd done it. Slate had gotten Benson's man to leave her alone.

A tap on her shoulder made her jump. She turned to see the conductor holding out her violin. Circles surrounded the man's eyes like he could sleep for a week. "You won't be wanting to forget this, miss."

She accepted her violin and hugged it tight to her body,

the case's scent of rosin and rosewood soothing. She'd been so desperate to get away, she'd left it behind.

Her vision blurred. "Thank you."

Even with the clouds moving over the sun, it was so bright outside. That must be why tears pricked her eyes.

Slate turned to her. And oh! The way he was looking at her.

Like she was precious.

A tear spilled over, but she quickly brushed it away.

"Did you hurt your ankle rushing off the train?" His words were a gentle echo of what'd passed between them before, when they'd been strangers to each other.

More tears rushed in. "I—don't know."

"C'mere. I can help you find the doctor's office. Unless you'd rather sit down."

His gentle hand cupped her elbow, and she jumped, her heart leaping into her throat.

With a gentleness that calmed her shaking, Slate led her to a bench against the station and supported her as she sat.

Slate sat next to her, his warm gaze embracing her. A gaze she wanted to lose herself in, but she was under no illusion that his actions came from anything other than a sense of duty.

True, he'd stood up for her. Even made the declaration she was under his protection, but she couldn't allow her bruised heart to jump to conclusions.

"Are you all right?"

She tried to shake her head, but a hiccup interrupted. "I'm fine."

He slanted her a look. So, maybe she wouldn't be able to hide how rattled she was.

The raw emotion she held at bay began to expand until she thought she might burst. "You came for me."

What had changed his mind?

It had to be duty. He was, after all, honorable.

He tilted his head, a softness in his eyes that made her ache. "You are worth coming after."

At that, her heart split open, and she held back a sob. Had he really found her worth standing up for?

His mouth opened, then closed. He glanced down and softly took her hand. "I'm sorry. I never should've left you with him. Never should've doubted you. You've shown me who you truly are. I know you never did those things he accused you of."

Lizzie drew in a large breath to regain her composure but failed miserably. "You believe me?"

His throat bobbed as he swallowed. He brushed his thumb over her hand. "Yes. And . . . I don't want to spend my life questioning whether I can trust every person I meet. Especially when that person shows me who they really are."

His words filled up her dry well and almost consumed her with a delight she hadn't experienced in so long. If ever.

Slate soothed all the wounds, all the hurts that no one had ever seemed to care about, in just a few words.

And he meant it. After all he'd been through, she understood what it took for him to trust.

She searched the gathering clouds above her, which promised more snow, trying to keep the pesky tears from flowing. "I thought you'd never trust me."

When Rykers had produced that newspaper, she'd thought for sure Slate would turn on his heel. But he hadn't.

So when he'd stood against Rykers and refused to let him take her without a warrant, she'd had to blink to make sure she hadn't imagined it.

"Well . . ." The intensity of his gaze became a caress. "Maybe you taught me to trust again."

Lizzie's cheeks warmed and she averted her gaze to the packed snow layering the platform. She didn't know why, but the statement seemed so heartfelt. Still, she shouldn't make too much of it.

It didn't seem fair. She could fully fall in love with this man. His honorable ways, his strength, his tenderness. But despite how he'd stood up for her, it didn't mean he would feel the same.

"Lizzie." Her name was but a whisper on his lips. "I allowed myself to become so jaded that I believed the worst. Can you forgive me?"

She nodded. He didn't need to ask that of her. "Of course. Thank you for being honorable."

The corner of his mouth quirked. "You think I did what I did only because of honor?"

He scooted a little closer. Close enough it sucked away her oxygen.

Everything in her stilled. Why else would he come after her? "Yes, honor. Duty. It's why you asked to see the warrant."

His eyes softened, and his fingers lifted to brush her cheek. "Lizzie, you are more than a duty to me."

She gave a sharp inhale. "Am I?"

What would he do if he knew all the emotion roiling through her stomach right now?

His hand on her cheek slid down her arm until he grasped her hand in both of his. "This morning, I had decided I was going to take you home, back to Calvin, with me."

Was going to. Her heart dropped. He'd changed his mind.

His expression turned cautious. Maybe even shy. He drew in a deep breath. "I still want you to come home with me. I have some friends who would help straighten out your situation. After that . . . if you still want to go to your friend, I'll take you."

Oh. She bit her lip against the tugging smile.

He gave a slight shrug. "Of course, you have the freedom to go anywhere you want."

She blinked. She hadn't had a chance to consider. It was true. She could go anywhere. Do anything. No one dictating what she did. The possibilities were endless.

A gentle snow began to dust his black coat in white flakes. They rested on his eyelashes. It could be an overwhelming thought, except, feeling Slate's warm hands around hers, maybe she knew what direction she wanted to go.

What if her direction was the same as Slate's?

She cleared her throat to keep her excitement from making it squeak. "I'd like that. Going home with you, that is."

At her answer, his hand moved from her hand to behind her back. "I was planning on spending Christmas with some good friends. I'm sure you could join us."

Her smile stiffened. "But I don't have a gift."

He leaned closer. His warm breath on her chin made

her shudder. "Don't you know, Lizzie? You are a gift. And that's enough."

She lost control of her tears, and they trailed down her cheeks. How could it be that this man would believe that of her?

Her heart overflowed. She wanted to tip her head up, just a little, and cross the distance to kiss him, but she couldn't quite force herself to make the move.

But then his smile fell, and he became serious.

Oh no. What had happened? Why the change of mood?

She almost pulled back, embarrassed, but his hand on her back held her firmly in place.

Hovering above her lips, he said, "I have heard that Calvin lacks a fiddler."

She tried to drop her smile to mimic his seriousness, but she couldn't do it, and a small laugh escaped. "We can't have that. I'm of the belief that every town needs a fiddler."

He raised his hand and rested it behind her head. Her stomach turned into a bowl of butterflies.

As the snow floated down around them, serene, peaceful, he closed the distance and brushed his lips against hers.

And she suddenly wanted to kiss him all her days.

He lifted away, as if asking her if he'd gone too far. With his lips only a breath from hers, she tilted her head. "Now, sir, isn't kissing a criminal in the gray area?"

He smiled, mischievousness in his eyes. A new side of him she had a feeling she was going to enjoy discovering.

His hands came up and cupped her cheeks, smoothing his thumb along her face. "You're not a criminal. Even if you were, I'm not sure I could resist."

Then his lips dropped to hers, strong and intentional. His mouth traveled over hers in a way that promised hope for tomorrow.

Just when she thought she might become lost in his kiss, a place she never wanted to leave, he pulled away and wrapped her more firmly in his arms until her chin pressed against his shoulder.

Behind them, hanging on the faded wall of the station, was the sign for the ticket booth.

Her heart swelled with joy. She could see her future.

And it started with a ticket to Calvin, Wyoming.

Acknowledgments

It's true. A book is a joint effort. I have an amazing team behind me that brought this book about. A team that encourages me, motivates me, and then nudges me to dig deeper.

First, thank you dear reader, for taking the time to read Lacy's and my novella, *Her Yuletide Protector*. With so many good books to read, you spent your time with Lizzie and Slate. Thank you!

Also, thank you to my wonderful family. To Trevor, for your continuous support and believing in me. To Nathan, Zachary, Seth, and Adalynn, my wonderful children. I'm so proud of you. To my parents and my parents-in-law. Without your willingness to help whenever needed, I wouldn't be able to write.

Thank you also to my amazing agent, Tamela. You are the best cheerleader I could ask for. Thank you for believing in me and being ready to offer an encouraging word.

To the entire Sunrise team. I can't thank you enough. You saw potential in this newbie and have offered me the chance to work with Lacy.

Now to Lacy, thank you for all the blood, sweat, and tears you have put into this story to help me bring it to life. I have grown so much as an author under your direction and for that, I'm eternally grateful.

THANK YOU

Thank you again for reading *Snowbound at Christmas*. We hope you enjoyed the stories. If you did, would you be willing to do us a favor and leave a review? It doesn't have to be long—just a few words to help other readers know what they're getting. (But no spoilers! We don't want to wreck the fun!) Thank you again for reading!

We'd love to hear from you—not only about this story, but about any characters or stories you'd like to read in the future. Contact us at www.sunrisepublishing.com/contact.

READ ON FOR MORE FROM THE

Spinster schoolmarm Merritt Harding is done waiting for the future she's always wanted. Which is why she answered a mail-order bride ad and is anticipating her groom's arrival on the eve of Christmas. She's about to get everything she's dreamed of…

Except the Jack who steps off the train can't be the same man who wrote her letters. That Jack was a steady, mild-mannered businessman. This Jack is an enigma with flashing eyes and a pirate's smile. He's too charming, too keen, too perfect to be real.

And too secretive. What exactly is he hiding?

Jack wasn't looking for a bride, only an escape from the danger chasing him. But the longer he stays in the small Wyoming town, the more he wants to stay. How can he, when his intended doesn't even know his real name?

One

December 1892

MISS HARDING, PAUL COPIED FROM my slate!"

Merritt Harding stood beside a school desk with one finger pointing at a line from *McGuffey's Eclectic Reader* while little Clarissa Ewing struggled to sound out a difficult word.

The tiny town of Calvin, Wyoming, had seen growth over the past years, and her one-room school was bursting at the seams with students.

"Miss Harding, he's copying my mannerisms again!"

With a prayer for patience slipping silently from her lips, she patted Clarissa on the shoulder and left the girl to sound out the words on the page.

Ignoring whispers from the front of the classroom, Merritt turned toward the back of the room, where the older students were seated.

Thirteen-year-old Daniel Quinn had his arms crossed and was glaring at twelve-year-old Paul Gowen, who was indeed sitting in an identical pose, down to the pinch in his lips.

"Boys, what are we supposed to be working on?" she asked.

Both boys swung identical mulish looks at her. She didn't know whether to laugh or cry.

"He's mocking me!" Daniel cried.

Indeed, Paul mouthed the very same words.

Daniel was new to her classroom this year, his parents having moved to town last summer. She'd taught Paul in this schoolroom since he was six years old.

The two boys were alike in nearly every way. She'd been stumped since the first week of school, unable to understand how they had ended up as rivals instead of friends.

The whispers from the front of the room had grown in volume. A glance in that direction revealed Clarissa with her head bent over her book, lips moving as she silently read. Her seatmate was distracted by whatever conversation was happening amongst the six students in the three desks in front of her.

Merritt tapped the desk in front of Paul. "Why don't you continue your arithmetic work from my desk? Take your slate and chalk with you."

For a moment, she thought he would argue, but he reluctantly stood up and tucked his slate beneath his arm to trudge to her wooden desk at the front of the classroom. There were thick books stacked on one corner of the desk and paintbrushes lined up along the opposite side, but the center surface was clear. He should be able to do his work there.

"Please keep working," she told Daniel before she walked to the front of the room. With every step, the whispers became more muted until she stood before the front two desks with her eyebrows raised.

"Would you like to share with the rest of the class?" she asked Harriet Ferguson. The eight-year-old was small for her age and hadn't joined the schoolroom until last school year.

Harriet flushed and ducked her head, folding her hands in her lap as if Merritt had meted out a grand punishment, not asked a simple question.

"We was wonderin' if it's time to start practicin' for the pageant yet." Harriet's seatmate, five-year-old Samuel Ferguson, was practically bouncing on the wooden bench.

The slate-gray winter sky outside the window was no help determining the hour. It had been threatening snow all day, but only an occasional flake had danced past the window today.

Merritt consulted the watch pinned at her shoulder. "We've another half hour of work at least." She made her voice loud enough for the entire class to hear.

She felt the collective sigh of impatience and heard one audible groan. Though her glance encompassed the entire room, she couldn't tell where it had come from.

The Christmas pageant was scheduled to take place in this very classroom on Monday evening, a mere seven days from now.

Christmas was three days after that.

Between the two events, it was no wonder her students were restless and distracted. After nearly ten years in her position as Calvin's schoolteacher, Merritt expected it. Just like the tradition of holding the pageant in the schoolhouse had been upheld since she'd sat in one of the desks as a student, it was also tradition that the closer the performance loomed, the more distracted her students would be.

She had her own reasons for being distracted. This day had stretched interminably long already. *How* much longer until dismissal?

She'd be happy if she could wrangle fifteen more minutes of work out of her students. Then they could all practice reciting lines. A glance at the nearly completed canvas backdrop leaning against the wall at the back of the classroom made her shoulders droop slightly. She'd meant to make more progress on that project over the weekend but had spent her time planning meals for the next few days, shopping for each one as the special occasion it was, and scrubbing and dusting her entire house from floor to ceiling.

The work will get done, she told herself.

But not tonight. Tonight she had an engagement.

"Miss Harding, what's this?"

Paul held up a folded piece of paper. One crossed with cramped handwriting in even lines. One that she recognized.

Paul must've opened the drawer in her desk and found the letter.

"That's personal—"

"Are you getting married?"

Her words tumbled over his blurted question. It was too much to hope that no one else had heard.

She felt sixteen pairs of eyes swing in her direction as she hurried toward her desk.

"That's private," she snapped.

Paul's eyes widened as she came to stand beside where he sat in the hard-backed wooden chair.

She rarely used such a tone with the children.

But as she took the letter from his hand and slipped it into the pocket of her skirt, she felt blazing heat in her cheeks and realized she was breathing hard, as if she'd run up here instead of walked.

"You're gettin' married?" Harriet asked in the sudden empty silence.

"Course she ain't." Bobby Flannery piped up from across the room. "Miss Harding is a spinster and everyone knows it."

His seatmate must've elbowed his side, because Bobby yelped. "What? My ma even said so."

"That ain't nice," Clarissa said. "Miss Harding is pretty enough to get her a man if she wanted one."

"Children—"

Merritt's attempt at regaining control of the class went unheeded. Two students began arguing about her looks while Paul said, "I thought you couldn't be our teacher anymore if you get married."

Little Samuel looked at her with sad eyes and a now-trembling lower lip. "You don't want to be our teacher no more?"

"Of course I do," she told him.

But it was more complicated than that.

"She's old!" A voice burst out from the middle of the room.

And Merritt felt her temper spark.

"Enough!" She rapped the edge of her desk with her ruler, and the children went silent.

Twenty-five might be a spinster here in the West—most girls married before they were eighteen—but Merritt wasn't *old*.

She bit back the words to defend herself, knowing that debating a ten-year-old would not be an effective use of her time. Though it was tempting.

"I was not planning to tell you this yet"—her heart pounded as she made her voice loud and clear—"but I am . . . possibly . . . considering getting married."

"To who?" demanded a single voice from the back before Merritt's raised eyebrow quelled any more noise.

"*If* you complete today's work diligently and make it through our rehearsal, I will tell you a bit more."

It had been years since she'd lost control of her classroom like this. Even longer since she'd had to resort to bribery. But these were desperate times.

Her plea worked, and the last hour of the day flew past—probably because she dreaded what the children would ask.

The inquisition was as terrible as she'd imagined, but she was able to shorten it a bit as she rushed the children into their coats and out the door.

"I have known him for months." Technically true, though she'd never met her intended groom in person.

"He is a businessman." John had told her about investing in the railroad, though she hadn't understood it all from his letters. There would be time to discuss it at length soon enough.

"No, he isn't from around here." They hadn't discussed where they would live, other than agreeing that she needed to stay and finish the school term as her contract stipulated.

"Where did we meet? I answered an ad in a newspaper."

These last words were said as she ushered the children out the door with her own woolen cape on and arms wide lest they dawdle any longer.

As she crossed out of the doorway, she caught sight of a familiar figure standing on the boardwalk just outside.

Drew McGraw. Her cousin and his three younger brothers owned a ranch well outside of town. She hadn't seen him in weeks, and he had a couple of days' worth of scruff on his jaw.

Her stomach was already twisty with anticipation and nerves as she crossed the boardwalk to him, watching the last of her students scurry toward their homes.

"What's this I just overheard?" He stretched out his arms as she walked toward him.

"What are you doing in town?" She asked the question as she joined in the affectionate hug. Maybe he'd be distracted . . .

But he was just as inquisitive as one of her students. He squeezed her shoulders, then stepped back to look into her face. "You met someone?"

She bit her lip and nodded. Icy wind bit at her cheeks but didn't cool the blush there.

"How come you haven't told the family?"

She saw the hint of hurt in his eyes and felt a pang of remorse. "I wanted to make certain that it . . . that he . . ."

She couldn't say the words aloud. There was still a part of her that worried that John would step off the train, take one look at her, and change his mind about the whole thing. Finding a husband to marry, bearing children of her own . . . her long-held dreams were coming true. Finally.

Drew didn't seem to know what to say to that, and that was all right too.

"Did you bring the children with you?" she asked.

Drew's thirteen-year-old son David, ten-year-old daughter Josephine, and five-year-old daughter Tillie were as close as if they were Merritt's own nieces and nephew, and Merritt missed them dearly.

"Not this time. Gotta grab a load of supplies and head back. Wanted to check if you're still coming for Christmas."

In the excitement of John's arrival, she'd forgotten about her promise to come and stay with the McGraw cousins for Christmas next week.

She'd be a married woman by then.

And John already knew how much her cousins meant to her. "I'll be there."

We'll be there.

The train whistle blew, the sound carried on a stiff wind, still far in the distance.

Her gaze flicked toward the end of town where the station was located. Her heart pounded.

"I've got to go," she said. "I'm meeting . . . him."

This was the moment her life would change forever.

"We're supposed to get married on Sunday. That's less than a week away. I mean, isn't it a lark? When I get off the train, she'll be looking for my hat and coat." He patted a red flower—a poppy?—in his lapel pocket.

Jack Easton didn't turn his head from where he sat in the railroad car. He didn't have to. Between the quiet, mostly empty compartment, a reflection in the glass window beside him, and the acoustics in the arch of the train car, the young man's conversation with an older gentleman who wore a neatly trimmed gray beard, in the seat across from him, carried perfectly to Jack's ear.

"She's a schoolteacher, been in the classroom for years," the young man went on.

"How many years?" Gray Beard asked.

Both men were dressed in suits—not the best quality, but a sign they were doing all right financially.

"Nine, I think." The younger man wore a bowler hat that made him look a mite foolish.

Jack favored a cowboy hat, but he'd lost his in a barroom scuffle a few days ago and hadn't replaced it yet. He riffled one hand through his hair at the empty feeling on his head.

"Nine years in the classroom?" Gray Beard sounded skeptical. Jack couldn't see his face in the reflection, but he had a clear view of the prospective groom's face. "Don't you think she's a little . . . long in the tooth?"

It was a rude thing to say, and Jack took offense on the unknown bride's behalf.

"She's twenty-five." But the groom suddenly looked uncertain.

"Or that's what she wants you to think. She could be lying. She might be forty."

It seemed to Jack that a schoolteacher would probably be someone upstanding in the community. Why would she lie? Especially when a lie about her age would be instantly revealed when the two met.

"What's wrong with her, anyway? Why'd she need to get a husband from a mail-order ad?"

The groom obviously hadn't considered anything like this, and Jack watched in the reflection as the man tugged at his shirt collar and then swallowed hard. "I've jumped into this, haven't I? Maybe I should've thought about it longer than I did."

Jack lost track of the conversation as he watched the landscape change outside the window. The woods and trees they'd been passing through opened up to a plain where everything was dusted with snow. The Laramie Mountains were visible in the far distance, purple shadows against the gray sky.

"Next stop, Calvin, Wyoming!" The conductor's voice called out, and then the man himself passed through the train car.

Jack had been all over the West in the past few years. Montana, Nevada, Colorado. He'd never stopped in Calvin. Passed through once and judged it too small.

But that'd been . . . three years ago? Maybe things had changed.

"Perhaps I should go home." The groom's voice sounded clear as a bell, and Jack saw that he'd loosened his tie now.

He took off his bowler hat and ran his hand through his hair, clearly agitated.

He'd be an easy mark across the poker table. His tells were as big as a brand on a cow's hindquarters.

"You don't want to meet her? What if she's a great beauty?" Gray Beard said. Was the man toying with the groom? He seemed to be playing devil's advocate now.

"It's almost Christmas," the young groom said.

Christmas.

Jack should find a game. Put aside a few dollars and hole up in a hotel room. Shops would be closed during the holiday. Restaurants too.

Jack didn't have a home to go back to. No one to celebrate with.

And he liked it that way. The nomadic life he lived suited him just fine.

He decided to stretch his legs. Standing up, he slipped his leather satchel over his head and shoulder. He had to hold on to the seat in front of him with one hand as the train swayed and rocked.

Jack strode through the nearly empty train car, then moved through the door at the end and into the next car over.

This one had a small water closet, its door slightly ajar, and was more crowded, with people in almost every seat. Many had packages around their feet or on their laps. Another sign of Christmas.

The conductor was calling out, and several people stood up in this train car, moving toward the door.

The brakes weren't screeching yet, but Jack could feel the slowing motion.

Looking down the car, he recognized the head of dark hair beneath a ten-gallon hat, the matching dark-brown mustache. The man was a head taller than most other travelers in the train car, and his lined face showed hard living.

Morris.

Jack turned to go back the way he'd come. He didn't have any desire to bump into Morris.

But two passengers blocked his way back into the other train car, and the only exit was to slip into the water closet.

Jack latched the door behind him.

He had a revolver at his hip, though he'd only had occasion to use it shooting cans off a branch or fence post. It was mostly for show, to keep other poker players from trying to rob him.

But Morris was a hired gun for the owner of a silver mine back in Colorado. Jack had judged him as unpredictable the last time he'd seen him.

The conductor called out again, his voice sounding just outside the water closet door. He must be returning through the compartment and re-entering the car Jack had left.

"I'm looking for a man named Jack Easton."

That was Morris's voice. He must've followed the conductor. Sounded like he was standing right outside the water closet.

"He's got some aliases," Morris went on.

Whatever the conductor said in response, it was muffled.

"He's got light hair. Wears a beard sometimes. Ugly as sin."

There was a tiny spotted looking glass high on one wall, and Jack glanced in it now. His nose had been broken once, a long time ago. It had the slightest bend in it. His eyes had crow's feet from being in the sun.

He wasn't ugly.

At least, not judging by the looks he got from the women who kept company in the saloons. He never took them up on the offers their eyes made.

Jack appeared a little disreputable, maybe, with the scruff on his chin—hadn't seen a barber in weeks. Not ugly.

"He stole five hundred bucks from a friend of mine. I'd like to get it back."

Jack watched in the looking glass as his reflection scowled.

He hadn't stolen a thing from Clark Henshaw. Jack had won at the poker table fair and square—without even a card up his sleeve.

He'd learned early on how cards made more sense than people. How to predict what was coming up next—ace or deuce or anything in between.

Reading people had come later, out of necessity. He'd learned to predict when a fist might come his way and that an empty bottle meant trouble.

He was good at reading people now. And he didn't drink much. Saw it as a weakness after what he'd been through as a child. Which meant that the longer the night went on at a poker table and the more drunk the men around him got, the sharper Jack's senses became.

He didn't have to cheat to win.

And the men he played could afford to lose. He didn't play otherwise.

"I'd like to get the money back to my friend," Morris said.

Good luck.

Jack had fifty cents in his pocket. He'd passed the winnings from Henshaw's table to a group of widows whose husbands had died in a mine accident. Henshaw had sent men into an unsafe shaft, and they'd been lost to a cave-in. The unscrupulous owner had made no reparations to the widows left behind—women who had children to feed but no source of income. Likely those women had paid overdue bank notes or settled up accounts at the local general store.

Jack had righted that wrong.

There was no money for Morris to collect.

And Jack didn't want to think about how the man might try to enforce the debt. He winced.

The train braked with a hiss and screech. The voices outside the water closet rose and fell as passengers disembarked.

Jack edged open the door to find the small vestibule empty.

He cautiously moved out of the water closet and tried to guess where Morris had gone. Would he get off the train at this stop?

Jack crept through the doors and back onto his original train car.

It was empty.

As he tried to guess whether Morris had gone through here, Jack rushed forward to see that both the young groom and Gray Beard were gone.

But the groom's coat and hat were abandoned on the seat. The coat was crumpled, flower hanging precariously.

The door opened at the end of the train car, and Jack's pulse pounded as if he'd drawn a pair of aces.

It wasn't Morris but a grandmotherly-looking woman. Short.

Over her head, Jack had a clear view of Morris's back, his head and shoulders, in the train car beyond.

And then Morris started to turn.

Jack ducked, instinct pushing him to don the abandoned coat. He quickly shoved his arms into the sleeves, hastily pulling the coat over his own. His satchel hung awkwardly between the coats, but he ignored it for now. He reached for the hat, mashing it low on his head. It wasn't much of a disguise, but maybe if he moved quickly, Jack would be all right.

He kept his back to where Morris had been and walked calmly away.

"All aboard!" the conductor called from the platform outside.

He couldn't stay on this train with Morris on board.

He stepped off the train and onto the platform. Another train would pass by. Maybe this afternoon or maybe tomorrow. He'd get on it and find a place to hole up for Christmas.

"John?" A feminine voice called out.

He turned on instinct and came face-to-face with a woman who was pretty as a picture.

Snow dusted her dark hair, pulled behind her head in a low bun. Her dark eyes were intelligent, and he saw a moment of hesitation pass through them before she took one step closer, her pert chin rising just slightly.

"It's me." She sounded the way he felt—breathless. Anticipation shimmered between them.

"I'm . . . I'm your bride."

USA Today bestselling author **Lacy Williams** is devoted to bringing her readers heartwarming love stories about cowboys and the women that tame them. She is the author of over fifty-five books, including the acclaimed Wind River Hearts and Sutter's Hollow series. Her books have been nominated for the RT Book Reviews' Seal of Excellence as well as finaled in RT's Reviewers' Choice Awards. She has been a puppy parent almost her whole life and often writes with one of her dogs snuggled in her lap. She is a mom of four and spends her non-writing time buried under piles of laundry and dishes.

Learn more at lacywilliams.net.

Wendy Galinetti grew up in Michigan's Upper Peninsula—the eighth of eleven kids in a town just big enough to have a library (thankfully). After high school, she saved $325, climbed into a small plane out of a cow pasture, and flew to Bible college in Oklahoma, where she met her husband of over 40 years.

Her books come with faith, laughter, a few tears, and a firm belief that faith, love—and really good coffee—can get you through anything.

Discover more at wendygalinetti.com.

Wendy Klopfenstein enjoys sunshine, sweet tea, and a good book, preferably all at the same time. Having always loved creating stories as much as reading them, she now puts the ones wandering around in her head on paper for others to enjoy. When she's not sitting on the porch reading or helping clients in the family business, you can find her working on her next novel.

Discover more at wendyklopfenstein.com.

Traci Summeril is a Colorado girl who loves exploring the Rocky Mountains she calls home. She spent her childhood summers on her grandparents' ranch, where her rodeo queen grandmother taught her to ride, planting the seeds for the rugged cowboy heroes she writes today. When she's not writing, Traci is a music teacher and mom to four amazing kids.

Discover more at www.tracisummeril.com.

Also by Lacy Williams

Christmas Bells and Wedding Vows (anthology)

Wagon Train Matches
A Trail So Lonesome
Trail of Secrets
A Trail Untamed
Wild Heart's Haven
A Rugged Beauty

Wind River Hearts series
Marrying Miss Marshal
Counterfeit Cowboy
Cowboy Pride
The Homesteader's Sweetheart
Courted by a Cowboy
Roping the Wrangler
Return of the Cowboy Doctor
The Wrangler's Inconvenient Wife
A Cowboy for Christmas
Her Convenient Cowboy
Her Cowboy Deputy
Catching the Cowgirl
The Cowboy's Honor
Winning the Schoolmarm
The Wrangler's Ready-Made Family
Christmas Homecoming
Heart of Gold

Wind River
MAIL-ORDER BRIDES

USA Today Bestselling Author *Lacy Williams*

Martha Hutchens, Wendy Klopfenstein, Wendy Galinetti, Traci Summeril

---

In the wild and untamed landscape of old west Wyoming, the McGraw brothers navigate the challenges of ranch life, unexpected love, and the transformative power of second chances. As each mail-order bride enters their lives, these steadfast men discover that love can bloom in the most unlikely places. Love comes softly in Wind River...

We solve the problem of what to read next.   Available on Amazon

YOU MAY ALSO LIKE...

When a blizzard strikes Deep Haven and Megan is overrun with catastrophes, it takes a former Ranger to step in and help. But the more he comes to her rescue, the sooner she'll move out... Come home to Deep Haven in this magical tale about the one who got away... and came back.

Still the One **by Susan May Warren and Rachel D. Russell**

Grace Howell leaves her life as a ballerina and returns to Heritage, Michigan, to heal. Teaching dance is just a temporary gig, until she finds herself unexpectedly charmed by small-town life and her growing attachment to Seth Warner, a man from her past with a troubled history of his own.

You're the Reason **by Tari Faris**

Dani Sullivan is determined to revive Jonathon Island's fading charm and reunite her fractured family. Her plan? Reopen the Grand Sullivan Hotel. But without the funds to restore the hotel, Dani's forced to accept help from Liam Stone—a big-city hotel developer whose sleek, modern vision is everything she's trying to avoid.

Meet Me at the Grand **by Lindsay Harrel**

We solve the problem of what to read next.

Available on Amazon

**WHERE EVERY STORY IS A FRIEND,
AND EVERY CHAPTER IS A NEW JOURNEY...**

Subscribe to our newsletter for a free book, the latest news, weekly giveaways, exclusive author interviews, and more!

follow us on social media!

@sunrisemediagroup

@sunrisepublish

@sunrisepublishing

Shop paperbacks, ebooks, audiobooks, and more at
SUNRISEPUBLISHING.MYSHOPIFY.COM